SHERLOCK HOLMES

The Will of the Dead

Also Available from Titan Books

Sherlock Holmes: The Breath of God
Sherlock Holmes: The Army of Dr Moreau
Sherlock Holmes: The Stuff of Nightmares

Coming Soon from Titan Books

Sherlock Holmes: The Spirit Box (June 2014)
Sherlock Holmes: Gods of War (August 2014)

SHERLOCK HOLMES

GEORGE MANN

TITAN BOOKS

Sherlock Holmes: The Will of the Dead
Print edition ISBN: 9781781160015
E-book edition ISBN: 9781781160084

Published by Titan Books
A division of Titan Publishing Group Ltd
144 Southwark Street, London SE1 0UP

First edition: November 2013
10 9 8 7 6 5 4 3 2 1

A CIP catalogue record for this title is available from the British Library.

Printed and bound in the USA.

What did you think of this book?
We love to hear from our readers. Please email us at:
readerfeedback@titanemail.com, or write to us at the above address.

To receive advance information, news, competitions, and exclusive offers online, please sign up for the Titan newsletter on our website.
www.titanbooks.com

SHERLOCK HOLMES
The Will of the Dead

FOREWORD

BY DR. JOHN H. WATSON, MD

In the interests of completeness I have included here, alongside my own record of the case, extracts from the testimonies of some of the key players in this most unusual of mysteries, outlining events that transpired whilst I was otherwise engaged.

I cannot, therefore, vouch for the accuracy of such accounts (and, indeed, would caution that in some instances they are most definitely unreliable), although where included they align with my understanding of how events unfolded, and work to shine further light on the myriad complexities of the case.

I do, however, put my full faith in the testimony of Inspector Charles Bainbridge of Scotland Yard, and believe that his account of the "Iron Men" investigation, in particular, represents a true and full picture of what actually transpired. Reassurance may be drawn from the knowledge that Inspector Bainbridge has given his full approval for his description of events – interpreted and recorded by me, Dr. John Watson – to be published here alongside my own humble narrative.

All that remains for me to say, then, is that, despite the

sometimes remarkable nature of these transcripts and the shocking events to which they elude, all of it remains true.

CHAPTER ONE

FROM THE TESTIMONY OF MR. OSWALD MAUGHAM

I woke to the sound of shattering glass.

Startled, I sat up in bed, my heart thudding. It was dark – well past midnight – and my first thought was that someone had put out a window and was attempting to enter the house.

I blinked the sleep from my eyes, waiting for my vision to adjust to the stygian gloom. The house was silent, save for the distant ticking of the grandfather clock in the hallway below. I held my breath, listening nervously for any sounds of movement. Nothing.

The moment stretched.

My thoughts seemed sluggish – whether from being dragged so unceremoniously from sleep, or from the copious amount of claret I'd consumed during the evening's festivities, I could not say. I closed my eyes, feeling the pull of unconsciousness. I told myself the sounds had been imagined. There was no need to get up, no need to trouble myself. A mere dream…

I was close to drifting off again when I heard movement on the landing – footsteps, accompanied by the low murmur of a mumbling voice. I sat up, knowing now that my earlier fears were not unfounded.

I am not, by nature, a brave soul, but I could not allow a potential intruder to go unchallenged. I slid from beneath my eiderdown, shocked by the sudden cold of the floorboards against the soles of my bare feet.

I crossed to the door, cautious and quiet. I paused for a moment, listening. There was more murmuring, coming from along the landing.

I turned the key in the lock and pushed the door open, cringing at the creak of the ancient hinges. I peered out. A shadowy figure stood at the top of the stairs, surrounded by a diffuse globe of lamplight. It turned at the sound of my movement, and I realised, with a sigh of relief, that it was only Uncle Theobald.

"Oh, thank God," he called, his voice wavering. "Is that you, Oswald? Lend me your arm, will you? I'm not sure what the devil's come over me tonight."

I pushed the door open and, pulling my dressing-gown around my shoulders and tying the sash about my waist, I emerged onto the cold landing. I saw Jemima, Uncle Theobald's black and white cat, dancing around his feet. She mewed noisily as she rubbed against his shins.

"Yes, yes, Jemima. Just a moment longer. Oswald's here to help."

I crossed the hallway, the floorboards creaking. "Uncle?" I asked, concerned. "What are you doing out of bed at this hour?" He looked haggard, his eyes lost in shadow. "You look unwell. Here, let me help you." I put a reassuring hand under his arm, supporting him.

Uncle Theobald was an elderly man, and his ailing health over recent months had been a cause of great concern for my cousins and I. Nevertheless, that night he seemed rather more out of sorts than usual. I took the lamp from him, holding it up so that I could see properly. His face looked pale and craggy, the myriad lines cast in stark relief. He narrowed his eyes at the sharpness of the light, and I lowered the lamp again.

"Thank you, my boy. Thank you. I'm feeling rather light-headed. I spilled my drink... I..." he faltered, his shoulders sagging. He expelled a long, heartfelt sigh. "I'm old, Oswald. Old and feeble." He sounded bitter, as if he were carrying a great burden, frustrated by his inability to carry out tasks that, only a few months earlier, had seemed like second nature.

"Uncle, those stairs are treacherous and you're clearly in no condition to attempt them unaided. You really should know better," I said, gently admonishing, but careful to avoid patronising him. "You could have called for Agnes. Or one of us." I sighed. "Look, I'll fetch you another glass of water myself."

Uncle Theobald smiled sadly. "You always were a thoughtful child, Oswald," he replied, patting my arm. "I've promised Jemima here some of that chicken, too. See to that, would you, while you're downstairs?"

"Chicken?" I asked, rubbing my eyes. I was still half asleep and desperate to return to my bed, but I couldn't allow Uncle Theobald to go running about the house in the dark.

"Quite so. The leftovers from the party. I had Agnes put some aside on a plate in the pantry." He grinned. "Didn't want Jemima to miss out, you see."

I glanced down at the cat, which was still mewling around his feet. "He spoils you, Jemima," I said with a chuckle. I stooped and ruffled the fur behind her ears. "I'll see to it, Uncle." I straightened up, taking his arm. "First, however, allow me to escort you back to your bed."

"Very well," he replied gratefully, allowing me to take some of his weight. We shuffled slowly across the landing to his chamber, where I ushered him towards his bed, careful to avoid any fragments of broken glass. The floorboards were damp where he'd dropped the tumbler, but the water had mostly drained away, leaving scattered shards of glass that shone when they caught the fleeting light.

Jemima had followed us, and jumped up onto the bed as Uncle Theobald pulled the heavy blankets over his legs, propping himself up on the pillows. She meowed loudly.

"I'm sorry, Jemima," said Uncle Theobald, conspiratorially. "You heard him. I'm under orders. If you go with Oswald, though, he'll fetch you that chicken I promised."

I hesitated for a moment, as if stupidly waiting to see if the cat would acknowledge what Uncle Theobald had said and follow me, but it seemed she was set upon haunting the poor chap all night. She didn't seem to want to leave his side, as if – and I realise this sounds ridiculous – she was exhibiting some sixth sense, some foresight of what was to come.

Of course, at the time I knew none of this, and put it down to the vagaries of the animal, who had always been Uncle Theobald's pet and no one else's, trailing around after him as he drifted from one empty room to the next, stirring up the dust and the memories in the old house. Sometimes, it was as if Uncle Theobald himself was a relic of the past, and Jemima his only reason for living.

"There. Now you make yourself comfortable and I'll return momentarily with a drink," I said.

I left the room and made for the stairs, holding on to the banister as I descended into the murky gloom of the hallway. It didn't seem worth lighting the wall lamps, so I made do with the flickering oil lamp, traipsing across the cold marble floor and along the passageway to the kitchen. The inky darkness was eerie, the only sounds the swishing of my dressing-gown, the soft thud of my bare feet and the rattle of my breath as I hurried through the kitchen and into the pantry.

I found the plate of chicken and placed it on the floor in the kitchen beside Jemima's water bowl. Then, leaving the lamp on the table, I filled a glass with water from the tap, and drained it. I then replenished it for Uncle Theobald. I collected the lamp and hurried back to the stairs, eager to return to my bed.

"I know, I know. I'm disappointed too, girl. Can't even fetch myself a ruddy glass of water without causing a fuss." Uncle Theobald was talking to Jemima when I knocked gently on his open door, and he looked up, beckoning me in. "Ah, thank you, Oswald. You're a kind boy."

"I haven't been a boy for many years, Uncle," I chided, grinning.

"No, no, of course not," he replied with a chuckle.

"Right. Here you are," I said, placing the glass on his bedside table. "We'll have Agnes clear this mess away in the morning." I indicated the remnants of the previous glass. "You get some rest, and be careful not to stand on any of this when you rise."

Uncle Theobald sighed. He reached for the water and sipped at it slowly. "Very well." He returned the glass to the bedside table and sunk back into his pillows, his eyes already fluttering closed. "Goodnight, Oswald."

"Goodnight, Uncle. Sleep well," I said, turning down the oil lamp. "And goodnight to you, too, Jemima." I crept from the room and along the landing to my own chamber, where I hastened to bed, and soon after fell into a deep, restful sleep.

I woke to the sounds of someone stirring; a door opening and closing, water running, footsteps on the landing. It was still early – around six o'clock, I estimated, and I groaned wearily as I propped myself up on one elbow, blinking away the last vestiges of sleep.

I started at the thud of something landing upon my chest, and looked down to see Jemima staring up at me with plaintive eyes.

"Oh, hello, Jemima. What are you doing here? Is it morning

already? I must have left the door ajar." I stroked the fur on the top of her head, and she mewled happily. "Where's Uncle Theobald, eh? Well, I suppose it's almost time for breakfast. Did you polish off that chicken?" She looked at me curiously, tilting her head to one side. I sighed. "Look, you've got me doing it now. Talking to a cat –" I stopped abruptly at the sound of a dreadful, ear-splitting shriek. It was perhaps the worst sound I have ever heard; the raw, terrified, primal scream of a woman.

"Agnes!" I called, throwing back the covers and sending Jemima sprawling on the bed. I ran out onto the landing. "Agnes?"

I could hear her whimpering in the hallway below, and I hurried to the top of the stairs. She was huddled at the bottom, her back to me, slowly rocking back and forth on her knees. I could see she was bent over something bulky, but it was obscured from view.

"Agnes? What's wrong? Whatever's happened?" I asked, with trepidation. I started down the stairs towards her. Behind me I could hear doors being flung open as the rest of the household, woken by the screaming maid, came rushing out to see what had occurred.

"Oh, Mr. Oswald, sir," gasped Agnes, between sobs. "There's been a terrible accident. Sir Theobald…" She drew a deep intake of breath, moving to one side so I could see. There, on the marble floor, lay the broken remains of my uncle. His head was resting at an unnatural angle and blood had trickled from his nose, forming a glossy pool beside him. One arm looked broken, and his eyes were open and staring. I felt a creeping sensation of dread in the pit of my stomach.

"Good God!" I cried, hurtling down the remaining steps to his side. "He must have fallen in the night!" I dropped to my knees, meaning to search for a pulse, but found I could not bring myself to touch him. He looked so pale, and I could see that he was no longer breathing. "Is he…?" I stammered, already knowing the answer.

"Yes, sir," sobbed Agnes, unable to control her tears. "He's… he's…" she whimpered. "Sir Theobald is dead."

CHAPTER TWO

Of all the many adventures of Sherlock Holmes that I have chronicled these long years, the mystery surrounding the death of Sir Theobald Maugham still lingers in my mind as perhaps one of the most unsettling, and certainly one of the most affecting.

For many years I had thought not to set it down, in part due to the sensitivities of that fateful family, but as much – in truth – because I could not even begin to see how to record such a complex web of betrayal and deceit.

I hope that perhaps, with the benefit of time, I may finally be able to present it here, if not only to once again demonstrate the deductive cunning of my friend and associate, but also to set straight the record of what truly occurred.

It began on a grey evening in late October 1889. Domestic duties had kept me away from Baker Street for nearly two full months, and the long summer had given way to a fruitful, mellow autumn. The streets were wreathed in a low-lying mist that curled around the gas lamps and softened the harsh lines of the city. I'm not ashamed to admit that I was happy and enjoying married life, and my thoughts had been far from murder, blackmail, or any of the other forms of criminal activity that typically punctuated the time I spent with Holmes.

Holmes himself, on the other hand, unable to find a case that could hold his attention, had once again retreated into one of his insufferable black moods. He had taken to lounging about the apartment in his tatty, ancient dressing-gown, smoking his pipe incessantly and indulging in his deplorable chemical habit. In his drug-induced lethargy, he had abandoned all sense of cleanliness and propriety. The apartment was cluttered with abandoned teacups, heaped plates and a landslide of discarded newspapers. Mrs. Hudson had, for the last week, refused to enter his chambers, and it had been her hastily scrawled missive that had brought me to town, and to Baker Street, that very morning.

I had bustled into the apartment with the intention of admonishing Holmes for his lackadaisical behaviour. Although I had learned from experience that my chastisement was unlikely to stir him from his ennui, I felt obliged to make the attempt all the same, both for his sake, and for that of the long-suffering Mrs. Hudson.

He had his back to me when I entered the room, propped up in his armchair by the fire. His bare feet were resting up on a small table, and he was drawing his violin bow steadily back and forth across the strings of the instrument in an apparently random fashion, causing it to emit a violent, disharmonious screeching – rather, I considered, echoing my own present temperament.

"Holmes?" I said, full of bluster. "What the devil do you think you're doing, man? Poor Mrs. Hudson is beside herself! Stop torturing that damn instrument for a moment, will you, and listen to an old friend."

To my satisfaction, the screeching came to an abrupt halt.

"Ah, Watson!" replied Holmes, delighted. "Yes, I was rather expecting you," he continued, in a more languorous manner.

This somewhat took the wind from my sails. "You were?" I said, a little indignantly.

"Naturally," replied Holmes, with a dismissive wave of his hand. He lowered the violin and turned about in his chair to regard me. I could see he was wearing his crimson dressing-gown over a tatty black suit, both of them pitted and pockmarked with tobacco burns and chemical stains. His eyes were hooded and lost in shadow; he was evidently not in the best of ways.

"Then you knew of Mrs. Hudson's letter?" I prompted, resignedly. The fight had already gone out of me. Now, I could think only of how I might assist my friend, to set him once again on the path from which he had strayed.

Holmes removed his feet from the table and set the violin down in their stead, fetching up his briar and tobacco slipper. He began filling the pipe, tamping the weed down into the bowl with his thumb. "Yes, yes, Watson. Mrs. Hudson is nothing if not predictable, and you, my good doctor, are a creature of simple habits. The letter was the least of the matter." He struck a match, puffing on the end of the pipe as the flame took to the tobacco with a dry crackle.

"What on earth are you talking about, Holmes?" said I, more than a little frustrated by his games. I wished to speak earnestly with him regarding his recent behaviour. I couldn't help but feel he was engaging me in such trivialities in order to distract me from my goal. "Stop being so dashed opaque. I haven't called in weeks. It could only be the letter that gave you warning."

"It really is a trifling matter. Hardly worthy of discussion," he said, with a shrug. Yet his tone of barely suppressed superiority belied his true intention – to toy with me.

"*Holmes…*" I said, testily.

He emitted a playful sigh. "Mrs. Watson is away visiting her mother in Sussex, is she not?"

"Yes…" I said, perplexed. "But… how did you know?"

Holmes laughed. "Really, Watson. It's a simple deduction. Was it not the happy occasion of your mother-in-law's birthday this last week? As it has been, on the twelfth of October, every year for the last seventy-three?"

"Indeed it was…" I confirmed.

"And since I am aware that you and Mrs. Watson were away taking the air in Northumberland last week – you mentioned your impending constitutional in your last letter – it seems only logical that Mrs. Watson should wish to pay a visit to her mother directly upon your return." Holmes took a long draw on his pipe, and allowed the smoke to curl from his nostrils as he regarded me. "Therefore," he went on, "knowing you are a conscientious man, and that you would feel obliged to return forthwith to your patients, it is but a simple leap to assume you would take the decision not to join your wife on her call."

"I cannot deny it," I said, with a shrug.

"Left, then, to your own devices, I'd wager that yesterday evening you dined alone at your club, enjoying the company of your fellow medical men. Then, this morning, having discharged your duties – and before you had ever set eyes on Mrs. Hudson's no doubt rather melodramatic missive – you had already decided to take the opportunity to pay a visit to your old lodgings, and to your friend, Mr. Sherlock Holmes." He finished his oratory with a flourish of his hand, before clamping his briar once more between his teeth and sinking back into the depths of his armchair, his gaze fixed upon the leaping flames in the grate.

I let out a heavy sigh. "As usual, Holmes, you explain it in such a logical fashion that it seems entirely obvious you should expect my call. But listen here, this destructive behaviour has got to stop. And as for that poison you insist on sinking into your veins… well, you know my feelings on the matter. I mean…

look at this place. Look at you!" I gestured around me in dismay, aware that the timbre of my voice had altered as I'd spoken. It was not often that I found myself raising my voice to another – particularly a dear friend – yet I believe Holmes understood that my agitation stemmed purely from my concern for his health and wellbeing.

Holmes took his pipe from his mouth, cradling the bowl in the palm of his left hand, as if weighing it. He glanced up at me, his eyes shining with amusement. When he spoke his voice was level, his manner genial, as if my outburst had already been forgotten. "Calm yourself, dear Watson. You wouldn't want to scare away our visitor. He's evidently a rather indecisive example of his class."

"Visitor, Holmes?" I mumbled, somewhat flustered.

"Indeed, Watson," replied Holmes, with a flourish of his pipe. "Your timing is, once again, impeccable."

"This is too much, Holmes. You mean to say you're expecting a caller? Other than myself, I mean." I found this somewhat hard to believe, given Holmes's careless appearance and the state of his rooms. I couldn't believe that even *he* would countenance admitting a client to the premises with the place in such disarray.

"In a manner of speaking. It is my belief that within the next few minutes a man will call at the door, seeking my advice. A man with a grievous problem indeed. He is around six feet tall, in his thirties, and walks with a limp. He was never a soldier, suggesting his leg was afflicted by a childhood illness or accident. He is indecisive and of a nervous disposition. Two days ago, something terrible occurred that has today caused him to take a cab across town to seek my assistance." Holmes had grown steadily more animated as he spoke, and was now sitting forward on the edge of his seat, clutching the bowl of his pipe between thumb and forefinger, eyeing me intently.

"You know this man?" said I, wondering at his game.

"Not at all, Watson," said Holmes, with a chuckle. "We have not yet been introduced."

"Then what gives you cause to anticipate his arrival?" I sighed, resigned now to indulging my friend in this little bout of sparring. At the very least, it had stirred him from his brooding. "Really, Holmes, your games can be quite infuriating."

Holmes grinned wolfishly. "All in good time, Watson. All in good –" He stopped short at the sound of the doorbell clanging loudly from the street below. He sprang from his chair, suddenly animated. "Ah-ha! There he is." He threw open his dressing-gown, thrusting his hands into his trouser pockets, his pipe clenched between his teeth. He paced back and forth before the fire for a moment. The doorbell rang again, and I heard the sound of Mrs. Hudson's hurried footsteps in the hallway below. A moment later the front door creaked open and the sound of a man's voice – indistinct but most definitely hesitant – followed.

Holmes almost leapt over a pile of heaped leather-bound tomes, crossed the room towards me, and clapped his hand heartily upon my shoulder. "Now Watson," he said, around the mouthpiece of his pipe, "be a good fellow and keep him busy for a moment, while I slip away and change."

"I… I…" I stammered, but to no avail; he was already making a beeline for the bedroom door. "But Holmes!" I cried after him, despairingly. "The state of the place!"

My pleas fell on deaf ears, however, and the door slammed shut in abrupt response, leaving me standing amidst a scene that felt more akin to the battle-scarred ruins of Kabul than a British gentleman's drawing room. I was surrounded by detritus, with the sound of our visitor's footsteps already starting up the stairs.

"Well, I suppose I'll just have to do it myself," I muttered, in abject consternation. I glanced around in dismay. I have never been one to relish domestic chores, and the condition of Holmes's quarters was decidedly shameful. Nevertheless, someone had to make the place presentable if Holmes was going to secure himself another case to investigate.

I set about hurriedly tidying away the filthy plates, stuffing them into the sideboard to hide them from view. I hoped that poor Mrs. Hudson would forgive me. I then gathered the abandoned newspapers into a large, irregular heap, and dumped them unceremoniously behind the sofa. There was very little I could do about the dust, but I crossed to the window and heaved it open, inviting a gust of cold – but clean – air into the room.

"There. That'll have to do," I muttered beneath my breath.

As if our visitor had read my thoughts, there was a polite rap at the sitting room door. I smoothed down the front of my jacket, took a deep breath and tried to dispel the harried feeling within me. I crossed to the door and opened it to see a man almost exactly matching the description Holmes had given. I smiled politely. "Oh, ah… come in," I said, standing to one side and ushering him past me.

"Mr. Sherlock Holmes?" he asked nervously, extending his hand.

"I rather fear not," I replied, with an apologetic shrug. "My name is Watson, Dr. John Watson, an associate of Mr. Holmes."

The newcomer looked relieved, and turned back towards the stairs as if to depart. "Oh. Then perhaps I should call another time…?"

"Not at all," I said, reassuringly. "Mr. Holmes will be along presently. Please, make yourself comfortable."

To my relief, I heard footsteps behind me and turned to see Holmes, looking immaculate in a black suit and white shirt. He smiled brightly. "Good evening to you, Mr…?"

"Maugham," replied the man, his shoulders dropping in what I took to be either relief or resignation. "Peter Maugham, sir."

"Well, Mr. Maugham," said Holmes. "Pray take a seat by the fire and warm yourself. Dr. Watson here will fetch you a drink for your nerves."

"What?" I said, caught off guard. "Oh, yes. Quite."

"Thank you, Mr. Holmes. I fear my nerves are, indeed, in tatters. I am close to the end of my endurance," said Maugham, unbuttoning his overcoat and handing it to Holmes. He lowered himself into the seat I had previously occupied, and I sighed.

I crossed to the sideboard and fumbled for a clean glass, hoping I wouldn't have to open the doors and reveal the terrible mess of dirty plates inside. Thankfully, there was a clean tumbler beside the decanter on a silver tray. I splashed out a measure of brandy and handed it to our visitor, before finding a perch amongst the detritus on the sofa. Holmes offered me an amused grin.

"Much obliged, Dr. Watson," said Maugham. He sipped at the drink and nodded appreciatively.

"Now, Mr. Maugham, I see that something is clearly preying on your mind. I can assure you that Dr. Watson and I will hear your case without prejudice, and we ask only that you speak frankly and with as much accuracy as you can muster," said Holmes, returning to his own chair opposite Maugham. "Leave out no detail, no matter how small or insignificant it may seem."

"I shall do as you ask, Mr. Holmes, for I am indeed in need of your help," replied Maugham, solemnly.

"Very good. Now, in your own time, would you care to elaborate on the reason for your call?" Holmes retrieved his pipe and settled back to listen.

Maugham cleared his throat. "Two days ago, Mr. Holmes, something terrible occurred to change my fortunes forever. I have lost everything. I am ruined." He took another sip of brandy, and I noticed that his hand was trembling.

"Two days ago, indeed..." Holmes shot me another glance,

with a raised eyebrow. "Pray continue, Mr. Maugham."

"It was the occasion of my cousin's birthday. The whole family, such as it is, was gathered at the home of my uncle, Sir Theobald Maugham. Sir Theobald is – *was* – a lonely man, with no children of his own. The Maughams, you see, have not been blessed with the sturdiest of constitutions. Sir Theobald's siblings all died some time ago – my mother from a severe dose of influenza, an uncle from a wasting disease, and another to the war in Afghanistan." Maugham looked pained as he listed the terrible fates that had befallen his relatives.

"An unfortunate family indeed," I said.

"Quite so," agreed Maugham. "As a consequence, Sir Theobald lived alone, rattling around in that big house of his. He doted on his niece, however – my cousin, Annabel – and on the occasion of her birthday he called us all together for a party.

"Well, we had a pleasant enough time of it, Annabel, Joseph, Oswald and I. Sir Theobald had become a rather eccentric figure in his dotage, but it pleased us all to see him in such high spirits. We retired late, each of us rather rosy-cheeked and merry, and I saw Sir Theobald to his bed." Maugham paused for a moment, as if collecting his thoughts.

"The next morning, however," he went on, "I was woken by the sound of the maid's screams. The same was true of my cousins, whom I encountered on the landing as I came barrelling out of my room. What we found was a sight none of us will ever forget. Agnes was at the bottom of the stairs, kneeling over the twisted body of my uncle, her face stricken with shock."

Holmes was silent for a moment, respecting the gravity of the man's words. "I'm very sorry for your loss, Mr. Maugham," he said quietly. "Can you tell me, was it deemed that he had fallen?"

"Yes," replied Maugham, gravely. "Yes, absolutely. The police doctor who came out to the house said that it was clear he'd fallen during the night. A terrible accident. We were always warning him about that staircase. It's particularly treacherous."

"You heard nothing to rouse you during the night?" asked Holmes.

Maugham shook his head. "No. But then I had been rather over-zealous with the wine. We all had. When the police found the empty bottles from the party they were quick to conclude that it was likely Sir Theobald had tripped and fallen in a drunken stupor. The doctor confirmed as much when he examined the body. He said there was clear evidence that he'd stumbled and banged his head, breaking his neck on the way down. The smell of alcohol upon him served to support the theory."

"But you doubt this conclusion?" I prompted. It was clear from Maugham's tone that he did not entirely agree with the police doctor's report.

"I don't know what to think, Dr. Watson," Maugham replied, unsure. "It's just… given the events that followed… well, to be honest, I simply don't know."

"Please, continue then, Mr. Maugham," said Holmes.

"As I've already explained, Mr. Holmes, my uncle lived alone, and my cousins and I were his only remaining relatives. He'd set it out in his will that the estate was to be divided equally amongst the four of us upon the occasion of his death." He looked at both of us in turn. "I hope you'll forgive me for discussing such vulgar matters, gentlemen, and I assure you that – at the time – thoughts of such matters were far from my mind. Nevertheless, my cousins and I have all grown used to living on my uncle's generosity, and my sole income these last years has been an annual allowance from Sir Theobald."

"We understand, Mr. Maugham," I said, glancing at Holmes, who appeared to be observing Maugham intently.

"Thank you, Dr. Watson." He sighed. "So it was that, later the same morning, once the police had removed my uncle's body, the family solicitor, Mr. Tobias Edwards, came to the house to offer his condolences and to begin the necessary proceedings."

"I assume that things proved not to be in order?" ventured Holmes.

"Quite correct, Mr. Holmes," said Maugham, with a sad smile. "Mr. Edwards discovered that the will had been removed from its place in my uncle's writing bureau. We turned the whole house upside down, but there was no sign of it." He drained the rest of his brandy, placing the empty glass upon the table.

"Surely Mr. Edwards must maintain a copy at his offices?" I asked.

Maugham shook his head. "I fear not. Mr. Edwards explained that my uncle was quite specific about the matter – the only copy of the will, the original, was to be held at the house." Maugham's shoulders sagged. "Without it, I am ruined. I stand to lose everything."

"Hmmm," murmured Holmes, thoughtful. "I imagine your cousins must likewise have been frustrated by this unexpected development, Mr. Maugham?"

"Oh yes, indeed," confirmed Maugham. "It is on behalf of us all that I sit before you today, Mr. Holmes, to beg for your assistance in locating the missing document."

"It is this missing document that gives you cause to doubt the claims of the police regarding your uncle's death?" asked Holmes.

"It is," replied Maugham.

"You believe your uncle's death and the missing will are connected, Mr. Maugham?" I queried, seeking clarification. "That the alleged thief is also a murderer?"

Maugham frowned. "No... Well..." he said, searching for words. His shoulders slumped in defeat. "Oh, perhaps, Dr. Watson. The trouble is, as much of a coincidence as it seems, I cannot see to what end the two things are connected. Only Joseph would gain from the loss of the will. Being the oldest surviving relative of Sir Theobald, he stands to inherit everything if my uncle dies intestate. Yet I cannot believe for a moment he was involved in my uncle's death, even if he did prove to be responsible for the theft of the will. Even then, it is most unlikely, for he was the one who most strenuously supported my proposal that we come to Mr. Holmes for assistance in retrieving it." He shook his head. "The entire matter is most distressing."

"I quite understand, Mr. Maugham," said Holmes. He stood, folding his arms behind his back and adopting a reflective pose.

I could see from the look on his face, and from the manner in which his brow furrowed in thought, that something about Peter Maugham and his story had captured my friend's attention. I did not yet know what it was – why Holmes should deem this family's affairs a worthy focus of his not inconsiderable intellect – but I knew at that moment that he would take the case on.

"Your story is certainly intriguing," said Holmes, removing the pipe from his mouth and holding it by the polished mahogany bowl.

"Then you'll take the case, Mr. Holmes?" replied Maugham, hopefully.

"Indeed I will." Holmes gestured in my direction with his briar. "First thing tomorrow morning, Dr. Watson and I will make haste to the morgue to inspect Sir Theobald's body, following which I should like to pay a visit to his house. Perhaps if you could arrange for us to be granted full and unequivocal access, Mr. Maugham?"

"Of course," replied Maugham. "I'll send word to Mrs. Hawthorn, Sir Theobald's housekeeper, to expect you."

"Very good. There we shall no doubt begin to get to the root of your problem," said Holmes.

The relief on Maugham's face was palpable. "My thanks to you, Mr. Holmes," he said, hurriedly. "It is a great comfort to my cousins and I to know you are investigating the matter on our behalf." He stood, extending his hand to Holmes, who took it and shook it firmly.

"Well, until tomorrow, Mr. Maugham," said Holmes.

"Yes, good evening to you, Mr. Holmes, Dr. Watson."

I helped Maugham into his heavy woollen overcoat and showed him to the door. The change that had come over him since his arrival at Baker Street was quite remarkable. Where earlier I had taken him to be a nervous, uncertain man with a timid disposition, now he appeared to be confident and assured. I marvelled at the impact of Holmes's brief statements, the effect he could have upon a person simply by agreeing to help. If nothing else, he had done this man a service.

I stopped Maugham by the arm, just as he was stepping across the threshold. "Mr. Maugham? One last thing, if you'll humour a medical man. May I enquire how you injured your leg? Did you see military action in your youth?"

Maugham laughed, for the first time since his arrival. "Military action?" he echoed. "Why, not at all, Dr. Watson. I fear I was afflicted by polio as a child. Why do you ask?"

"Oh, curiosity, that is all," I replied, avoiding eye contact with Holmes. "Good evening to you."

"Good evening, Doctor. And thank you once again, Mr. Holmes."

I closed the sitting room door behind him and returned to my seat on the sofa. A moment later we heard footsteps on the stairs, and then the front door banged shut as Maugham took his leave.

Holmes laughed, at first softly, and then more vigorously, throwing back his head as he revelled in his amusement. I felt myself flush. I knew it was at my expense. I allowed him his moment of triumph.

"Well, Holmes. You were right," I admitted. "On every count. But how the devil did you know two days had elapsed since the incident in question?"

"Don't look so startled, Watson," he replied, playfully chiding. "You know my methods. The man had been pacing back and forth along Baker Street all afternoon. He's indecisive, unsure of himself. I reasoned it had most likely taken a couple of days for him to pluck up the nerve to consult me."

"A guess!" I exclaimed.

Holmes grinned.

"And what of the fact you knew he wasn't a military man? I assume that had everything to do with the manner of his step?" I prompted.

"Very good, Watson!" said Holmes, surprised. "That and the fact a military man would never have been so indecisive."

He was pacing back and forth before the hearth, animated and restless.

"I see you have that familiar gleam in your eye, Holmes. Something about this case has captured your attention," I said. "Although I'm damned if I can see what it is."

"Indeed," replied Holmes. "Tell me, Watson – do you suspect that Mr. Peter Maugham is entirely what he seems?"

"I take it, then, that you do not?" I asked.

"Indeed I do not. Lies and falsehoods, Watson. Those agitated gestures were, I believe, the result of more than a simple nervous disposition. There's more to that fellow than meets the eye. Mark my words: this is a dark business we're embarking on." His words were ominous, and I had no doubt they were the truth.

"So what now, Holmes?" I asked.

"Now, Watson?"

"Well, yes. I'd rather hoped Mrs. Hudson might be persuaded to set an extra place for dinner. If it's not too much of an imposition, of course? With Mrs. Watson away… Well, I suppose I could always head back to the club if you plan on making a start on the case."

Holmes laughed again, kindly. "My dear Watson! The corpse will keep until morning. I'm sure Mrs. Hudson will be only too happy to oblige her favourite culinary critic. And besides, I wouldn't have it any other way."

"Thank you, Holmes," I said, with a satisfied sigh. I pulled myself up off the sofa. "I suppose in that case, then, I better ask Mrs. Hudson to see to those dirty dishes."

CHAPTER THREE

I felt overcome by a sense of weary inevitability as our hansom hurtled through the misty, rain-lashed streets towards the morgue the following morning. I'd called for Holmes early, only to find him setting about a hearty breakfast of coffee, toast and marmalade, and had consequently spent half an hour waiting around while he saw to his morning ablutions. At least, I considered, he was making an effort.

Holmes had, I discovered, spent much of the evening digging through his records, searching out references to the Maughams, researching the family's history. The evidence of his investigations had still been spread haphazardly across the sitting room floor when I'd arrived: swathes of newspaper clippings pasted into leather-bound ledgers, now marked with neat little slips of paper; old, hand-drawn family trees, annotated in scratchy black ink; scrawled notes on scraps of yellowed notepaper. I'd found myself wondering if the chaotic nature of this display did not in some way represent the strange and incomparable processes that took place inside his head.

Holmes had also, it transpired, sent ahead to arrange our visit to the morgue. We were to meet with a delegate from Scotland Yard upon arrival, namely an Inspector Charles Bainbridge. I'd had occasion to make the man's acquaintance once before, during the fateful affair of the Persian Teardrop, and he seemed like an amiable, competent fellow.

I'd also gathered from Holmes's manner that he'd volunteered me to inspect the body. As we trundled through the busy streets in the rear of our hansom, I must have been frowning as I considered such work, for Holmes turned to me, an amused gleam in his eye. "I'd have thought you'd have grown used to the morgue by now, Watson, given the nature of your profession," he said, with a single arched eyebrow.

"I made a pledge to save lives, Holmes," I replied, somewhat tersely. "Not to wallow in death. I'm quite capable of examining a cadaver – as you well know – but I most definitely reserve the right to exercise my distaste for such endeavours."

Holmes threw back his head in sudden, raucous laughter. "Quite right, dear Watson," he said, pushing aside the blind in order to peer out of the window. "Quite right."

We lapsed into silence for a time as the hansom rolled on through the bustling streets of the capital. Holmes sat with his head bowed and his eyes closed, distracted by his own thoughts. I, on the other hand, couldn't help feeling a little affronted by his dismissive attitude towards my obvious discomfort. Nevertheless, as we rolled on I found myself growing resigned to the thought that I would shortly find myself examining Sir Theobald's corpse. There was nothing else for it; Holmes would never accept the word of the police surgeon without further examination of our own. We trundled on, jostled and jolted as the cab bounced over the uneven cobbles.

"Incidentally, Holmes," I said after a while, breaking the

silence in an effort to dispel the solemn atmosphere that I sensed had settled over us, "what do you make of this damnable 'iron men' business?"

Holmes looked up from his meditation. "Ah – so I see you made good use of your time at Baker Street this morning, Watson, scanning the day's headlines."

"Quite so," I said, almost adding that he had left me with little else to do. I decided to refrain from such recriminations, however; I had long ago learned that getting flustered with Holmes did not in any way precipitate a productive conversation. "It sounds like a remarkable – if regrettable – state of affairs, does it not?"

"Indeed, Watson," replied Holmes. "Most unusual."

The "iron men" robberies had become something of a plague upon the rich households of the capital in recent weeks. They'd begun with the most outlandish of reports – of terrifying men forged of iron, who lurched out of the fog-shrouded night to smash their way into people's homes.

The descriptions in the newspapers would have had one believe the machines had been conjured from the fiery pits of Hades itself: glowing eyes; a jerking, mechanical gait; razor-sharp talons; and inhuman strength. Hot coals burned in braziers on their backs, and scalding steam hissed from vents at their elbows and knees. By all accounts they possessed a keen intelligence, although they never spoke or communicated in any way. They would simply force their way into the chosen property, and, taking no heed of any protestations from the homeowners, would march directly to where the lady of the house stored her most precious jewellery and claim it as their own, marching off again into the night.

At first I'd assumed the reports to be an elaborate hoax, or else the wild imaginings of the traumatised victims, but the incidents had continued to increase in frequency, and soon enough the sheer number of recorded sightings lent credence to those initial accounts. My friends at Scotland Yard had confirmed the truth of them, too; a lone bobby had tried to tackle four of the machines as they quit the residence of a Mr. Humphrey Scott, an architect, and had received a sharp blow to the head for his troubles. The force of it had hospitalised him for three days.

That very morning, as Holmes had presupposed, I had read the latest account in the morning edition of *The Times*, detailing the theft of Lady Godfrey's pearls during the night. It seemed as if this epidemic of robberies was unlikely to cease any time soon, and from what I gathered, the Yard had no obvious leads.

"Have you not considered lending them a hand? The Yard, I mean," I ventured. I found it somewhat odd that Holmes had not yet seized upon the matter with his customary zeal, particularly given the recent paucity of interesting cases and his resulting doldrums.

He gave a dismissive wave of his hand. "I think, Watson, that the matter is not for me," he said. "And besides, here we are on our way to the morgue to engage ourselves with another enterprise. If Mr. Maugham's assertions are correct, I believe this case will demand our full attention. I shall leave these fanciful accounts of 'iron men' to the police." With that he closed his eyes and returned to his contemplative state.

Sighing, I leaned back in my seat and watched the city rush by the window.

Presently the hansom trundled to a stop, and glancing up I recognised the familiar entrance to the police morgue. "Right, well – here we are," I said, collecting my hat from the seat beside me. "Let's be on with it."

Holmes inclined his head in acknowledgement and I opened the door, clambering down from the carriage. Driving rain lashed my face, but the inclement weather had not dissuaded the multitudes from going about their business. The sounds of the city assaulted me from all directions: brash newspaper salesmen pitching their wares; barrelling hansom cabs; and the chatter of pedestrians as they bustled about beneath their umbrellas. Beside me, the horses were whinnying and stamping their feet impatiently. I handed the driver a couple of coins, and then turned to see Holmes already disappearing into the building.

It was not without some resignation that I followed him into that house of death. The morgue was a cold, clinical sort of place, filled with the rich aromas of blood and decay. I admit I couldn't quite repress a shudder as we stepped over the threshold and were confronted with all the varied sounds of the butcher's art.

Inspector Bainbridge was waiting for us in the foyer, leaning heavily on an ebony cane. He was a wiry-looking fellow in his mid-thirties, with prematurely greying hair and a wide, bushy moustache. He offered us a weary smile in greeting, as if in anticipation of the unpleasant business to come.

"Morning Mr. Holmes, Dr. Watson," he said genially.

"Good morning, Inspector Bainbridge," replied Holmes, with far less reserve than I'd come to expect from him when addressing policemen.

"Indeed. Thank you for coming to meet us, Inspector," I said. "I fear it is not the most pleasant of circumstances in which to meet again."

"Quite so, Dr. Watson," said Bainbridge. "But for the life of me, I cannot understand why you are here. Surely it's a cut and dried case? The poor man took a tumble down the stairs in the night, and broke his neck in the fall. That's about the size of it."

Holmes waved a dismissive hand. "I'd prefer not to leap to any conclusions until I've seen the body for myself, Inspector, or before my colleague here has had a chance to examine it. I'm sure you understand…" His tone was firm, but not cutting.

"As you wish, Mr. Holmes," said Bainbridge, nodding. "It wouldn't do to colour your opinion on the matter. This way, then."

He turned and beckoned for us to follow him, leading us along a corridor lined with smooth porcelain tiles that had once been white, but were now discoloured and yellow with age. We trundled behind silently in single file as he showed us to the small antechamber – really no more than a partitioned-off area of the passageway – where the remains of Sir Theobald awaited us.

I smelled the corpse before I saw it, a thick, cloying stink that seemed to stick in the back of my throat. Like all cadavers left unburied for more than a couple of days, the early stages of decomposition had begun to set in. I set my jaw in determination, resolving to get this over with as swiftly as possible.

The body rested on a marble slab, covered by a thin cotton sheet. Holmes turned up the gas lamps while Bainbridge stepped forward and peeled away the shroud. He wrinkled his nose in distaste as he did so. "Here we are, then. I'll warn you, gentlemen – it's not a pretty sight."

"You're certainly right about that, Inspector," I said, appalled by the gruesome countenance of the victim. The man's face was a bruised and bloodied pulp, his head resting at an awkward angle, the neck clearly broken. The pale flesh of the torso was covered in deep, purple contusions, and the bones of the left forearm had snapped in at least two places. "Look at him, Holmes!" I exclaimed. "I'm amazed the family was able to recognise him at all."

Holmes approached the slab, peering intently at the cadaver. "Yes…" he said, clearly concentrating. He began to circle the body, his footsteps echoing in the enclosed space. "Remarkable, isn't it? It appears as if his cheekbone has been broken by the impact. And there, around the orbit of the left eye – the skull is completely shattered."

"Yes, a severe blow to the face if ever I've seen one," I confirmed.

"I'll remind you, gentlemen," interjected Bainbridge, "that Sir Theobald *did* take a tumble down a rather hazardous flight of stairs."

"Quite," said Holmes, a little dismissively. "His neck is broken, too." He glanced up to see Bainbridge frowning. "Just as the Inspector suggested," he added. "What do you make of it, Watson? In your opinion, could a fall down a flight of stairs in the dark have caused such a severe set of injuries?"

I considered the question for a moment, joining Holmes beside the corpse. Grimacing, I turned the head from side to side, examining the wounds. The face was swollen and damaged beyond what I would have expected. Could a fall down the stairs really have led to this?

I cast my gaze over the torso, searching for a pattern in the injuries. There was no obvious story to set out, no quick explanation I could offer to describe what might have occurred. Shrugging, I turned to Holmes. "It's certainly possible. I hesitate to commit, but I don't think I can rule it out."

I lifted the right arm, turning it over to examine the hand. "Hold on!" I exclaimed. "Look here, at his hand, Holmes."

"Ah, yes! I see it Watson!" said Holmes, animated. He lifted the other, broken arm, and rotated it in the same manner, holding it up for me to see.

"See what?" said Bainbridge, from over my shoulder. "What is it?"

"It's typical in cases such as these, Inspector," I explained, "that the victim puts their hands out before them in an effort to break their fall. It's an involuntary reaction."

"And?" prompted Bainbridge.

"Well," I continued, "with injuries as severe as this I'd expect to see evidence of just that – bruises and scratches on the hands and forearms where Sir Theobald attempted to save himself. Probably even a broken wrist, judging by the condition of his face."

"As you can see, Inspector," added Holmes, "the victim's hands, however, are entirely unblemished."

"What of the broken arm, then?" asked Bainbridge.

Holmes ran his hands along the dead man's arm, applying pressure. "The breaks are clean and appear to have been caused by the arm being trapped beneath him as he fell," replied Holmes. "The radius and ulna have sheared, but the wrist remains undamaged. Thus, he did not attempt to put his hands out before him as he fell." He gave a satisfied smile.

"Yes, Mr. Holmes," conceded Bainbridge. "But if Sir Theobald had imbibed as much alcohol as the reports suggest, his senses would have been considerably dulled. If he fell in a stupor he may not have been able to react in time. Is it not true that his head might have struck the stairs before his hands did?"

"Watson?" said Holmes, deflecting the question. I could see by the look in his eye that he already knew the answer, but was looking to me to debunk Bainbridge's theory.

"It's a good theory, Inspector," I said, "but even so, he'd have had to be practically unconscious to be quite so unresponsive. So inebriated, in fact, that he wouldn't have been able to walk across the landing in the first instance."

Bainbridge's face fell.

"What, then, is your assertion, Watson?" asked Holmes.

"Even a cursory glance at the cadaver suggests that Sir Theobald was most likely unconscious before he was pitched down the stairs. Either he blacked out near the top as the result of a seizure or heart attack – which remains a possibility – or else someone gave him a helping hand," I replied.

"Precisely!" said Holmes, a little too gleefully for my liking.

"You're suggesting murder, Dr. Watson?" asked Bainbridge. He sounded weary.

"I'm suggesting the *possibility* of murder, Inspector, which is a very different matter," I replied.

"Quite so, Watson," said Holmes. "Yet it nevertheless confirms my fears that Sir Theobald's death might well have been engineered." He reached out to turn the corpse's face towards him, and then stopped, glancing up. "May I, Dr. Watson?" he asked, courteously.

"What? Oh, be my guest, Holmes," I replied, retreating from the side of the mortuary slab to stand beside Bainbridge.

We watched for a few moments as Holmes set about examining the body in minute detail. He withdrew his magnifying glass from his pocket and leaned in so close that his own face was nearly touching that of the dead man. He peered at it closely for a few moments.

Next he pulled a small paper bag and wooden toothpick from a leather wallet and began scraping beneath the man's fingernails, catching any resulting detritus in the bag.

Bainbridge leaned closer, lowering his voice to a whisper. "What's he doing, Doctor?"

"Oh, don't worry, Inspector," I replied, laughing. "This is quite typical of Holmes. Volunteers me to do the examination but can't resist taking a look himself."

Holmes had begun muttering beneath his breath. "...no obvious signs of poison, no puncture wounds, no –" he stopped suddenly, beckoning me over. "Ah, Watson! Look here! Bruises on the upper arms."

"The poor chap is covered in bruises, Mr. Holmes," said Bainbridge. "I really can't –"

"No, indeed you can't, Inspector," interrupted Holmes, brusquely. He abandoned his examination of the corpse and strode across the room to where Bainbridge stood watching. "Your police surgeon has once again offered up a slapdash job. The bruises here are entirely consistent with two people grasping hold of Sir Theobald, their hands beneath his arms, just so..." He reached out and grabbed Bainbridge, hoisting him up onto his tiptoes and causing him to splutter and flush in consternation.

"Yes," I said, intrigued now by Holmes's findings. "You can see how they must have taken his weight."

"Meaning?" said Bainbridge, smoothing down the front of his suit and eyeing Holmes nervously.

"Meaning the case is not quite as cut and dried as it at first appeared," said Holmes. "Wouldn't you agree, Inspector?"

"It certainly sounds that way, Mr. Holmes," replied Bainbridge, with a heavy sigh. "Although I admit, I rather wish it wasn't. I have my work cut out as it is, what with this iron men business. Let alone another murder enquiry."

"The iron men case," said Holmes, "how interesting."

"Oh, believe me, you're welcome to it, Mr. Holmes, if the matter's taken your fancy," said Bainbridge, with feeling. "It's a damnable business, make no mistake."

Holmes smiled. "I fear not, Inspector. I deal with men, not phantoms. Such as the men who saw to it that Sir Theobald fell to his death." He appeared to make a decision. "Watson, I think we've seen enough. Let us make haste to St. John's Wood, and the late Sir Theobald's home."

"Right you are, Holmes," I said.

Holmes was already making for the door, and I rushed to keep up with him. "Er… my thanks to you, Inspector," I called over my shoulder to Bainbridge, who stood watching us leave, wearing something of a bemused expression.

"Right! Yes. Good day to you, Doctor," he called in response. "It sounds as if I'll be seeing you again very shortly."

He did not seem overly amused by the idea.

CHAPTER FOUR

The late Sir Theobald Maugham's house had once been grand, but was now dilapidated and rundown, like so many of the former great houses of the capital. Such was the curse of the very rich: dilettante children who cared little for the upkeep of their father's estates, born into riches and intent only on spending them.

The same wasn't true of Sir Theobald, of course. His was rather the opposite problem. He had no children upon which to prevail, dilettantes or otherwise, so in his later years he had been forced to abandon many of the more challenging aspects of maintaining a large house. It appeared neither his niece nor his nephews had been forthcoming in taking on the administration of any of the work, and, as soon became apparent to Holmes and I, the house had been very much neglected.

Nevertheless, it was still a rather impressive abode, and it was clear that Sir Theobald had been wealthy, if not scrupulous in the care of his property.

Holmes and I learned from Mrs. Hawthorn – the dour housekeeper of middling years – that Sir Theobald's niece and nephews had all returned to their own homes in the city, and that the door to Sir Theobald's study had been locked, everything left in situ as directed by Inspector Bainbridge. Holmes had been delighted by this news, and I knew he was impressed with Bainbridge's foresight. In his experience, Scotland Yard was wont to trample over the scene before he'd had a chance to examine it for any clues. He had often bemoaned as much to me, and I'd seen evidence enough to know it was true. The police were not, however, the simpletons that Holmes often made them out to be. It was simply that they were ignorant of his methods, and so could not see the value in such things. Bainbridge, it seemed, was a rare exception.

Holmes began by interviewing the poor maid, Agnes, who in every way corroborated the story told to us by Peter Maugham. She was clearly still distraught by the whole affair and had very little to add to that most unpleasant of tales.

Next, Holmes set about his examination of the hallway, scrutinising the treads on the impressive staircase, carrying with him an oil lamp in an effort to dispel the gloom. It cast his face in sharp relief as he muttered to himself, running his fingers back and forth across the wooden treads and the runner.

He found what he was looking for almost immediately.

"Blood, Watson. Here on the treads," he announced triumphantly, indicating a step almost halfway up to the first floor.

I hurried to join him, the ancient wood creaking under my weight.

"What do you make of that?" he said, straightening his back and peering expectantly. I took the lantern from him and stooped to examine the step in question. Dark, dried blood was spattered unevenly across its worn surface, emanating from a single point in one corner, where Sir Theobald had clearly shattered his skull during the fall.

"Yes, that would be consistent with the injuries sustained by Sir Theobald, Holmes," said I, returning the lamp to him.

"Quite so," he said, in that manner that told me he had already drawn the same conclusion and was presently preoccupied with some other matter pertaining to the case.

"You sound troubled, Holmes," I prompted, eager to offer any assistance I was able.

"Not troubled, Watson, no…" He glanced at me, as if sizing me up. "You weigh, what? A hundred and sixty-five pounds?"

"Well, more like a hundred and sixty," I blustered.

"Come now, Watson. A hundred and sixty-five, I think," countered Holmes.

"I… well – what the devil's it got to do with anything, anyway?" I demanded.

"Humour me, Watson, if you will?" said Holmes, with a wry smile.

I shrugged. "I don't suppose I have a great deal of choice."

"That's the spirit! Now, follow me…" said Holmes, as he charged energetically towards the landing above.

Sighing, I followed as he climbed the rest of the way to the landing.

It was dark at the top of the stairs, and turning back towards the steep incline, I began to get a sense of how a man might easily lose his footing in the dark, particularly a man in his dotage, such as Sir Theobald. "It does look rather perilous from up here, doesn't it?" I ventured.

"Particularly if one has been rendered unconscious in advance of tackling it," said Holmes.

"Well, quite." I mused for a moment on the implications of his words. If Sir Theobald really had been rendered insensible and thrown down the stairs, wouldn't someone have heard? "What?" I started suddenly at the sensation of someone grabbing me from behind, thrusting both hands beneath my arms and grasping me around the chest. "Now, hold on just a minute, Holmes!" I bellowed, shocked by his sudden imposition. "What the devil are you up to?"

"You're quite safe, Watson," replied Holmes, his voice loud in my ear. "Now, if you would simply relax in my arms."

"If I'd *what*?" I cried, struggling to free myself from his impertinent embrace.

"Allow me to take your weight for a moment, Watson, so that I may judge the manner in which you would fall," said Holmes, sounding exasperated.

"Don't be preposterous, Holmes!" I countered, but I knew it was a losing battle. He had me pinned, and if I were to struggle any more vigorously, we should both tumble down the stairs to our deaths.

"I would be terribly obliged," said Holmes, as if making the most reasonable request in the world.

"Very well," I snapped, feeling thoroughly put out. "But I feel like a damn fool. And be warned, Holmes – if you drop me, I'll damn well come back to haunt you."

I relaxed in his grip, and he grunted as he hefted me, swinging me back and forth on the landing as if preparing to launch me into the abyss. Then, after a moment, he dragged me back to safety and set me down.

I slumped as he retreated, dropping to one knee.

"Very good, Watson. You may stand," said Holmes, dusting his hands.

"Oh, may I?" I offered, sarcastically. I stood, giving an embarrassed cough. "Right. Well then…" I stammered, only to see that Holmes was already off, heading towards one of the doors that opened off the landing.

I followed my companion to a room that transpired to be

Sir Theobald's bedchamber. It was a musty place, with dark, heavy curtains of red velvet and a large four-poster bed. Ancient portraits crowded the oak-panelled walls, staring down at us as if sitting in judgement. A glass case filled with a diorama of colourful stuffed birds rested upon the small mantelpiece above the empty fireplace.

Holmes must have spent half an hour picking the place apart, examining every inch of the walls, the windows, the floor beneath the bed. At one point, on his hands and knees before the bedside cabinet, he gave a brief exclamation of triumph, producing a fragment of broken glass from between two floorboards and proclaiming that a glass of water had been spilled in the vicinity in recent days. I admit that I had no notion of the import of what appeared, at the time, to be a triviality, but later, as Holmes surely knew it would, that tiny fact would help to corroborate his theory.

Unable to be of any real assistance – and chastised for prompting Holmes with too many questions while he worked – I made my way to the drawing room to talk to the maid, who elaborated a little on the events surrounding Sir Theobald's death.

Her story confirmed all that Peter Maugham had told us – namely, that she, Agnes, had been the one to discover Sir Theobald's body that fateful morning, and that her distraught cries had woken his niece and nephews and brought the other servants running.

The police had been sent for immediately, and within a few hours the doctor had been and the body had been taken away to the morgue. It was then that Mr. Tobias Edwards, Sir Theobald's solicitor, had discovered that the will was missing.

I recorded all of this in my notebook for later reference, knowing that the girl's testimony might prove useful if, later, there was any confusion over the sequence of events.

Holmes joined us a short while later and urged Mrs. Hawthorn to unlock the door to Sir Theobald's study.

The room was in some disarray, despite all that Bainbridge had done to preserve it. Papers were scattered across the desk and the bureau hung open, its contents spilt across the floor as if it had spontaneously decided to divulge all its secrets. It smelled damp and musty, as if the place hadn't seen much use in recent years.

"I see the family really did have a thorough search of the place," I said, closing the door behind me and taking in the chaos.

"It was only to be expected, Watson. Despite the best efforts of the Inspector," observed Holmes.

"But to leave it in such a state… I suppose they must have been desperate." I could see no good reason to leave everything on the floor in such disarray. Holmes, of course, was hardly a scion of tidiness himself, but at least his own particular brand of chaos had some degree of order about it.

"Desperate is *exactly* the word, Watson. Desperate indeed. Without that will, they stand to lose everything. Or at least, all but one of them does." Holmes stooped to examine a landslide of files by his feet. They appeared to contain archives of letters and personal papers.

"Joseph Maugham?" I prompted a moment later, when it seemed he had decided not to elaborate. "You think he might have something to do with it?"

"I do not wish to hurry to conclusions, Watson. I'll need to speak with him. I'll need to speak with them all. One thing is clear, however. I'm convinced you were right about the means of death. There's foul play there."

Somehow, those words filled me with a terrible sense of foreboding.

I watched as Holmes set about examining the lock on the writing bureau, studiously ignoring the raft of personal papers it contained. He did not appear to be looking for evidence of the will itself. In that, it seemed, he was satisfied to take the word of the family. Personally, I wondered if they had not simply misplaced the document amongst the chaotic mess they'd created in their haste to retrieve it. I wondered if the solicitor, Tobias Edwards, had also been involved in the search.

Holmes, evidently finished with the lock, crossed to the fireplace and snatched up a poker from the metal bucket. He used it to stir the remnants of a fire in the grate, turning over the cold ashes.

He knelt down by the hearth and reached in, rubbing a pinch of the ash between his thumb and forefinger. He sniffed it, and then stood again, wiping his fingers on a white handkerchief that he withdrew from his pocket.

Finally, clearly deciding he had seen enough, he came to stand beside me once again.

"Well?" I asked, anxious to hear his conclusions.

"I think it's time we paid a visit to the office of Mr. Tobias Edwards," said Holmes, neatly side-stepping my question. "I should very much like to hear his account of the events leading up to his discovery that the will was missing, and the details of what he knew it to contain." He paused, tapping the index finger of his right hand upon his chin. "Not to mention his explanation as to why he had no copy of the document in his possession."

"Very well," I said, "I shall speak to Mrs. Hawthorn and make enquiries as to his address."

Holmes shook his head. "No need, my dear Doctor. I believe you will find he maintains his office in the suite of rooms above a bookshop at 112 Charing Cross Road."

I admit I was quite taken aback by the boldness of this statement. "Holmes, once again you astound me."

"One makes it one's business to know the address of London solicitors, Watson. And besides, it's a very good bookshop."

"You old devil, Holmes," I said, laughing. "Come on. Let's

away." And with that, we left the austere, faded home of the late Sir Theobald, and set off in search of a cab to take us to Charing Cross Road.

CHAPTER FIVE

Holmes, of course, had been right about the location of Tobias Edwards' office. It was a relatively small set of rooms above what I took to be a reasonably busy esoteric bookshop, selling – I gathered from a quick glance in the window – a rum variety of occult grimoires, pagan treatises and astrological almanacs. I decided to afford the place a wide berth.

The firm, known as *Barker, Smith & Edwards*, appeared to employ at least three other people: a secretary and two further solicitors, each with their own, modestly sized offices. I assumed these to be the titular Barker and Smith, whose names adorned the plaque alongside Edwards' on the street door below.

The secretary was a tall, softly spoken man in his mid-twenties, with a willowy, pale look about him. He glanced up from his desk as we entered, offering us a thin smile. "Good day, gentlemen," he said, placing his pen neatly in the inkwell and standing. "How may I be of assistance?"

"We're here to speak with Mr. Tobias Edwards," said Holmes, matter-of-factly.

"And you are…?"

"Sherlock Holmes," replied Holmes, glancing dismissively out of the window at the busy street below.

"Ah," said the man, coming round from behind his desk. "If you would like to follow me, gentlemen, I shall show you directly to his office."

I grinned at Holmes as I fell in behind him. Upon hearing Holmes's name the secretary had not so much as hesitated, or thought to question us as to the nature of our visit. It was almost as if Sir Theobald's solicitor had told him to expect us. Either that, or Holmes's reputation had yet again preceded him.

Edwards himself was sitting behind a large mahogany desk and he stood to greet us, beckoning us in. He was a severe-looking man, with a hard stare and raven-black hair, which he wore swept back from his forehead. He was thin, about six feet tall, and had a smouldering pipe clamped between his teeth. His complexion was pale, and his eyes were red-rimmed through, I presumed, tiredness. I placed him at around forty years of age. I noticed he was missing three fingers on his left hand.

The office itself was sumptuously appointed, with two Chesterfields, a drinks cabinet, a safe and a portrait hanging on the wall behind the desk. The man in the picture bore the same severe expression as Edwards and was standing in the foreground of an impressive landscape, on the banks of a river.

Holmes removed his hat, and we both took a seat.

"I must say, Mr. Holmes, what a pleasure it is to make your acquaintance," said Edwards, with surprisingly upper-class inflection. "And you, of course, Dr. Watson," he added quickly, as if as an afterthought. Holmes flashed me an amused smile. "Would either of you care for a drink?"

"No, thank you, Mr. Edwards," said Holmes, with a dismissive wave of his hand. "I wish to ask you some questions regarding the late Sir Theobald Maugham, if it is convenient."

"I've been expecting your call," said Edwards. "I received a visit from Peter Maugham this morning and I was cheered to hear he'd set you on the trail of his uncle's missing will. It is such a sad state of affairs." He averted his eyes. He seemed quite stricken with grief.

"Then you knew Sir Theobald well?" I asked.

"Well enough to call him a friend, Dr. Watson. I should think he might have said the same of me. As unlikely as it seems, the two of us had forged a strong bond over the course of the last two years." His voice cracked as he spoke, and I felt a deep sympathy for the man. He seemed genuinely affected by the loss of his client, unlike Peter Maugham who had appeared more concerned with his own situation than the death of his uncle.

Holmes paused for a moment while Edwards collected himself. "I fear I may need to try your patience a little, Mr. Edwards, by asking you to give account of what occurred that morning at Sir Theobald's house."

"Not at all, Mr. Holmes," said Edwards, with a sad smile. "I'm only too glad to be of service."

"Then pray continue," said Holmes.

"I fear there will be little I can add to the tale, Mr. Holmes, other than that which you have already heard from Peter Maugham. Nevertheless, I shall try," said Edwards, taking a sip from a glass of water before continuing.

"I arrived at the house just after ten. The whole place was in disarray. Servants were running about all over the place, and Annabel Maugham was wailing so pitifully that I barely knew what to do. Her brother had moved her to the drawing room in the hope that a stiff drink might help with her shock.

"Annabel's two cousins, Oswald and Peter, were both as pale as bedsheets, standing over Sir Theobald's corpse like lions protecting a kill. They'd covered him with a sheet and were waiting for the police. I recall feeling terribly disconcerted at the sight of the blood stains seeping through the white cotton.

"I'd only been at the house for a few minutes before Inspector Bainbridge arrived from Scotland Yard, along with a veritable army of uniformed constables. No sooner than he had arrived, order was restored. He co-opted the library and conducted brief but efficient interviews with everyone who had been at the house the previous night. He inspected the body, and then sent for the police surgeon, who arrived a short while later. He made his pronouncements and arranged for Sir Theobald to be swiftly removed to the morgue."

Edwards sighed. "I don't mind telling you, Mr. Holmes, that I was more than a little shaken up by the time Inspector Bainbridge left. Simply being in the house at that time was a dreadful strain on my nerves, but I wished to offer my support in any way I could."

"Your sense of duty does you credit, Mr. Edwards," I said.

"I had given my word to Sir Theobald that I would ensure his estate passed into the right hands upon the eventuality of his death," he went on. "There was no question that I would not have been there to see it through."

"What of the will?" prompted Holmes. "At what point in proceedings did you establish the document was missing?"

"It was Peter Maugham, I believe, who – after the police had taken his uncle's body away – urged me to retrieve the will," replied Edwards. "At his insistence I went directly to Sir Theobald's study, where I knew I should find the necessary papers. It was then that I discovered the will to be missing. I called for the others, and we searched the place from top to bottom. But the will was gone."

"There was no evidence the lock on the bureau had been tampered with?" suggested Holmes.

"No evidence whatsoever, Mr. Holmes," replied Edwards.

"As I understand it, however, the bureau was rarely locked. Sir Theobald was a trusting man. Some would say a little too trusting at times."

"Indeed," I said, glancing at Holmes. He was observing Edwards intently, reading the man's every movement and expression. I'd seen him like this before; he was summing the solicitor up, weighing the truth behind his words.

"Was the bureau locked when you went to retrieve the will, Mr. Edwards?" said Holmes.

"No," came the slightly exasperated response.

"But you do have a key?" prompted Holmes.

"Yes, I do. I keep it in the safe, just here." Edwards rose from his seat on the other side of his desk and crossed the room to where a small, stout safe sat beside a cabinet. He withdrew a ring of keys from his jacket pocket, squatted for a moment, and carefully unlocked the safe. He fumbled around inside for a few seconds, withdrew a small cream envelope and then locked the safe, before returning to his seat. "There. This is the one," he said, handing the envelope to Holmes, who folded open the unsealed flap and tipped the key out onto the surface of the desk. It clattered noisily upon the lacquered surface: a dull-coloured, ornate little thing about the size of my forefinger. I noticed the envelope, discarded by Holmes, had the legend: MAUGHAM written upon it in neat copperplate.

"I didn't have it with me when I went to the house that morning. I'd gone there directly from home, having received word from Peter Maugham as to what had occurred in the night," said Edwards, regarding Holmes, who had picked up the key and was turning it over in the palm of his left hand.

"Yet you still went to find the will," said Holmes. It was a statement of fact, rather than a question.

Nevertheless, Edwards felt the need to respond. "At the behest of my clients, yes, Mr. Holmes. I suspected the bureau would be unlocked, as I have already set out. It was."

"Were you alone, Mr. Edwards?"

Edwards bristled slightly at Holmes's question – and the potential implications behind it – but Holmes's demeanour had not changed. He was simply establishing the facts. There was no judgement in his tone.

"Yes. Until the point at which I realised the will was missing and I called for the others to join me," replied Edwards, with a shrug. I had the sense that the casualness of the gesture was somewhat affected. Clearly, he was concerned that Holmes might suggest some wrongdoing on his part; that he had not been as thorough in upholding his duties as perhaps he should have.

"Forgive me, Mr. Edwards, but is it not standard practice for a gentleman's solicitors to maintain copies of his will at their offices, in case of any such eventuality?" said Holmes, with the wrinkle of a frown. "Surely it is but a simple matter to look out the copy?"

"Indeed, Mr. Holmes, and if you care to inspect the cabinet behind you, you will see that is exactly the policy of this practice." I turned at Edwards' insistence to see a tall, glass-fronted cabinet containing row after row of neat files, each clearly labelled. "However, Sir Theobald had a mind to manage his own affairs, and engaged me only to offer legal advice. The key was the only article with which he entrusted me, in case it became necessary for me to recover the will on behalf of the family."

Holmes nodded, although his frown deepened. "Nevertheless, you knew the content of the will, I presume?"

"Quite so," said Edwards, reaching for his glass of water. "Sir Theobald's three nephews and niece – Joseph, Oswald, Peter and Annabel – were each to inherit equal amounts, one quarter of the estate's worth and a share of the property."

"There were no… irregularities?" Holmes paused, and I

admit, I could not for the life of me see what he was getting at.

"Such as…?" prompted Edwards, apparently as bemused as I.

"Names that you did not recognise or instructions that you had to query with Sir Theobald? Bequests of an unexpected nature?" said Holmes, leaning forward, as if he were beginning to lose patience with the man.

Edwards shook his head emphatically. "No, Mr. Holmes. Not at all. It was a very straightforward document, with little room for misinterpretation."

"Thank you, Mr. Edwards. Your recounting of the events has proved most useful." Holmes sat back in his chair, wearing a contemplative expression.

"I do hope so, Mr. Holmes. I wish to uphold my promise to Sir Theobald to do what is right," said Edwards, visibly relaxing now that Holmes's questions had come to an end.

"What will happen now?" I asked Edwards, anxious to clarify the consequences of the missing will.

"Unless the will can be located, the entire estate will pass into the hands of Sir Theobald's oldest living relative," said Edwards, with a shrug.

"Joseph Maugham?" I said.

"Indeed," confirmed Edwards.

I sighed. "Will he do the right thing, Mr. Edwards?"

"If you mean, Dr. Watson, will he abide by the intentions of his uncle and divide the estate – then no, I don't believe that he will. I imagine he would extend his new fortune to his sister, Miss Annabel, but Joseph is not the most… thoughtful of men. He'll care little for what becomes of his cousins." Edwards shook his head in resignation.

"Just as Peter Maugham feared," said Holmes.

"Yes. As things stand, he and Oswald stand to lose their entire inheritance," replied Edwards.

We sat in silence for a moment, as if the weight of the news lay heavy upon us all. Eventually, Holmes stood, and I took my cue, levering myself up out of the chair and straightening my jacket.

"Very well, Mr. Edwards," said Holmes. "Dr. Watson and I will take our leave. Again, my thanks."

Edwards reached out and clasped first Holmes's hand, and then my own. "Please, do not hesitate to call again if you have need. I am at your service, gentlemen. I am as anxious as the family to see this situation resolved."

"Good day, Mr. Edwards," said Holmes. "We shall speak again."

I followed Holmes out through the reception area, and then quickly down the narrow staircase and out onto the bustling street below.

The light was beginning to fade as we sought out a cab, and the air was damp and redolent of coming rain. Everywhere about us, people were hurrying home, barely taking note of one another as they bowed their heads and tramped away into the evening, or stared blankly from the windows of passing carriages.

"Well, Holmes, what next?" I asked, turning up the collar of my coat against the chill.

"Dinner, Watson, followed by a little Bach. Would you care to join me?" Holmes seemed in somewhat high spirits, which, after a moment's consideration, I concluded to be the result of his being engaged, finally, on a new and intriguing case.

"For dinner? Absolutely," I said, with gusto. "But I think I'll skip the performance, if I may?"

Holmes turned to me, grinning, as a cab slewed to a stop just before us, its wheels sending a spray of foul gutter water up over the kerb, narrowly missing my boots. "Really, Watson," he said, nodding to the driver and pulling himself up onto the footplate, "it's a most splendid concerto…" He hauled himself into the back of the cab, disappearing completely from view.

Sighing, I pulled myself up behind him, wondering once again what he was up to.

CHAPTER SIX

The following morning Holmes seemed bright and energetic, as we met once again at Baker Street with a view to spending the morning visiting each of the Maugham cousins in turn.

He'd clearly enjoyed the concerto the previous evening, for he was sitting at his dining table humming a repeating melody when I arrived. He was slicing open a heap of envelopes with his old – but dangerously sharp – dagger, slowly extracting the contents of each, and then tossing the letters aside with barely a second thought.

"Aren't you going to read those, Holmes?" I said, pulling out a chair and reaching for the coffee pot.

"What? Ah, hello, Watson! Good morning," he replied, as if he hadn't quite heard my question. He tossed another letter to the floor. I watched it flutter aimlessly, finally settling atop its fellows. The floor was covered with them, his chair a tiny island in a sea of discarded paper. All of them unread.

"I say, Holmes. Whatever are you doing? There might be something important in one of those letters," I said, frowning.

Holmes ceased his humming and glanced up at me. "What's that?"

"The letters, Holmes," I stressed. "You may wish to consider reading them?"

"Not at all, Watson. Bills, bills and more bills. All terribly commonplace. I have no time for bills. These postmarks, however, are an altogether different proposition." He held up one of the envelopes to illustrate his point, indicating the black, inky smudge over the stamp. "One might learn a great deal from the study of postmarks." He reached for another envelope, readying his dagger, and resumed his melodic humming.

Sighing, I sloshed coffee into an empty cup and sat back in my chair. Clearly, it was going to be a long morning.

A few hours later we stood on the doorstep of Oswald Maugham's residence in the drizzling rain. I'd turned my collar up in an effort to stave off the damp, and Holmes was brandishing a large black umbrella. He rapped briskly on the door.

At first I thought we'd come in vain, as the door remained decidedly shut, but just as I was about to give voice to such thoughts, I heard the muffled sounds of footsteps from inside, and suddenly the door swung open and a short, thin man peered out. He had beady, darting eyes and sand-coloured hair drawn back in a neat parting. He was wearing a black suit that was a little worse for the wear, thinning at the elbows and with a stain down one lapel. He looked up at us curiously.

"May I help you, gentlemen?" he said, unsure. His voice was thin and tremulous, but his enunciation spoke volumes about his upbringing and education.

"Mr. Oswald Maugham, I presume?" asked Holmes.

"Yes," said the man, clearly put out. He glanced back over his shoulder as if he was anxious to get back to something. "What of it?"

"My name is Mr. Sherlock Holmes," said Holmes, with as patient a tone as I had ever credited him with, "and this is my associate, Dr. Watson."

Oswald Maugham's demeanour altered almost immediately, his expression softening. He smiled, and opened the door a little wider. "Oh, I do apologise, Mr. Holmes. My cousin Peter told me to expect your call, but with everything that's been going on, I fear I've allowed myself to become somewhat distracted." He stepped aside and gestured for us to enter. "Please, do come in."

I went ahead of Holmes while he shook out his umbrella, unbuttoning my drenched overcoat and handing it gratefully to Oswald. I looked around, summing the place up.

The apartment was on the ground floor of a large terraced house – not at all the type of property one would associate with the nephew of a man as wealthy and well appointed as Sir Theobald. Compared with the rooms maintained by his cousin, Peter – which we had visited earlier that morning – Oswald's apartment seemed meagre.

Our interview with Peter Maugham had been brief, during which he had simply reiterated his account of the events surrounding his uncle's death, confirming he had indeed insisted that Tobias Edwards make haste to secure the will that morning. I had mentioned to Holmes afterwards, as we'd struck out across town to Oswald Maugham's residence, that this insistence so soon after the death of his uncle suggested to me a lack of trust amongst the cousins, and perhaps that Peter Maugham even secretly suspected one of them of wrongdoing.

Holmes, however, had been largely withdrawn since the interview, and had sat in the back of the brougham, staring out of the window in silent thought as we'd trundled through the busy streets of the metropolis.

Now, in Oswald Maugham's apartment, I could once again see the glimmer of interest in his eyes.

Oswald led us through to the sitting room, which was dominated by a large mahogany dining table, its scuffed surface covered by a vast array of chemistry equipment – bottles, rods, vials and burners – many of which formed a vast and complicated network, through which variously coloured fluids bubbled and dripped. The stench was positively sulphurous, and the noise of the liquid simmering on the still was most off-putting as we tried to talk.

"Please, forgive the state of the place," said Oswald, apologetically. "I'm something of an amateur chemist, and I've been dabbling again this morning. I live alone and tend not to receive many visitors, so think nothing of putting the dining table to what I consider to be much better use."

I could see from Holmes's expression that he agreed wholeheartedly with this sentiment. Indeed, I knew that if it were not for Mrs. Hudson or the need to keep at least one of his Baker Street rooms suitable to receive visitors, he would long ago have done the same. "It's a most impressive arrangement you have here, Mr. Maugham. I see that you do yourself a disservice. You are far more than an idle dabbler."

Oswald raised an eyebrow. "Do I take it you have an interest in chemistry, Mr. Holmes?"

"A little," replied Holmes, and I had to turn away to hide my smile.

"How excellent to meet a fellow enthusiast," said Oswald. "It's been my passion for many years."

"Indeed," agreed Holmes. "A most interesting and worthwhile pursuit. Nevertheless, I fear the reason for our call is somewhat graver, and far less savoury."

Oswald's good humour dissipated almost immediately. When

he spoke, his voice had taken on a morose timbre. "Ah, yes. Poor Uncle Theobald. I suppose you have innumerable questions for me, just like the police?"

"Perhaps," said Holmes. "But I should like to begin with your account of the events leading up to the death of your uncle."

"The party?" exclaimed Oswald, surprised.

"Just so," replied Holmes.

"Very well, but I find it difficult to understand how that might assist you in your enquiries, Mr. Holmes," said Oswald, who appeared genuinely perplexed.

"I find it essential in these circumstances to have the full picture, Mr. Maugham," said Holmes. "Sometimes even the slightest detail, often considered too trivial to mention, might help to shed light on the events that came after. If you could provide us with as full and frank account as you are able?"

"Of course," said Oswald. "Whatever I can do. Now," he gestured for us to move through to the sitting area on the other side of the room, "please take a seat, both of you."

We did as he suggested, Holmes perching on the edge of the sofa while I took a chair by the window. Oswald joined us, sitting on a tatty-looking armchair by the fire. It seemed to dwarf him somewhat, and I was reminded again how diminutive a fellow he was.

"The party was in honour of my cousin Annabel's birthday. Uncle Theobald rather doted on her, you see, and it was at his absolute insistence that we came together on the occasion to celebrate." He glanced from one of us to the other as he spoke. "Well, it was a pleasant enough affair, and we all partook in an excess of wine and sherry. Even Uncle Theobald. Annabel enjoyed being the centre of attention, even if – I suspect – the whole gesture was rather lost on her."

"How so?" prompted Holmes.

"I fear Annabel rather believes the world owes her attention," replied Oswald. "She's always been the same, ever since she was a little girl, and Uncle Theobald's intolerable doting only made matters worse. She enjoyed the party, true enough, but only in as much as she'd probably been expecting it. It wouldn't surprise me if she'd ordered a new dress for it before ever Uncle Theobald thought to organise the gathering."

Oswald gave a sudden, startled cry. "Oh, do forgive me. I've been terribly remiss. Would either of you gentlemen care for a drink?" He started to rise from his chair, and I felt a pang of sympathy for the man. Clearly, he was telling the truth when he spoke of his lack of visitors, and in his haste to relate his story had forgone the usual social niceties.

"Fear not, Mr. Maugham," I said, raising my hand to prevent him from getting up. "Do not trouble yourself. We both had tea before our cab ride."

I glanced at Holmes, who smiled and fractionally inclined his head in acknowledgement of my white lie. "Pray continue, Mr. Maugham," he said.

"Very well," said Oswald. "As I recall, Peter saw Uncle Theobald to bed at around eleven o'clock. The rest of us stayed up a while longer, drinking in the drawing room. A while later – sometime after twelve – tired, and losing patience with Annabel's self-aggrandisement, I turned in for the night."

"And that was all?" said Holmes. "Nothing else until morning, when you woke to find Sir Theobald dead?"

"Not entirely, Mr. Holmes," corrected Oswald, with a shake of his head. "I woke at the sound of a disturbance in the night: the sound of breaking glass, followed by a heavy thump. I lay there in bed for a while, listening for any sounds of movement, and when I heard a voice on the landing I climbed out of bed and went to investigate. I fully expected to find one of my drunken cousins stumbling about on their way to the lavatory."

"And yet?" prompted Holmes.

"Well, it was Uncle Theobald. He'd spilled his water, knocking the glass off the bedside table. Being the considerate old fellow he was, he'd chosen not to wake Agnes – the maid – and was about to tackle the stairs to fetch himself another. Of course I stopped him and sent him straight back to bed. He was complaining of dizziness, and I didn't want him taking a fall." Oswald paused for a moment, dropping his eyes. I could see he'd been deeply affected by the loss.

"Well, he listened to me, that time at least," he went on. "He returned to his room. I fetched another glass of water for my uncle myself. Then I went back to bed. The next thing I knew it was morning, and Agnes was screaming the whole house down."

Holmes nodded thoughtfully, assimilating the facts. "Most interesting, Mr. Maugham. So, let me be clear. You prevented Sir Theobald from fetching himself a fresh glass of water, sending him back to bed and bringing him one yourself?"

Oswald seemed a little unsure of the question. "Precisely so, Mr. Holmes. Is that important?"

Holmes smiled. "As I explained, Mr. Maugham, in a case such as this one, *every* detail is important, no matter how small it may seem." He rubbed his chin, studying Oswald intently. "Now, is there anything else you'd like to add? Any other details you believe I should be aware of?"

Oswald shook his head. "Not that I can think of, Mr. Holmes. I'm sure Peter has given you a full account of the events of the following morning."

"Indeed he has," said Holmes, levelly.

"To be honest, I'm still not clear exactly *what* happened in those few hours after Agnes discovered the body. It all passed in such a blur." Oswald sighed forlornly.

"Shock will do that to a man," I said. I knew this from years of experience on campaign. A man's memory can play terrible tricks on him when it's fractured by a sudden shock. The field hospitals in Afghanistan were proof of it.

"I…" Oswald started, and then trailed off.

"Go on," said Holmes, not unkindly.

"I only hope you can assist us in locating my uncle's will, Mr. Holmes," said Oswald, hesitantly. "Without it, I fear I'll be ruined."

"I believe I'll soon be able to bring matters to a satisfactory conclusion," said Holmes. His expression gave little away. "Now, if you'll excuse us, Mr. Maugham, I believe we have everything we need. At least for now." He stood, and I followed suit, beginning to wish that I had requested a warm drink, after all; the rain had started up again and was battering against the windowpane.

"Of course," said Oswald, fetching our coats from the stand in the hall. "Allow me to show you out."

We made our farewells and ventured out into the inclement weather. We huddled beneath Holmes's umbrella on the pavement as we waited for a passing cab, and I took the opportunity to pose a question which had been playing on my mind. "Did you mean what you said, Holmes? That you'll soon bring everything to a satisfactory conclusion?"

Holmes laughed, freely and loudly, and I caught a glimpse of that familiar, manic gleam in his eye as he turned to regard me. "Oh yes, Watson," he said, darkly. "I'm convinced of it. We shall have our satisfaction. Cabbie!" He called out suddenly, startling me and causing me to step backwards into a puddle. I cursed loudly as the icy water spilled into my boot.

I looked up at Holmes, thinking to admonish him for giving me such a fright, but he was already clambering up into the brougham and barking instructions to the sodden driver. Sighing, I followed my companion.

CHAPTER SEVEN

FROM THE TESTIMONY OF
INSPECTOR CHARLES BAINBRIDGE

I was dragged from my bed by a rap on the door at around six o'clock that morning. With a low groan, I pulled back the sheets and reached bleary-eyed for my dressing-gown. The house was icy cold, and I noticed with dismay that the sun had not yet begun to peek around the curtains.

Beside me, Isobel barely stirred. We'd been married for some months, and already she'd grown used to her lot in life: marriage to a policeman brought with it disturbances in the night, unsociable hours and frequent, unexpected absences.

I watched her for a moment, dreaming easily, her placid face upon the pillow. She wore the burden well. I felt a momentary pull of envy. Then the rap sounded again from the front door, more insistent this time, and I jammed my bare feet into my boots and bustled from the room, down the stairs and along the hallway in the gloaming, with only the ticking of the clock to accompany me.

With a sigh – for I anticipated the nature of the call – I slid free the bolts and pulled the door open. Cold, damp air swept in, and I stamped my feet to stave off the sudden chill.

True to my expectations, it was a uniformed man who awaited me, Constable Harris from the Yard. "Morning, sir," he said, as bright as a button.

"You could at least do me the honour of appearing a little sheepish for having dragged me from my bed at so ungodly an hour," I said, but not unkindly.

Harris grinned. "Yes, sir. Sorry, sir." He cleared his throat. "The thing is, sir, there's been an incident."

"An incident?" I echoed.

"Yes, sir. Another of these 'iron men' robberies, over in Belgravia. A house belonging to a banker named Mr. Hillingsborough. All of his wife's jewellery's gone, just like before. You're needed, sir." Harris glanced at his boots as he spoke, as if he somehow expected them to help him state his case.

"Very well, Harris," I said. "I must get over there straight away."

"Yes, sir. I have a carriage waiting," replied Harris, with a satisfied nod.

I adjusted the collar of my dressing-gown, wishing I were already dressed in my usual suit and coat. The cold was penetrating, chilling my bones. "Tell me, Harris," I said. "Was anybody hurt?"

"Well, sir, I have it on good authority that Mr. Hillingsborough took it upon himself to attempt to defend his home from the attackers, and has a lump the size of a cricket ball on the back of his head for his trouble," said Harris. He was a portly man, with bushy whiskers and red cheeks, and I knew him for his reliable cheerfulness, even in the face of such overwhelming horror as was faced almost daily by the men of the Yard. Yet now he looked serious, distracted, and I feared for what that might signify.

"But we're not looking at a murder enquiry?" I asked, perhaps a little too hopefully.

"No, sir. Not that," replied Harris. His smile returned, as if in understanding of my sudden relief. The so-called "iron men" crimes had yet to escalate to anything more serious than robbery and assault. I hoped it would stay that way, but experience told me it was only a matter of time before their *modus operandi* changed. These "iron men" – or whatever they were – would grow greedy, or else they would find themselves in the position of needing to cover their tracks. How they might respond to such eventualities remained to be seen.

Frustratingly, I had no idea what these things might be, where they had come from, or the nature of their ultimate aim. Someone had to be behind the business, pulling their strings – either literally or metaphorically – but I was damned if I'd been able to ascertain any clues as to who that might be.

I left Harris waiting in the lobby while I returned to the bedroom and dressed hurriedly in the dark; another skill swiftly perfected by a married policeman if he wished to maintain harmonious relations with his spouse.

We left a few minutes later in the police carriage, hurtling through the streets as the dawn slowly began to rise over London. By the time we reached Belgravia the city was cast in a weak half-light, and, as I clambered down from the carriage, I felt at last that I had started to regain my wits, and to cast off the last vestiges of sleep.

The house itself was just off Pimlico Road and was a suitably grand target for a robbery; three stories of exquisite townhouse in one of the most fashionable – and thus expensive – districts of London. It was well maintained, with tall sash windows and a white-painted exterior, now dulled by the constant attentions of the weather. I could see a scattering of uniformed constables guarding the entrance, deep in conversation. I glanced over my shoulder to see Harris speaking with our driver. He rapped on the side of the cab with the palm of his hand, and the carriage clattered off down the street, the horses whinnying as the driver struck their flanks with his whip. His lantern, dangling on the end of a staff like a bowed fishing rod, bobbed wildly as they bounced off into the dull morning.

"Come along, Harris," I said, impatiently, as I started towards the house. I could see that the curtains were still drawn in all the windows, but assumed the household had been fully roused by the night-time incursion. At first I thought the front door was hanging open, too, but then realised that the door itself no longer existed – or rather, the remains of it hung from the frame in splinters.

"Good Lord," I said, as I took in the extent of the damage. Harris came to stand beside me, also regarding the wreckage.

"It seems the iron men simply smashed their way into the property, sir," said Patterson, one of the other young constables I recognised. "As brazen as you like. Just battered it until it shattered, and then forced their way inside."

"That's some show of strength," said Harris, with a low whistle.

"They're growing in confidence," I muttered, concerned by where such boldness might lead. Perhaps they had already begun to escalate matters.

I stepped over the threshold, using the edge of my boot to push aside fragments of painted wood that still lay scattered upon the marble floor of the hallway. The door had once been a glossy, regal blue. There was barely any of it left intact.

The hall itself was narrow but grand, and seemed mostly in order; aside, that is, from a mahogany walking stick which lay on the floor, and a tall vase of dried flowers that had been overturned and shattered, the debris from which had been gathered into a neat pile but not yet cleared away. There was a faint tang of oil and steam in the air, such as one might encounter on a railway platform.

The butler, a pale-looking fellow in his late fifties, dressed in an immaculate black suit, his balding pate gleaming in the lamplight, was standing at the bottom of the stairs. He looked up as I entered. "Inspector Charles Bainbridge," I said, by way of introduction.

"Ah. Yes, sir. Peters, sir," he replied in a dolorous voice that nevertheless quavered slightly as he spoke. Understandably, the man was still quite shaken from his ordeal, but he was doing his best to maintain a stoic facade. "Here to assist you in any way I can," he finished.

"Thank you, Peters," I said. "I may need to interview you, but first, I think, I should like to talk to the family. Would that be possible?"

"Yes, sir," said Peters, enthusiastically. "They're in the drawing room. Allow me to show you the way." I nodded and waved for Harris – who had remained in the ruined doorway, talking in a low voice with his colleagues – to join me. We followed the butler along the side of the staircase and down a passageway that led to the drawing room. He knocked briskly on the door to announce our arrival. It seemed strangely formal given the circumstances, but I understood that this was how people coped in these most desperate of circumstances, taking comfort in the familiar. He held the door open for us to enter, and then retired, returning to his silent vigil in the hall.

In the drawing room, Mrs. Hillingsborough sat beside the fire on a chaise longue, her two young children – a boy and a girl, neither older than five or six – gathered around her. She looked up as we entered and offered me a weak smile. She was a pretty woman in her early thirties, with long blonde hair and striking blue eyes. Her husband, Mr. Hillingsborough, was at least ten years her senior, and stood beside the fireplace, his arm on the mantel. He was wearing an expression of deep concentration. I noticed his left hand kept returning unconsciously to what I assumed to be the tender spot on the back of his skull.

"Good morning Mr. Hillingsborough, Mrs. Hillingsborough. My name is Inspector Charles Bainbridge of Scotland Yard. I understand you've been the victims of a most unfortunate incident during the night," I said, diplomatically.

Mrs. Hillingsborough issued a short, nervous laugh. "That seems quite an understatement, Inspector," she said, "although I imagine you probably find yourself in these sorts of situations quite frequently."

I smiled in acknowledgement, but decided to avoid being drawn into that particular conversation. "I wonder if I might speak with you regarding the events?"

"Yes, of course," said Mr. Hillingsborough, suddenly stirring into action. I was momentarily taken aback by his American accent. My untrained ear placed it as New York, but it might well have been from further afield. "Margaret, take the children to the nursery. I shall talk with the inspector."

"Very well," she said, and her relief was palpable. "Come along, children." She swept them up into her arms and hurried out of the room.

"Please, take a seat, gentlemen," said Hillingsborough. "Although I hope you won't mind if I stand. I'm still a little woozy from the blow I received to my head."

"Not at all," I replied, taking a seat in one of the most uncomfortable chairs I had ever had the displeasure to encounter. "But tell me – has anyone sent for a doctor? It would be an advisable precaution."

"Yes, yes," said Hillingsborough, with a dismissive wave of his hand. "I believe one is on the way." He had begun pacing back and forth before the fire, his hands clasped behind his back. He looked tired and gaunt. "Now, what do you need to know?"

"As full an account of the events as you can give me, Mr. Hillingsborough," I said, "including as many details as possible.

As you may or may not be aware, this attack on your property represents the latest in a series of incidents involving these so-called 'iron men'. So far, the perpetrators of these crimes have eluded us. I would be grateful for anything that might aid our investigation. Even the slightest detail might help to complete our understanding of these unusual villains."

"So you don't hold much hope of retrieving my wife's stolen jewellery?" asked Hillingsborough, levelly.

I sighed, glancing at Harris, whose face gave little away. "I'll be honest with you, Mr. Hillingsborough. I suspect it is unlikely. However, if we could get to the bottom of precisely who or what these 'iron men' are, then perhaps we'd have a hope."

"I understand," said Hillingsborough. He continued to pace before the fire, stopping occasionally to warm his hands. "This country of yours is a cold one," he said, feigning jollity.

"I'll see to it that your door is secured within the hour, sir," said Harris. Hillingsborough nodded gratefully.

"Very well then. I shall relate to you everything that I remember. The household was asleep. This was—" he glanced at his pocket watch "—two and a half hours ago." I indicated at Harris, who took out his pocket notebook and began taking down the details.

"Everything in the house was silent, and I'd been asleep for some hours when I was startled by a loud banging from downstairs, as if someone was hammering urgently on the front door. Roused from sleep, I rose from my bed to investigate. I took up a lamp and fetched my dressing-gown."

"Would it not be the role of your butler to answer such an early call?" I prompted.

"Typically, yes," replied Hillingsborough, "but the insistence with which the caller was knocking suggested that there was an emergency of some kind. And so I hurried down the stairs, only to find Peters doing the same. I called out, 'Yes, yes, we're coming!', but the thumping continued unabated. At first I thought they couldn't have heard us calling to them, but then, to my horror, one of the door panels splintered.

"I bellowed for them to desist as Peters rushed to unlatch the bolt, just as a gauntleted fist burst through the door, flailing and grasping at the air." Hillingsborough's face had taken on a haunted expression. He was staring into the distance as he recited his tale. It was as if Harris and I were no longer there.

"I called again for them to stop, but it was clear by then that we were under attack. Furthermore, it soon became clear that there was more than one assailant. Our attackers had walked right up to the front door and were brazenly battering their way inside.

"Peters and I fell back, aghast, as the door finally gave way beneath the force of the blows and we were afforded our first true glimpse of our attackers. They were metal men." Hillingsborough paused here, running a hand over his face.

"Describe them for us," I prompted, utterly engrossed in his tale.

"In every respect they seemed to jerkily mimic the form and movements of a real man: two legs, two arms, a head upon a set of square shoulders. Yet in the same breath, they were like something from a feverish dream. Their appearance was bulky and they appeared to be constructed from a series of interlocking iron plates. Two large exhaust pipes jutted from each of their backs, emitting constant gushes of white steam, which, I assumed, was the power source by which they were animated. Their faces were smooth metal plates with two menacing holes for eyes, and a thin slot for a mouth. What struck me most about them, however, were the glowing, crimson lights behind their eyes, and the impassive expressions upon their terrible, inhuman faces." Hillingsborough shuddered as he recalled the details of his horrifying ordeal.

"There were three of them. They marched noisily into the hall, stinking of machine oil and steam. They showed no concern for subtlety, nor did they appear in any way to be mindful of being captured or deterred from their goal.

"As you might expect any man to do when presented with such interlopers in his own home, I took up what arms I could – a stout wooden cane from the stand at the foot of the stairs – and made ready to defend my property.

"The metal monsters marched forward, either ignorant of our presence, or simply unconcerned by it. I went at their leader, swinging the cane wide and striking him solidly across the chest, but it rebounded from the iron plating without so much as leaving a dent, and causing me to wince in pain as my wrists absorbed the shock of the blow. The iron man did not so much as turn to regard me as he batted me away with a swipe of his left hand, hitting me hard in the ribs and sending me sprawling across the floor. Peters rushed at once to my aid and helped me, breathless, to my feet, but by then I knew we were impotent. I possessed no weapons that could defend us against such armoured brutes.

"The trio of iron men appeared to know exactly what they were about. They took to the stairs, ascending towards the first floor with so regimented an approach that they might have been marching soldiers. I shouted for Margaret to take cover, and heard her footsteps at the top of the stairs, followed by a shriek as she saw what was happening. I called to her again and she rushed immediately to gather up the children, as Peters and I cautiously followed the iron men up the stairs, unsure what else we could do."

Hillingsborough fixed me with a look of absolute sincerity. "I don't mind telling you, Inspector, that I feared then for the lives of not only myself and Peters, but for those of my wife and children. How could even I – a prize boxer in my youth – take on three men of iron? They had the run of my home, free to do whatever they wished without fear of reprisal. I was absolutely powerless.

"Thankfully," he went on, "it transpired that these metal monsters did not have murder in mind. Assuming, that is, they even have minds of their own. One thing is certain: they appeared to know the exact layout of my home. They marched directly to my wife's dressing room, where one of them began scooping up handfuls of her jewellery, throwing open drawers and tipping out their contents on the floor. I watched as he crushed a walnut box in his fist, before finding nothing of use to him inside and tossing the fragments away without a second thought.

"The remaining two iron men stationed themselves outside the door to the dressing room, keeping Peters and I at bay as their leader went about his business inside. I watched all of this unfold, unable to do anything to prevent it, frustrated and angry.

"Within minutes it had quit the room, my wife's jewellery clasped in both fists. I decided to make one last attempt to stop it, irrespective of the consequences. By this point I was so enraged by the sheer gall of these man-machines that I could see nothing but the red haze of anger before my eyes. I rushed forward and threw myself upon him, scrabbling for a ruby necklace that dangled from his metal fingers. But again the iron man simply batted me aside, bashing me hard across the back of my head and rendering me immediately unconscious.

"When I came round they had gone, and Peters had sent for the police. Margaret and one of the maids had fetched cold flannels, and the swelling on the back of my head was the size of an egg. The jewellery, or at least the valuable stuff, had all gone." Hillingsborough rubbed his bruised skull unconsciously again as he talked. He had visibly slumped as he'd recited his tale, as if the weight of his failure to defend his home was visibly bearing down upon his shoulders. Clearly it pained him greatly that he'd been unable to protect his family from this dreadful invasion.

"You did everything you could, Mr. Hillingsborough," I said, in an effort to reassure him. "You were the victim of a most terrible intrusion, and I have made it my business to get to the bottom of the matter. Tell me, did you have a sense that these iron men were being controlled in some way from afar? A remote operator?"

Hillingsborough shook his head. "I…" he faltered, and sighed. "I simply don't know, Inspector. They were so inhuman, and yet mimicked in almost every way the actions of an intelligent man. The strength of them, though, to be able to brush me aside so easily – they were far more than men."

"Quite so, sir," I agreed. In truth, Hillingsborough's tale was already familiar to me from at least three other similar incidents, where exactly the same pattern had been observed. A trio of iron men would smash their way into a home, always with apparent foreknowledge of where to find the most valuable belongings. They would take them and disappear, leaving a swathe of destruction in their wake. They had not yet, however, inflicted any serious harm on any of the inhabitants, and when they had raised their hands in violence, it had only been in response to the machines themselves coming under attack. I wasn't yet sure if this was indicative of an attitude, or simply a degree of pragmatism on the part of whoever was controlling them.

"Thank you for your most lucid account, Mr. Hillingsborough," I said. "May I take a few moments to examine the scene of the robbery?"

"Of course, Inspector," replied Hillingsborough. "Peters will show you to my wife's dressing room. I fear it is still in some disarray. Her private belongings have been exposed for all to see."

"Fear not, Mr. Hillingsborough. You and your wife can both count on my discretion," I said.

Hillingsborough inclined his head, and Harris and I both stood and left the room. Peters was waiting for us outside. He showed us upstairs, to a landing with a series of doors on either side, flanked by large potted plants, and decorated by innumerable paintings of English landscapes.

There was no sign of the struggle on the landing, but the dressing room was immediately apparent. The door was hanging off the hinges, and there was evidence of the disturbance within. I crossed the landing, stepped over the threshold and stood for a moment amongst the chaos, taking it all in. Drawers had been pulled from the chest and overturned on the floor, their contents spilled haphazardly across the carpet; brightly coloured fabrics, animal furs, scarves and underwear had been cast aside as the iron man searched for the jewellery.

"This place is a damned mess," I muttered, beneath my breath. "Harris?"

"Yes, sir?"

"Make sure you get a list of what's missing. As comprehensive as possible."

"Yes, sir."

"Mrs. Hillingsborough will be best placed to assist you in that regard, sir," said Peters, who was lingering behind Harris, clearly anxious to help in any way he could. "Allow me to take you to her now." He gestured across the landing to one of the other rooms.

I turned and nodded in agreement to Harris, and with an almost imperceptible sigh, he left with Peters.

I stood in silence amidst the ruins of the woman's private dressing chamber. I had no leads. No motive. No means of even beginning to understand who might be behind this plague of robberies and the dreadful metal monsters. Yet there and then, despite everything else, despite the numerous other matters vying for my attention, I resolved to bring an end to this reign of terror. I would find a way to stop these iron men before anyone else got hurt.

CHAPTER EIGHT

From the Testimony of Miss Annabel Maugham

My brother Joseph had always suffered from a disagreeable temperament, and recent events had inspired more than one tempestuous outburst. Despite the fact he was expected to benefit dramatically from the death of our uncle and the loss of the will, Joseph still found reason to complain. Indeed, his complaining was the least of the matter: he was given to violent episodes, during which his anger appeared to consume him utterly.

I admit I often found him terrifying during such outbursts, and more than once I'd been forced to retreat to my room and lock the door in fear that he might strike me in his rage. He would often overturn a table in a fit of pique, or dash a vase against the wall, and he would frequently injure himself, on one occasion breaking two of his fingers as he beat his fists against a wall.

It was all I could do to keep the servants from handing in their notice in the aftermath of such miserable events, and our life together at that house was far from peaceful. I longed to marry and be away from the brute, but such was the weight of his overbearing presence that I'd begun to think that any man who might show an interest in me would be dissuaded by the prospect of Joseph as a brother-in-law.

The morning we received the letter from Hans Gerber, Joseph's temper had been relatively subdued. We'd breakfasted together in the conservatory and discussed our plans for the day ahead. I'd even begun to hope that the worst of it had blown over, and with the impending funeral of Uncle Theobald, matters might be swiftly drawn to a close.

The letter, of course, put an end to such ideas. Within moments of reading it he was up out of his chair, his face reddening, his coffee cup crashing to the floor. "The goddamn gall of the man!" he bellowed, slamming his fist upon the breakfast table and sending the crockery crashing to the tiled floor.

"Calm yourself, Joseph!" I interjected hastily, attempting to calm the situation. "These wretched outbursts will get us nowhere! We need to consider –"

"Listen to me, *little sister*," he cut in, through gritted teeth. "Do you realise what's at stake? You might not feel so disposed to sit there and *consider* if you had any real concept of what we stand to lose."

My own anger flared. "I assure you, *brother*, that I understand all too well. This letter is quite clear on the matter."

"The letter is the least of it," he barked, spittle flecking his lips.

"What would you have me do, Joseph?" I asked, exasperated. "This man is a stranger to us. Before we act rashly we should send for Mr. Edwards."

"Edwards!" Joseph nearly spat the name. "What use is he? He can't even manage to look after a bloody will!"

"At the very least we need to know whether this 'Hans Gerber' has a legitimate claim on our money," I said, trying to keep my tone calm.

Joseph lashed out, toppling a nearby aspidistra. There was a loud crack as the pot shattered, and soil spilled out across the tiles. "How *dare* he! The gall of the fellow! He doesn't know us. He isn't part of this family. No matter what he says in his letter."

"I know that, Joseph," I said, soothingly. "I know that."

"He wouldn't have a leg to stand on if Edwards hadn't lost that will. He should be liable." He flopped back into his chair, his rage beginning to dissipate.

"There's still time," I said. "This could still work out. For all of us. And if it doesn't, well, the loss of that will could be good for us too, Joseph. For you and I."

"Not if this Gerber has anything to do with it," he said, morosely.

There was a loud rap at the door. I knew the servants would have made themselves scarce at the first sounds of Joseph's outburst, and so I stood to answer it.

"Tell them to go away, Annabel," said Joseph. "Whoever it is. I can't face anyone now."

"Very well," I said.

At the door I discovered a portly, smartly dressed man in a bowler hat, accompanied by a tall, gaunt man with a hooked, equine nose.

"Miss Annabel Maugham?" enquired the latter, studying me with bright, intelligent eyes.

"Yes?" I replied, a little flustered. I had no idea who these people were, or for what reason they might be calling. I didn't wish to anger Joseph any further by lingering on the doorstep.

"I see that we've called at a difficult time, Miss Maugham, but I would appreciate a short interview. My name is Mr. Sherlock Holmes, and this is my associate, Dr. Watson. Your cousin Peter has engaged our services on behalf of the family, and I would speak to you regarding the death of your uncle, Sir Theobald." Mr. Holmes smiled genially. "I assure you, it won't take very long."

"Well, I suppose you'd better come in," I said. "But I warn you, it's not a good time." I stood back, holding the door open and ushering them in. Dr. Watson removed his hat, and they followed me through to the sitting room, which adjoined the conservatory at the rear of the house.

"Joseph?" I called to him, knowing he'd be unhappy about this unannounced intrusion. "I think you should join us through here."

"Didn't you listen to me, Annabel?" came his hasty – and rather fiery – response.

Dr. Watson gave Holmes an embarrassed look.

"Excuse me, gentlemen," I said, my face burning. I walked hurriedly through to the conservatory, pulling the door shut behind me. "No, Joseph," I said in a strained whisper. "It's that detective fellow, Mr. Sherlock Holmes. He has Dr. Watson with him. Peter sent them round to talk to us about Uncle Theobald."

"What? Oh, very well. If we must," he replied, scowling. He pulled himself up out of his chair, kicking at the shattered remains of the plant pot near his feet.

"Mind your temper, Joseph," I said, as I led the way back to the sitting room with some trepidation. "And mind your words, too."

All I wanted was to get the interview over and done with as quickly as possible, and get the detective out of our house before Joseph said or did something we both might regret. And yet I admit that a part of me was intrigued to learn what Mr. Holmes had discovered in the course of his investigation, and exactly what he might make of the letter we'd received from the mysterious Mr. Hans Gerber.

CHAPTER NINE

Upon our arrival at the home of Joseph and Annabel Maugham it was immediately clear that there had been a disagreement. The tension was palpable, and I glanced at Holmes, wondering for a moment if we might not be better served by retreating with a view to recommencing our interview the following day under more salubrious circumstances.

Holmes, of course, was having none of it. There was a case to be solved, and he was damned if he was going to let a familial argument get in the way of his investigation. Indeed, I imagined he was reading great significance into the situation, filing it all away for later consideration as he followed Miss Maugham into the sitting room, his jaw set firm, his eyes narrowed.

I was aware the fact the two siblings had been at loggerheads might simply have been a symptom of the acute grief they were suffering following the death of their uncle, but I also anticipated Holmes's alternate train of thought – that perhaps there was some other, related cause for their disagreement. Getting to the bottom of what that might be, of course, was another matter altogether.

We stood in the sitting room for a few moments while Miss Maugham went to fetch her brother from the conservatory. It was decorated in an austere fashion, which to me suggested impeccable taste on behalf of the young lady. It was, however, clear that she suffered from inadequate means by which to properly do it justice: the furnishings were unusually sparse, with very little in the way of vases, candelabras, picture frames and the like.

The woman herself seemed amiable enough, although it was clear from the strained look on her face when she answered the door that she wished for nothing more than Holmes and I to leave. I could hear her arguing with her brother in hushed tones through the adjoining doors, although it was difficult to catch more than a few words. A moment later, a big man came barrelling into the sitting room, his face like thunder.

"Mr. Holmes, Dr. Watson, this is my brother, Joseph," said Miss Maugham hurriedly, darting into the room behind her brother. He was tall and broad, with dark hair brushed back in a parting, and striking blue eyes.

"Good day to you, Mr. Maugham," I said.

"Thank you for making time to talk to us," said Holmes. "I understand these are distressing times."

"I fear that is a grave understatement, Mr. Holmes," said Joseph, with a scowl.

"Indeed?" prompted Holmes.

"We're in receipt of a letter, Mr. Holmes," replied Annabel, when it appeared Joseph was not going to respond. "It came this morning, addressed to me. Its contents place us in a rather precarious position."

"I'm most sorry to hear that," said Holmes. Miss Maugham waved us to the sofa, and we both took a seat. Joseph remained standing. "If there is anything I can do to be of assistance, please do not hesitate to ask. After all, I have been engaged by your cousin on behalf of your family…"

"Peter?" spat Joseph, angrily. "His thoughts are not for the family, Mr. Holmes, but only for himself."

"Joseph!" admonished Miss Maugham. "Peter is as distraught as the rest of us over Uncle Theobald's death."

"But particularly over the loss of the will. You know he blames me, Mr. Holmes? He might say otherwise, but he's intimated as much. He thinks I took the ruddy thing to steal his inheritance." I noticed Joseph was clenching his fists by his sides in barely contained frustration.

"And did you, Mr. Maugham?" asked Holmes, levelly.

The result was like lighting a touch paper. Joseph Maugham's face flushed red, and he took a step towards Holmes, raising one of his fists. "I most certainly did not!" he barked. He glowered at Holmes, and I feared any further questioning would result in a violent rebuttal.

Apparently seeing this too, Miss Maugham stepped forward and placed a restraining hand on Joseph's arm. "I think, Mr. Holmes," she said, deftly changing the subject, "that it's best if you examine this letter. It may be pertinent to the matter in hand, and it would offer me some comfort to know that a man of your keen intelligence had looked it over."

She produced the document and passed it to Holmes. He accepted it with a slight inclination of his head, and then turned his attention to examining the handwriting upon the cream-coloured envelope, the postmark and the notepaper within. He did this for a full minute, while we all looked on in silence. Then, clearing his throat, he began to read out loud:

Dear Miss Annabel Maugham,
It is not without considerable sadness that I write to you this day. Having been made aware of the news of my uncle's death

– our uncle's death – in the obituary pages of *The Times*, I nevertheless felt compelled to reach for my pen.

It has been many years since Sir Theobald shamefully cast out his sister, my mother Frances, forcing her into a life of near-poverty. She never forgave him for this slight, and for abandoning her in such a way, simply for following her heart. She carried that sense of abandonment to the grave.

However, I now feel it is appropriate, upon the occasion of Sir Theobald's passing, that the two halves of our family make reparations and are finally reconciled. As the oldest living nephew of Sir Theobald, I understand that it falls upon me to take on the upkeep of his not inconsiderable estate, and to manage the sizeable inheritance that comes with it. I shall therefore make haste to London at once to see to all of the necessary arrangements.

You may expect a call from me presently.

Yours,

Mr. Hans Gerber

Holmes folded the letter and returned it to the envelope. He passed it back to Miss Maugham, who was looking to him expectantly.

"Good grief," I muttered, under my breath. The gall of this fellow was quite exceptional, whatever the truth behind his claim.

"How dare he!" exclaimed Joseph, his temper flaring once again, this time – I felt – with good cause.

"So this Gerber chap is actually your cousin?" I asked.

"He is no cousin of mine!" snapped Joseph.

"Yet what he says is true," admitted Miss Maugham. "My uncle did have a sister named Frances, although he never spoke of her. She was disinherited many, many years ago for secretly marrying a German salesman. My uncle – as then head of the family – felt it was his duty to cast her out for marrying beneath her station, as much as I believe it pained him to do so." She sighed. "This, of course, was before Joseph and I were born, when Frances was still a young woman and before our father was killed abroad. We knew that Frances and Mr. Gerber had indeed had a son, but that is all. If Uncle Theobald knew any more than that, he kept it from us."

"And now this! He picks his time to introduce himself. Like a vulture circling the corpse of his dead relative." Joseph finally dropped into a chair, as if the fight had left him.

"As you can see, gentlemen, the contents of this letter have us deeply concerned," continued Miss Maugham.

"Have you consulted your solicitor on the matter?" asked Holmes.

"Not yet," replied Miss Maugham. "It was received a mere half an hour before your arrival, Mr. Holmes."

"Then I suggest you contact Mr. Edwards directly. He needs to be made aware of Mr. Gerber's claim, so that he may advise you on the appropriate course of action. I am sure he'll be able to offer you some comfort," said my friend.

"Thank you, Mr. Holmes," said Miss Maugham.

"Tell me, Mr. Maugham. Do you believe this man's claim to be related to the sudden disappearance of your uncle's will?" asked Holmes, leaning forward in his chair.

"I cannot say. Yet it seems too much of a coincidence not to be," replied Joseph, with a shrug.

"Quite so," said Holmes.

"So you think it to be the case, too?" prompted Miss Maugham.

"I believe it bears further investigation, Miss Maugham," he replied. "I should very much like to meet this Hans Gerber."

"As would I, Mr. Holmes," said Joseph, darkly. "As would I." The inference was not lost on me.

"I can see, Mr. Maugham, that today's events have greatly

disturbed you," said Holmes. "Dr. Watson and I will take our leave so that you may consult Mr. Edwards. I trust that we may call again at a more suitable time?"

"Of course, Mr. Holmes. And once again – thank you," said Miss Maugham. She started to rise from her chair, but I put a hand out to stop her.

"Oh no, don't get up, Miss Maugham. We'll see ourselves out," I said.

"Thank you, Dr. Watson. And good day," she replied, with a weak smile.

"Good day to you both," I said, accompanying Holmes into the hall, where we gathered our coats and hats, and took our leave.

By this point I was anxious to discuss this most unusual new development with Holmes, to discover what he made of this Mr. Hans Gerber, but frustratingly he seemed unwilling to open up, despite my questions. The letter had obviously given him much to consider, and he claimed he needed to retreat to Baker Street to think. I knew this for the euphemism it was. He intended to lose himself in a drug-induced fug, to retreat inside his own skull in search of answers. I could not be party to that.

With a heavy heart I dropped Holmes at Baker Street and took a cab home so that I might spend the afternoon reviewing my patients' notes. I hoped the following day would bring with it some answers. In the event, I was soon to discover, it would bring only more questions.

CHAPTER TEN

I rose early the next day to attend the funeral of Sir Theobald Maugham. Holmes, restless, had set his mind on remaining at Baker Street to continue his research into the history of the Maugham family, as well as the mysterious "Hans Gerber" character whose letter we had come across the previous day.

It was at times such as these that I had learned to stay out of his way. There was little I could do while he had his nose buried in notebooks and files of newspaper clippings, and experience warned me I'd likely find myself frustrated by his persistent silence and misuse of chemical stimulants.

Holmes knew this too, of course, and so dispatched me to Sir Theobald Maugham's funeral to both pay our respects and to keep an eye on the interactions of the cousins. Of course, it was not like Holmes to be truly altruistic; I knew that he also wished to get rid of me so that he might concentrate on his work without distraction.

So it was that I found myself standing on the side lines of what transpired to be a rather intimate family affair, far smaller and quieter than I had expected for such a venerable old man as Sir Theobald.

It was a miserable morning to be buried. The graveyard was veiled in a thin, wispy mist, and rain lashed the headstones, turning the soft loam into a sticky morass beneath my boots. Birds crowed forlornly from the jagged treetops, as if heckling the sodden vicar, who stood beside the grave, giving forth his sermon in a low, sonorous voice. My mind wandered, and I imagined shapes hulking in the mist, watching the small, quiet assembly as they lowered one of their own into the earth.

It would soon transpire that those shapes were not only born of my imagination, however.

The family hardly spoke to one another. Annabel and Joseph Maugham stood apart from the others, their faces hidden behind the angle of their umbrellas. Peter Maugham stood beside his cousin, Oswald, in silent vigil. Behind them, a small gathering of servants and friends of the late Sir Theobald filled out the ranks of mourners, stark silhouettes in black suits and long veils.

Tobias Edwards, the solicitor, stood alongside me, well back from the others. He was wearing a heavy woollen overcoat, similar to my own, and a wide-brimmed bowler hat, from which the rain ran in a steady cascade, pattering upon his shoulders.

"A rather poor show for the old man, isn't it?" he said, with a heavy sigh.

"I must say, I did expect more people," I replied. "I'd have thought a man of such standing would have attracted a greater turnout, despite the rain."

"Sir Theobald was a lonely old man, Dr. Watson. He had no one, save for his servants and the ungrateful children of his late siblings," said Edwards, regretfully.

"And you, of course, Mr. Edwards," I countered, stamping my feet in an effort to stave off the cold.

"Well, yes. I suppose you're right. Not that it's done him much good," said Edwards.

"Then you know of the claims of this Gerber chap, of the letter he sent to Miss Annabel?" I prompted.

Edwards turned away from the graveside to glance at me. I could tell from his expression that the subject was weighing heavily upon his mind. "Not only Annabel, Doctor," he said, wearily. "Peter, Oswald and Joseph have now received letters of their own. They informed me of the fact before the service. I fear, Dr. Watson, that Mr. Gerber intends to press the matter."

I stared at him for a moment, appalled. "Good grief. I judge from your tone that you're convinced Gerber has a real claim on the estate?"

"I fear so, if he can prove his identity and his lineage to Sir Theobald. His birth, of course, is a matter of record. I received a letter from Gerber myself this very morning, asserting his claim. I fear there is very little anyone can do to disprove it." He shrugged, but his face betrayed his frustration.

I shook my head, incredulous at the audacity of this Gerber fellow. "And you'd never even heard of the man until now?"

"Indeed not. There was no provision for him in Sir Theobald's will, and he was never mentioned during the many occasions upon which we discussed such matters," confirmed Edwards.

"But still you think the man might have a claim?" I asked.

"Without the will, Dr. Watson…" Edwards trailed off, as if to underline his point. "If Gerber can prove he is Sir Theobald's oldest living relative, there is no argument to be had. As things currently stand he'll inherit everything. The entire estate."

"What of the others? Of their allowances?" I knew from listening to Peter Maugham what dire circumstances the surviving Maughams faced if the situation could not be satisfactorily resolved.

Edwards shook his head. "Mr. Gerber will be under no

obligation to honour such arrangements."

"Then they shall be ruined, unless he can be reasoned with," I said.

"That will be no easy task, Doctor," replied Edwards. "Mr. Gerber has yet to show himself, and has not provided any address. I had thought we might see him here today, but it seems not."

"Happy enough to take his uncle's money, it seems, but doesn't deem it necessary to attend the man's funeral," I muttered, in disgust.

"Ours is not to judge, Doctor," said Edwards, quietly. He turned to regard the assembled family, and I realised the service had come to an end whilst we'd been talking.

"Well, I see that things are being drawn to a conclusion here," said Edwards. "I shall be on my way. Good day to you, Dr. Watson. I am sure we shall speak again shortly."

"Good day, Mr. Edwards. I imagine Holmes will be in touch to enquire after this letter you've received," I said, by way of forewarning.

"By all means," replied Edwards, before turning and trudging away across the muddy graveyard.

By this time the mourners had begun to drift away in small clusters, disappearing slowly into the enveloping mist. It was then, just as I was about to leave in search of a hansom, a pipe and a hot drink, that I caught sight of a lone figure, wreathed in mist and standing beneath the cover of a large tree about fifty feet from the graveside. He – for I presumed from the height and build it was a man – was wearing a black woollen overcoat and top hat, the brim of which was pulled down low so as to obscure his face from view. When he saw me looking, the man reached up and touched the brim of his hat in acknowledgement. I wondered how long he had been lurking there on the periphery, hidden by the mist. Had he been present for the funeral proceedings? Were the family aware of his presence?

Tobias Edwards' words of a few moments earlier came back to me, then. The solicitor had expected Hans Gerber to be in attendance. It was a reasonable enough assertion. Was this man, then, the same man who had written those letters? Was this lurking figure the long-lost nephew of Sir Theobald Maugham, come to claim his fortune?

Unsure what else to do, but unwilling to miss this opportunity to confront the man, I started towards him. The figure, as if startled by this new development, turned and strode away into the mist, disappearing from view.

Unperturbed, I pressed on, thinking I could catch up with the man. I picked up my pace, jogging across the sodden graveyard, my boots squelching in the sticky turf. The rain was still pelting down from the heavens, drenching my clothes and obscuring my vision, but still I pressed on, intent on my goal.

Within moments I had crossed the graveyard and reached the tree beneath which the man had been standing. I set off in pursuit, taking the path I had seen him take through the foliage, but there was no sign of him, and in the thickening fog and inclement weather my luck was out. Frustrated, I paused, listening for the sound of his footsteps on the wet earth, but alas, he was gone. I knew it would be hopeless to pursue him any further, and so, with a heavy heart, I quit the graveyard.

Within minutes I was ensconced in my waiting cab and rattling home towards Baker Street, dripping wet and convinced that I'd just caught my first glance of the elusive Mr. Hans Gerber.

CHAPTER ELEVEN

When I arrived at Baker Street an hour later, I found Holmes sitting contemplatively in his armchair before the fire, puffing away on his pipe. He seemed lost in thought, and barely acknowledged me as I divested myself of my overcoat and poured myself a large measure of whisky. Within a few moments I had deposited myself in the chair opposite him to dry off by the grate. My clothes were sodden, and my collar stuck uncomfortably to the back of my neck. The warmth of the crackling fire was most welcome, however, and I sunk into the chair's embrace with a heartfelt sigh.

Holmes seemed hardly to have moved since I'd seen him last, late the previous evening. I wondered if he'd even eaten; a tray of untouched food on the sideboard suggested he had not. It was times such as this that I felt considerable sympathy for Mrs. Hudson, who had clearly gone to a great deal of effort to prepare a meal for Holmes, only to have her endeavours resolutely ignored. This had been the order of things for as long as I had known Holmes – often taking the poor woman for granted while lost in the intricacies of his investigations. He was an infuriating man to live with; both Mrs. Hudson and I could testify to that.

Holmes was presently sitting with his hands steepled upon his lap, his pipe drooping from the corner of his mouth and his head lolled back against the upright back of his chair. His eyes were closed and his breathing was regular and even. For a moment I even wondered if he hadn't drifted off to sleep, but the sudden crease of a frown upon his forehead told me he had not. He was musing on something, and no doubt he would choose to enlighten me later, when the opportunity presented itself for maximum dramatic effect.

I took a long draw of my whisky, enjoying the fiery warmth upon my palate as I swallowed it down, and then, unsure what else I should do in the face of such apparent apathy at my arrival, I took up Holmes's discarded copy of the *Evening Standard* from the table.

It was only by doing so that I became aware of the new events that had transpired in the other matter that still played somewhat on my conscience – the case of the "iron men" and their on-going campaign of criminal activity across the city.

It seemed they'd been busy during the small hours of the morning – there were new reports of three burglaries at the homes of various socialites and peers, including eyewitness reports of the metal monsters forcing entry into a house in Belgravia by simply smashing down the door and marching inside.

The descriptions of the machines were almost identical to those given previously: the things took the form of a man, but were bulky and sheathed entirely in iron plating. Their eyes glowed crimson in the gloom as they came out of nowhere, clanking and stomping, making no attempt at stealth. It was almost as if they wanted to draw attention to themselves, or perhaps simply that their creator – tucked up somewhere safely at home, with no means of being associated with the crimes – was so confident in his inventions that he did not concern himself with thoughts of failure.

Indeed, as I read on I learned that a footman in the home of Sir Marshall Hargreaves had attempted to take on one of the intruders with a wooden hockey stick belonging to one of the daughters of the house. It seems his efforts were to no avail, as the metal man simply shrugged off the attack, and the footman was left with nothing but a painful wrist injury caused by the vibration of the wood as he'd struck the villain. In this particular instance, the iron men had marched straight into the dressing room of Lady Hargreaves and had made off with her diamonds before the police had even been alerted to the incident.

I marvelled at the audacity of whoever was behind this campaign of terror. Clearly a similar thought had occurred to Holmes, for he had circled the article in thick, black ink, underlining a handful of choice words and phrases: "form of a man", "bulky" and "diamonds". I wondered if he planned to intercede, or to offer Bainbridge his services.

Presently, however, there seemed little chance of him interceding with anything. He had not altered his posture in the slightest as I'd finished reading the article, although it was clear that he knew I was there. I decided to broach the matter with him directly. "If you're going to ignore me all evening, Holmes, I should rather head home for an early night. This bothersome weather has left me feeling damned uncomfortable." I did not attempt to disguise the note of annoyance in my voice; he had not yet deigned to so much as look at me since I'd arrived.

"What?" he murmured, distractedly. He inclined his head a fraction and regarded me through half-open lids. "You're wet, Watson. And spattered with mud. Evidently, you were ill-treated by the elements at Sir Theobald's funeral." He closed his eyes again, as if that were the end of the matter.

"Indeed," I sighed, made impatient by his games. "But what of you, Holmes?"

Holmes offered me a wry smile. "Not at all, Watson. I have taken every precaution to avoid the inclement weather."

"*Holmes*," I said, exasperated. "Did your research bear any fruit?"

"Indeed it did, Watson," he said, with a most annoying chuckle at my expense. "Indeed it did." He leaned forward in his chair, and at last it appeared as if I had his full attention. He took his pipe from the corner of his mouth and held the bowl in the palm of his right hand. "This Hans Gerber character appears to be genuine. Miss Maugham was quite correct in the details of her tale. According to my information, Gerber is the only child of Frances Maugham, Sir Theobald's disinherited sister. The man is as real as you or I, it seems."

I couldn't resist a quiet chuckle of my own. "I could perhaps have saved you some time, Holmes," I said. "I saw him today, this Gerber chap. He was at the funeral. Or at least, I'm convinced it was him. A tall chap, dressed in a thick woollen overcoat, who was lurking on the periphery, watching the funeral from afar."

Holmes stabbed the stem of his pipe in my direction, urgent now. "Did you speak with him, Watson?" I saw there was fire in his eyes. His interest was piqued.

I shook my head. "I fear not. He fled when I approached him. I gave chase, but regret to report that I lost him in the damn fog."

Holmes frowned, and took a long, thoughtful pull on his pipe. He allowed the smoke to curl from his nostrils, and for a moment his eyes glazed over and he stared away into the middle distance. Then, all of a sudden, he snapped back to attention. He turned his gaze upon me once again. "Then it was surely him," he declared, assuredly. "Who else would flee in such a way?"

"Precisely my thought," I said, containing my small grin of triumph.

"So he's in town," said Holmes. "That changes things."

"How so?" I asked, spreading my hands before the fire as I attempted to imbue them with warmth; the effects of a morning in the freezing rain had taken more of a toll on me than I'd imagined. I was feeling my age. "You fancy him for the murderer, Holmes?"

"It's a possibility, Watson, but a remote one. I rather think, however, he may have something to do with the disappearance of the will," said Holmes, somewhat cryptically.

"If only I'd been able to catch him," I said, airing my frustration.

"Fear not, Watson," said Holmes, not unkindly. "You'll have your chance yet. We shall know Hans Gerber before this case is out. Mark my words."

I nodded, reaching for my glass, only to realise it was already empty.

"Fetch another, Watson. And pull your chair closer to the fire. You must remain here until you've dried off." The sudden change in Holmes was remarkable. One minute he'd been lackadaisically resting in his chair, lost in dream-like thought, the next he had uncoiled like a spring and was up pacing the room as if suddenly charged with a bolt of lightning. He stood by the window for a moment, holding aside the curtain and staring out at the rain-drenched streets, and then he was at the door, calling for Mrs. Hudson to bring food. "Are you hungry, Watson?" he said, with a grin.

"Well… yes." I suddenly realised I'd not eaten since breakfast, and my belly was grumbling at the thought of warm food.

"Excellent! Then we shall encourage Mrs. Hudson to prepare one of her excellent meals. I'm sure she'll be delighted to oblige."

"I'm sure she will," I replied, knowingly.

Holmes had returned to pacing the room, his hands clasped behind his back.

"I see there have been further developments in the matter of these 'iron men,'" I said, proffering the newspaper.

Holmes gave a single nod of his head in acknowledgement.

"It's becoming quite an epidemic," I continued. "I wonder how Inspector Bainbridge can manage, juggling two high-profile cases at once." I eyed Holmes as he sought out his Persian slipper from beside the fire and began extracting little tufts of tobacco with which to fill his pipe. "Have you considered volunteering your services?" I ventured.

Holmes fixed me with a sharp, disapproving gaze, causing me to wince at the sudden alteration in his demeanour. Then his features softened, and he offered me a gracious smile. "No," he said, with a dismissive wave of his pipe. "No. I must remain focused on the case in hand." He balanced the pipe between his teeth and fetched a wooden spill from his dressing-gown pocket, stooping to light it from the fire. He straightened up and presented the flame to the bowl of the pipe, puffing steadily until the tobacco took. He discarded the still-burning spill into the grate. "Besides," he went on, jovially, "I have every confidence in Inspector Bainbridge. He seems like a most able chap, wouldn't you say?"

"Well, yes. I would. But nevertheless…" I stammered, unused to hearing such words of praise from Holmes, particularly for a policeman. I was quite thrown for a moment, and found myself unable to voice an objection.

"Well then. That's settled." Holmes exhaled slowly, fountains of smoke billowing from his nostrils. "Ah, and here comes the indubitable Mrs. Hudson. Let us hope it bodes well for lunch."

I sighed in exasperation, and, still feeling a trifle damp and uncomfortable, set about pouring myself another drink.

CHAPTER TWELVE

From the Testimony of
Inspector Charles Bainbridge

"Coincidence and luck, that's all it was." Lord Roth, Commissioner of the Metropolitan Police, twirled the thin, sickly, sweet-smelling cigar in his fingers and glowered across his desk. "Nothing has ever been clearer to me."

He paused, as if waiting for me to refute his statement. When I didn't, he continued. "And now this. Your lack of progress in this matter is embarrassing, Bainbridge. I may even be forced to hand the investigation to Lestrade, and you know how much that would gall me."

I bunched my fists, but forced myself to remain calm. Lord Roth was not a man renowned for his restraint, nor for keeping his thoughts on any given matter to himself.

I was clear, for example, regarding his feelings towards me – he considered me an upstart, promoted above my station despite his best efforts to the contrary. His hand had been forced by the Home Secretary, who'd been impressed by my handling of the Curzon matter, during which I'd apprehended the members of a sordid ring of prostitute murderers, including a high-ranking

Member of Parliament, Harold Curzon. The Home Secretary had seen to it that I was rewarded with a promotion to the rank of inspector, despite Roth's protests over my lack of suitability.

Consequently, Roth did everything in his power to assign me the thankless cases, the investigations no one else wanted – the crimes he deemed unsolvable or difficult. I believe he hoped to prove my inadequacy through such underhand means, in order to effect a demotion, or at least to discredit me to his superiors.

The problem for Roth, of course, was that I kept solving them. Whatever he threw at me, I bounced back and gave him the results. This was a reflection of nothing more than my sheer tenacity and willingness to roll up my sleeves and get on with the hard work – more than could be said of Roth himself, or many of the other inspectors in his employ. This is what set myself – and to some extent Lestrade – apart from those others. We got things done, despite the difficulties, and Roth detested us for it.

The iron men situation, however, was a different matter altogether. I barely knew where to start. I was floundering. Whoever was behind these crimes was not only brazen and bold, but knew how to cover their tracks. My only hope lay in the possibility that an industrialist by the name of Percival Asquith might be able to offer me a lead.

It had come to my attention that the man had called at the Yard the previous week, claiming to have been the victim of a robbery, during which four prototype automatons – or "artificial men" as he called them – had been stolen from his workshop. His complaint had been duly recorded by the desk officer, but no further action had been taken regarding the matter. Yet it seemed too much of a coincidence. I had sent word a few hours earlier that I wished to make an appointment with Asquith for later that afternoon.

"I need results, Bainbridge," said Roth, viciously stubbing out his cigar in the cut-glass ashtray on his desk. "I mean, these 'iron men' – they're the talk of London. Plaguing my sort of folk in their sleep. Take the men at my club, for instance. They can't rest. Don't know whether to barricade the doors or send their wives away to the country. They're all worried they're going to be the next target. And for goodness sake – what am I going to tell the Prime Minister, hmmm?"

I sighed inwardly. So, that was Roth's real concern. He wasn't so much concerned with apprehending the villains for the sake of upholding the law, but rather to save face amongst his peers. "Please assure them," I said, as levelly as I could, "that you have your best man on the case, and that he's giving the matter his full attention."

Roth raised both eyebrows dramatically. "Best man?" he scoffed, as I'd known he would. "Full attention? Is that so, *Inspector*? Then what of this little rebellion over the death of Sir Theobald Maugham?" He stared at me angrily for a moment. "Isn't it time you put that little *quest* of yours to bed?"

"I'm not sure that I understand, sir," I said, feigning ignorance. I knew it wasn't wise to bait him in such a manner, but at the time it felt as if it were the only way of retaining some measure of dignity.

"Of course you don't, Bainbridge," Roth said. "What I'm saying is that the matter is clearly a case of accidental death. There's no need for all this ridiculous complication. The old fool had obviously over-indulged on the claret and fell down the stairs. We've seen it all before."

"There is, of course, the missing will to consider," I said, trying – but failing – to keep the exasperation from my voice.

Roth waved a hand in a dismissive gesture. "There's nothing to it. He most likely squirrelled it away in a safe place and failed to tell anyone where to find it. You know how these old people get, absent-minded and doddery." He leaned across the desk towards me. "If that meddling amateur, Sherlock Holmes, wishes to waste his time pursuing the matter, then let him. You, however, have more serious matters to attend to. Be mindful of your priorities, Bainbridge, and your allegiance. I want an end to this iron men business within the next week."

"A week?" I echoed in disbelief.

"You heard me," replied Roth, a smile twitching at the corner of his mouth. "Otherwise I'll hand the matter to Lestrade, and you'll be back to walking the streets of Whitechapel in uniform." He reached for his cigar box. "Best place for you, in my view," he added, muttering smugly under his breath.

I fought the urge to stand up and strike the man.

"Now, leave. I have work to do," said Roth, indicating the door with a fresh cigar. He began pointedly shuffling papers on his desk.

Disheartened, frustrated and not a little angry, I left his office.

Harris was waiting for me in the hallway outside, wearing a somewhat anxious expression. "Ah, Inspector…" he said, almost as soon as he saw me.

"Yes, Harris?" I replied, wearily. I needed time to consider how I was going to resolve the iron men robberies within the next few days. Anything else would have to wait.

"You have a visitor, sir," he said.

"A visitor? Please tell me it's someone wanting to give themselves up and provide a full confession for the iron men crimes," I replied, as cheerfully as I could muster.

Harris looked at me as if I'd just escaped from a lunatic asylum. "Not exactly, sir. It's Percival Asquith, the industrialist."

"What?" I said, frowning. "He's here?"

"Yes, sir," replied Harris.

"But I only sent word this morning that I intended to call on him," I said.

"He's evidently very anxious to see you, sir," said Harris, with a grin. "He says it's to do with the iron men."

"Right," I said, feeling buoyed, and thinking that perhaps, for once, my luck had changed. "Lead on, Harris."

I followed Harris through the winding, echoing corridors of Scotland Yard. As we walked I felt my mood lifting, as if simply being in the vicinity of Roth's office was enough to cast a dark cloud over my day. Presently, we came upon a small interview room close to the main reception.

Harris held the door open for me, and I entered to find a fidgeting Percival Asquith sitting at a table. He looked up as I entered the dimly lit room, and then stood, offering his hand with a nervous smile. He was a thin, wiry man in his late thirties, dressed smartly in a black tailored suit, with a yellow silk cravat. His blond hair was foppishly long, and I noted that he had a habit of constantly brushing it out of his eyes. I decided this was probably a nervous tic, rather than a simple affectation.

I took his slender hand in my own and shook it. "Mr. Asquith," I said, pulling out a chair. "Thank you for your haste in coming here to see me. I had intended to call upon you at your home, later this afternoon."

"Ah, yes, Inspector," he replied, in a thin, reedy voice. "Your man told me as much. In truth, however, I'm just so glad to be heard that I found I couldn't wait. I hope you don't see it as an imposition. It's just that I've been anxious to give a full and proper account."

I must have been frowning, for he sighed and gave a little shrug. "Ah, I see that perhaps the matter is unrelated," he said. He looked crestfallen.

"Please, go on, Mr. Asquith," I said, lowering myself into the chair. I glanced at Harris, who was hovering by the door. "Harris, a pot of tea, I think."

Harris nodded and quickly left the room, pulling the door shut behind him.

Asquith returned to his seat and sat forward, forming a steeple with his hands. "This, Inspector Bainbridge, is my second visit to Scotland Yard in as many weeks."

"Indeed?" I asked, fully aware of the facts.

"And yet your colleagues think my situation a trifling matter, unworthy of investigation," he continued.

I admit my interest was piqued now, and although I had pressing questions for Asquith, I felt that by letting him speak, I might win his confidence and perhaps draw the best out of him. Moreover, Harris had said Asquith's visit was related to the iron men crimes, and so I hoped he might help to shed some further light. "Well, if you'd care to outline the situation for me," I said, "I'll certainly see what I can do to help."

Asquith brightened immediately. He sat back in his chair and offered me a winning smile. "Thank you, Inspector. Most satisfactory." He withdrew a silver cigarette case from his jacket pocket, popped the clasp and proffered it to me. I refused, but he withdrew one of the cigarettes and put it to his lips, lighting it with a match while I waited, patiently, for him to continue. "Well, here's the long and the short of it," he said after a moment, pluming smoke from his nostrils. "My property has been stolen, and I *must* have it back."

I was beginning to think that the two matters might be related, after all. "Go on," I prompted.

"My family, as you are no doubt aware, are industrialists of some standing," said Asquith, without a hint of irony.

"Quite so," I acknowledged.

"Since I inherited the business from my father three years ago, I have been working to establish new methods of automation, with a view to developing a machine which I might export to other businesses or private buyers throughout the Empire," he said.

"And what is the nature of this machine, Mr. Asquith?"

I asked, although I was sure I could already follow where the conversation was leading.

Asquith became animated as he talked. "It's an automaton, an artificial man, powered by a steam furnace and a series of intricate clockwork engines. I have great ambitions, Inspector, and I am very close to a breakthrough. My automata will revolutionise industry. No longer will men be forced to toil in fields, labour in factories or wait tables for others. In the future my automata will serve that function for society."

There was a polite knock at the door, followed by the appearance of Harris, bearing a tea tray. He set it down on the table, and then retired quietly to wait by the door in case I had further need of him.

"But your prototypes have been stolen?" I prompted Asquith.

Asquith's face fell. The change was remarkable – from the evangelical only moments before, to the thoroughly downhearted. "Quite so. Four of them, almost complete. They were stolen from my workshop two weeks ago, and now I fear they are being put to nefarious use. I have seen the stories of the iron men in the newspapers."

"Indeed," I said.

"You see, the truth is, Inspector," said Asquith, nervously, "I've ploughed everything I had into those machines. The whole family fortune. Without them I'm ruined. I don't even have the necessary funds to build another prototype, and the bank won't extend me a loan, not without evidence I can guarantee a return. Everything I own, everything my father built up, rests in your hands. Without those prototypes, I have no business."

"I assure you, Mr. Asquith, that I am doing everything in my power to resolve the matter of the 'iron men' as swiftly and efficiently as possible," I said, in a reassuring tone. "If I can recover your automata, I will." I paused, weighing my next question. "Tell me, Mr. Asquith – is there a way to stop them?"

"To stop them?" Asquith looked thoughtful, and then sheepish. "I think not, Inspector. The key is not in stopping the automata themselves, but the villain who is giving them instructions. Nothing short of artillery guns or other, more developed automata could stop them once they've been given a task."

I nodded. I'd anticipated as much from the many reports. "Do you have any idea who might be behind the thefts?"

Asquith shrugged. "A rival industrialist, perhaps? A criminal gang? I understand from the newspapers that my machines have so far been employed in a series of burglaries," he said, pursing his lips in disgust. "That speaks only of a stunning lack of imagination on the part of the villain. To reduce my automata to *that*…" he trailed off, shaking his head. "They're capable of so much more."

"I see it pains you enormously, Mr. Asquith," I said, in a placatory manner.

"Anything I can do, Inspector, anything at all, just ask." Asquith gave a heavy sigh. "I'll happily show you my workshops if it would prove useful, give a statement to the press – anything that helps."

"Thank you, Mr. Asquith. I'll certainly bear that in mind," I said.

"I *do* intend to speak to the press," said Asquith, fixing me with his bright, blue eyes. "It's imperative that I protect the name of my family and business, you understand. If it were to get about that these iron men belonged to me… well, the ramifications… I think it best that I address the matter directly, and explain to the public that these machines were intended only to be put to servile use, and not to be abused in such a way. I wish to make it clear," he went on, "that whoever stole these machines is misusing them."

"Very well," I sighed, already anticipating the wrath of Lord Roth, the expression on his face when he read such an article in

The Times. Nevertheless, I could not justifiably prevent the man from protesting his innocence and protecting his reputation.

"I'll be in touch, then, Mr. Asquith, as soon as I have news to report, or further need of your help," I said.

Asquith looked momentarily confused. "But Inspector – wasn't there something else? The reason for your message this morning?"

I chuckled, rising to my feet. "No, no, Mr. Asquith. I find we are entirely aligned in our concerns. I wished to question you regarding your missing automata and any possible links they might have to these notorious iron men. You answered my questions even before I asked them."

"Very good," said Asquith, standing and smoothing down the front of his jacket. "Here's my card," he said, handing me a small cream-coloured square of board. "You can usually find me at my club, if I'm not at the workshop."

I proffered my hand, and Asquith shook it vigorously. "I'm gratified to know that my case is finally being heard, Inspector Bainbridge. Thank you."

Harris opened the door and ushered Asquith through. "I'll show you out, sir," he said, leading Asquith away down the passage.

When they'd gone I let out a heartfelt sigh and withdrew my pocket watch from my waistcoat. It was approaching five o'clock. Not long, then, until I could unburden myself to Lestrade over a brandy. The thought was cheering, despite the knowledge that, in his office, Roth was most likely checking his own pocket watch, waiting for his opportunity to make his point and send me back to the old Whitechapel beat from whence I'd come.

I hoped I wouldn't be able to give him the satisfaction.

CHAPTER THIRTEEN

FROM THE TESTIMONY OF MISS ANNABEL MAUGHAM

It was early evening, but the light was already beginning to fade and I'd drawn the curtains to keep the warmth from escaping. Joseph was in town on business – although on what business, I could not testify. He revealed very little to me regarding his comings and goings, and I had long ago learned that if I wished to maintain a relatively peaceful existence, I should not provoke him by enquiring.

Consequently, I had eaten a light meal of pea soup and, trying to place aside my concerns over my present situation – although I admit I remained somewhat preoccupied by considerations of a financial nature – I had taken up my knitting needles and planned to spend the evening in quiet contemplation before the fire.

It was a shock to me, therefore, when, at around seven o'clock, there was a brisk rap at the front door. I heard Martha, our housemaid, run quickly to answer it.

"Is that you, Joseph?" I called, sighing. "Have you forgotten your key again?" I didn't expect a response, and so, a little exasperated, I placed my knitting on the arm of my chair and rose stiffly, stretching my aching back. I hurried down the hall, beckoning for Martha to move out of the way.

"I don't know, Jo –" I stopped short at the sight of an unfamiliar man, standing before me in the doorway. He was wearing a long black overcoat – a little threadbare around the elbows – with a wide-brimmed hat pulled down low over his face. He had an imposing, hook-shaped nose, a wiry moustache and green eyes that gleamed in the fading light. "Oh, I do apologise," I said, attempting to recover from the surprise. "I wasn't expecting any callers. How may I help you?"

The stranger smiled gregariously. "Good evening, Miss Maugham," he said, in a thick German accent. "My name is Mr. Hans Gerber." He studied my face, as if searching for my reaction. I remained outwardly calm, although inside I felt my stomach lurch. So, this was the mysterious Hans Gerber, the man who would steal my inheritance. He had quite a nerve, to come to my door in such a manner. "May I come in?" he asked, taking a step towards me, as if expecting me to make way.

"Well, I…" I said, unsure for a moment on the best course of action. There was a part of me that wished to discover more about this mysterious man, to question him on the nature of his claim, to challenge him, even, on his temerity. Here, before me, was the man who had threatened to ruin my cousins, Joseph and myself as an act of revenge against a slight carried out by a prior generation. I wondered if perhaps I might even be able to reason with the man, to make him see what he was doing, and discuss whether we might be able to reach some sort of compromise. After all, Uncle Theobald had been a rich man, and there was plenty of money to go around. Perhaps if he were to understand the implications of his actions, he might be better disposed towards a mutually satisfying solution.

My good sense told me, however, that I should not risk

allowing such a man – a stranger who might well wish me ill – into my home whilst I was without a chaperone. And besides, his business was as much with Joseph, and I could not speak on my brother's behalf.

I made my decision, and remained resolutely where I was standing, blocking the doorway. "I think perhaps you should call again, Mr. Gerber, when my brother is at home. It would be improper for me to invite you in while he is out on business. I am sure whatever you have come to say would be best heard by the both of us."

Gerber grinned. "Come now, Miss Maugham," he said, his tone slightly threatening. "We are, after all, family."

I felt my ire rising. "I assure you, Mr. Gerber, you are no family of mine." I began to close the door, but he caught it with his boot, forcing it open. I almost screamed in frustration, wishing I were stronger. "You are not welcome here," I said firmly. When this didn't seem to move him, I offered him a warning. "My brother will be back from town shortly."

"Ah. Excellent. Then perhaps I could wait?" he said, as if none of the unpleasantness of the last few moments had occurred. "I come only to discuss certain arrangements with you, Miss Maugham, regarding the future of my estate."

I could hardly believe the sheer audacity of the man. "Of *your* estate, Mr. Gerber!"

"Quite so, Miss Maugham. Within a matter of days I shall be taking up residence at Sir Theobald's house," he said, matter-of-factly. "I came here to discuss the return of your belongings. I understand you kept a room at the house?" He looked at me expectantly, and I nodded in confirmation. I found I was unable to speak for the sheer anger blossoming inside of me. "Such a room, of course, shall no longer be required," he went on. "Arrangements will need to be made for you to collect anything you wish to keep."

"How *dare* you," I said, sharply, flicking out my wrist and striking him hard across the cheek with the flat of my hand. He reeled back, his hand going to his face, and I felt a surge of panic. I'd struck out without thinking, driven by his audacity and rudeness. Now, I feared retaliation.

"Now, Miss Maugham!" he said, quietly. "There is no need for such unpleasantness. I have every intention of being reasonable about this. A week, at least, before you need to remove your things. Plenty of time to make the necessary arrangements."

"Reasonable!" I bellowed in disbelief. "*Reasonable*! You have some nerve, Mr. Gerber. I'll give you that. You wait until Joseph hears about this!"

"Excellent," replied Gerber, calmly. He was smiling again, my earlier assault on him already forgotten. "Your brother will no doubt be able to make all of the necessary arrangements." He stepped back, releasing the door.

"Goodnight to you, Mr. Gerber," I said, fighting back tears of frustration. "Do not come here again."

I slammed the door violently and hurriedly turned the key in the lock.

I waited until I heard his footsteps receding down the garden path as he strode off into the evening, and then slumped back against the wall. The sobs came in fitful, gasping bursts. Martha, who had been loitering in the hallway, ready to offer her assistance, came rushing to my side, but I batted her aside in embarrassment.

All of my life I had known security and safety, and I had always known that, when my uncle finally passed on, I would become a woman of independent means.

Hans Gerber was going to ruin everything. He was going to spoil all my plans, all my hopes for the future. That odious wretch who called himself my cousin was about to destroy everything I'd dreamed of, and I was powerless to stop him.

CHAPTER FOURTEEN

The following morning, events began to take a more sinister turn. I'd agreed – once again – to meet Holmes at Baker Street, although I'd promised myself I would return to my surgery later that afternoon. I feared that my patients would be feeling so neglected that I might as well have gone to Suffolk with my wife after all.

My plans were soon to be dashed, however, as these things often are when a man counts Mr. Sherlock Holmes amongst his closest friends.

Holmes was waiting for me when I arrived, even though, as a conscientious man, I was five minutes earlier than arranged. He nearly leapt out of his seat when I came bustling through the door, and I could see immediately that something had hold of his attention. He had that wide-eyed, frenetic look that only ever came upon him in the midst of a case, when something new or unexpected had occurred, throwing fresh light on the matter or introducing previously unanticipated levels of complexity.

"Ah, Watson! As punctual as ever." I realised Holmes was already wearing his overcoat and scarf, and was clutching his hat in his hand, as if ready to leave.

"Forgive me, Holmes," I muttered. "I wasn't aware that you were waiting for me, or I should have come sooner. Whatever is the matter?"

"Word from Inspector Bainbridge, Watson. Our villain has shown his hand," said Holmes. As he had been the previous evening, he seemed full of nervous energy, fidgeting with his hat and restless to get moving.

"Gerber, you mean?" I said, unsure.

"In a manner of speaking…" replied Holmes, once again falling back onto his predilection for ambiguity.

"Oh, not this again, Holmes," I said, with a note of warning in my voice. "Please, do enlighten me – without any cryptic comments."

Holmes frowned, but continued. "There's been a murder, Watson. Another death."

"Good Lord!" I exclaimed. "Go on!"

"Peter Maugham has been found dead in his sitting room, a knife in his chest. The telegram from Bainbridge said it was quite a spectacular mess." I did think that Holmes might have imparted this information without so much relish, but I knew it was not the poor man's death that had so excited him, but the prospect of a deepening puzzle.

"My word. The plot thickens, Holmes. What the devil is going on? Why would anyone have it in for Peter Maugham?" I admit, I could not see what motive the elusive Mr. Gerber might have for taking such extreme measures.

"That, Watson," pronounced Holmes, "is precisely what I intend to find out." He placed his hat upon his head decisively. "Now, don't remove your coat or hat," he went on. "We're to go directly to the scene. Bainbridge has arranged for everything to be left precisely as it was found."

He ushered me towards the door, and, at his insistence, I took the stairs two at a time, hurrying towards the street below. Holmes produced his whistle from his coat pocket and gave forth a shrill blow, duly summoning the nearest hansom.

So it was that we found ourselves hurtling across town in the back of a cab, towards yet more evidence of murder, intrigue and revenge. Holmes was positively alive with nervous energy, and I could see even being confined in the back of the cab was too much for him. He was like a hound that had caught the scent of the hunt, and he wanted to be at the scene, in the thick of it, engaging his not inconsiderable mind. It was a pleasure to see him once more himself.

I sat back in my seat, resolute in my mind that when we finally caught up with Mr. Hans Gerber – who I was already sure must be responsible for this latest tragedy – I would take great pleasure in seeing him put before a judge.

My patients, it seemed, would have to wait for my attentions a little while longer.

The residence of Peter Maugham was a modest, terraced house in a reasonably fashionable street just off Cheyne Walk, close to the river. The small front garden had a single raised bed, planted with roses, and a black cast-iron railing that ran parallel to the road. Three steps led up to the front door, which stood ajar, with a uniformed constable standing guard to one side.

Holmes, brazen as ever, strolled directly past the waiting policeman and in through the front door without knocking, causing the man to start after him, calling out in concern.

"Mr. Sherlock Holmes and Dr. John Watson to see Inspector Bainbridge," I said, catching the man's arm in an effort to avoid a scene. He was a young constable in his mid-twenties, with a pencil-thin moustache and a mess of dark hair poking out from beneath his domed helmet.

He looked at me suspiciously. "Sherlock 'olmes?" he asked.

"Yes," I confirmed. "And Dr. Watson." I offered my hand, and he took it, shaking it warily. "Please forgive my friend," I said. "Once he has hold of a scent…"

The bobby, evidently deciding that I wasn't attempting to pull the wool over his eyes, heaved a sigh of relief. "I've heard that about him, Dr. Watson, from the other men on the force." He lowered his voice. "They say he's a blinkin' nightmare, to be honest, always swanning in and shouting at everyone."

I laughed heartily. "Well, you're not wrong," I said. "And if I'm not mistaken, he'll be up to his usual tricks within the next few minutes."

"In that case," said the young man, "I'm glad to be out here."

I patted him on the shoulder and, still chuckling, followed Holmes into the house.

It took a moment for my eyes to adjust to the gloom inside. Bainbridge was standing in the hallway, leaning heavily on his cane. His clothes were a little crumpled, as though he'd pulled them on hurriedly in the dark, and I noticed he had forgone his usual bowler hat. He looked tired – haggard, even – and I saw instantly that the pressure of simultaneously overseeing two major investigations was taking a toll on his health. He looked as if he'd hardly slept, and I suspected that he'd probably been up most of the night working on the other case, only to be called away from his bed early that morning to Peter Maugham's house.

A murder was clearly the last thing he needed; the tangled web being weaved by the Maugham family was complex enough as it was, without this new, gruesome development. Additionally, there was now no room for dispute regarding the death of Sir Theobald. Even if it could be proved that the old man's death was an accident – something both Holmes and I very much doubted – the murder of Peter Maugham, along with the mysterious reappearance of

Hans Gerber, meant that Scotland Yard's investigations into the Maugham family were only just beginning. Added to that, of course, was the fact that the iron men crimes continued to increase in both frequency and boldness.

"Good morning, gentlemen," said Bainbridge, jovially, as we entered the hall. "Something told me I'd be seeing the two of you again shortly."

"Once again, Inspector, we meet under less than salubrious circumstances," I said, offering him a warm smile.

"Where's the body?" said Holmes, sharply, and I turned to glare at him for being so indelicate.

Bainbridge sighed. "Straight down to business then, Mr. Holmes."

Holmes raised both eyebrows in a gesture of complete incomprehension, as if to say "what else?" Then, realising his directness might well have caused offense, gave an impatient sigh, before going on. "There's little time to waste, Inspector, if we're to derive as much useful information from the scene as possible. Every second that passes, valuable clues are lost to us. Spilled blood thickens, fingerprints are disturbed…"

Bainbridge nodded in understanding. "Very well, Mr. Holmes." He turned and, cupping a hand to his mouth, called along the passageway. "Mitchell! Clear the way for Mr. Holmes."

"Thank you, Inspector," said Holmes. I stood back as he jostled his way through the gaggle of uniformed policemen that had formed in the doorway of the sitting room.

Bainbridge boomed at the men to get out of the way, and soon enough they had skulked off to the kitchen *en masse*, away from his acerbic gaze. I was impressed by the manner in which he handled his men; they appeared to have a respect for him that was far from the simple, begrudging loyalty typically paid to senior officers by the men under their command.

I waited in the doorway with the Inspector while Holmes set

to work, withdrawing his magnifying glass and setting about the scene, picking over everything in exacting detail.

Peter Maugham's body lay sprawled on the rug before the hearth. He was dressed in a black evening suit, and the white linen of his shirt was stained a deep crimson with spilled blood. It had pooled on the floor around him, congealing into a sticky morass. His face was pale and twisted into a visage of horror such as I had rarely seen. His lips were pulled back from the teeth in a terrified snarl, and there was rage in his expression, as if he'd died in the midst of committing a violent act of his own. His eyes were still open and seemed to stare right at me, as if even in death he remained defiant. I noted they had taken on a cloudy, milky sheen. Experience told me he'd been dead since the previous night, for at least twelve hours, perhaps more.

The manner of his death had been exceedingly brutal. His chest had been punctured by multiple stab wounds, and from what I could see of his hands and forearms they had been slashed to ribbons where he had attempted to defend himself. The murderer's choice of weapon was not in any dispute: it still protruded rudely from the victim's chest, from just below the heart: a long-bladed huntsman's knife.

Blood had liberally spattered the hearth and surrounding furniture during the violent episode, and had trickled down the walls, staining the paper with dark, gruesome tributaries.

We stood in silence as Holmes dropped to his haunches beside the body, studying the man's grisly visage with fascination.

"What do you make of it, Watson?" he said, his voice low and even.

"It's a damn mess, is what I make of it, Holmes," I replied, privately ruing the moment I had agreed to forgo my day in the surgery to accompany my friend. "This was more than a simple execution or a bungled robbery. Whoever killed this man had a deep-seated hatred of him. That's evident from the sheer ferocity of the attack."

"Very good, Watson!" exclaimed Holmes, evidently impressed with my reasoning, if perhaps a little patronising. "And do you see here?"

"What's that?" asked Bainbridge, stepping further into the room.

"A partial footprint in the blood," said Holmes. "A man's boot, size nine…" He trailed off, before turning and rising once again to his full height. "Inspector, is there any sign of forced entry?"

Bainbridge nodded. "Indeed there is, Mr. Holmes. The sash window in the kitchen has been jimmied. The maid discovered it this morning when she rose to clean the house. The poor woman must have been working for an hour before she discovered the corpse. It seems she always begins her chores in the kitchen." He shook his head in apparent dismay.

"She thought nothing of the forced window?" I said, incredulous. "She didn't think to raise the alarm, or at least to raise the issue with Mr. Maugham?"

"It's a professional job, Dr. Watson. On first appearance it seems that the window has only been propped open to air the room. A casual inspection would not show where the wood had splintered under the duress of a crowbar." Bainbridge was not in the least bit defensive as he offered up this explanation for what I saw as a grave oversight on the part of the maid. It was hardly the weather to be airing the room at that time in the morning. I simply couldn't see how the woman had failed to note anything suspicious. Nevertheless, it was what it was.

Holmes stepped carefully over the blood stains on the hearth rug, and I stood aside to let him pass, following him into the kitchen where the four uniformed constables stood in a huddle, discussing the circumstances of the crime in hushed tones.

"Is this just as it was found, Inspector?" asked Holmes, approaching the window.

"Quite so, Mr. Holmes," said Bainbridge, nodding. "The maid assumed that Mr. Maugham must have opened it earlier that morning."

"Very good," said Holmes. "Has anyone been around the rear of the premises?"

"No," replied Bainbridge. "We've confined ourselves to the house."

"Excellent!" said Holmes. "Excellent."

Bainbridge, the four constables and I all watched with increasing interest as Holmes stepped up to the window, running his index finger around the wooden frame, stopping to examine where the wood had split around the latch.

Then, almost nonchalantly, he hoisted himself up onto the ledge, swinging his legs out of the open window and dropping out into the garden beyond.

"Holmes!" I started in surprise.

"Just a moment, Watson," came his muffled response, followed a moment later by an exclamation. "How interesting!"

"What is it, Holmes?" I called.

"More footprints, Watson, here in the mud."

I dashed over to the window and leaned out, to find Holmes crouching over the flowerbed, sifting amongst the weeds and pansies.

"You see here, Watson?" he said. "They bear the same tread as the shoe that left the imprint in the blood in the sitting room."

"So only one of them, working alone?" I ventured.

"Yes," said Holmes, standing and straightening his back. "One person, short, wearing size nine boots and surprisingly strong given their slight build. They came over the back wall, landing here in the flowerbed. They crossed to the window, wiped their feet and then discarded this cigarette-end before setting to work with their crowbar." He held up the remains of a small, crushed cigarette for me to see. "They forced entry through the kitchen window as suggested by Inspector Bainbridge."

He paused for a moment, as if to ensure I was paying attention. "Once inside, the killer went directly to the sitting room, where they must have known Peter Maugham to be taking a whisky following his return from town. They surprised him there, and I'd wager he must have attempted to reason with them for a few moments, pacing back and forth and spilling his drink on the hearth rug. Our killer, however, so enraged, lashed out at him with their knife, stabbing him first in the stomach, then in the chest. Maugham attempted to defend himself, of course, as proved by the wounds to his hands and wrists, but by then it was already too late, and the third and fourth strokes of the knife penetrated his heart, killing him instantly."

He nodded to himself, as if approving of his brief soliloquy – for I knew from past experience that, as much as Holmes was setting out the sequence of events for me, he was also speaking it aloud in order to set it straight in his own mind. "The killer was immediately remorseful," he added, "and fled the scene via the front door, leaving the corpse to be discovered the following morning."

"How do you know that, Holmes?" I asked, frowning. "That the killer was remorseful, I mean. The rest I can go along with, but how can you presume to know what the killer was feeling?"

"They abandoned the murder weapon, Watson, leaving Maugham where he fell." Holmes looked thoughtful. "Either that or they were panicked by the violence of their own actions. The murderer, contrary to what Inspector Bainbridge intimated, was no more a professional killer than you or I."

"And they left via the front door?" I asked, unsure.

"Yes. There are no signs that they exited the building via the same means they entered. I have no doubt that a momentary inspection of the front door will prove there are traces of blood on the handle," said Holmes.

"Precisely!" I said, realising that Holmes had hit the nail on the head, explaining my unease with his postulation. "Wouldn't the killer have been covered in blood? Just look at the mess in there… they could hardly have been inconspicuous."

"Indeed, Watson," replied Holmes. "Inspector Bainbridge and his men will need to mount a search for a blood-spattered coat, which I imagine has been dumped in the near vicinity. Find that, and we're one step closer to finding our killer."

I stepped back from the windowsill to allow Holmes to re-enter the kitchen. Bainbridge was leaning on his cane a few feet away, watching us both with interest.

"Forgive me, Mr. Holmes," he said, "but I couldn't help overhearing your conversation with Dr. Watson just now. From what you said, am I right in thinking that you believe the victim knew his killer? The fact he tried to reason with them, that the killer was so incensed by what he said? These things point to a familiarity between the two."

"Without question, Inspector," replied Holmes, clearly impressed with Bainbridge's deduction. "The killer was known to Peter Maugham. What is more, this small, discarded cigarette-end may help to point us in the right direction."

"How so?" I asked.

"It is of a very particular brand, Watson. A German brand," said Holmes.

"Hans Gerber," I said, with distaste.

"Hans Gerber?" echoed Bainbridge, perplexed. "Do you know this man?"

"Not yet, Inspector," replied Holmes, "but I should very much like to make his acquaintance."

Holmes, in a most animated fashion, took a moment to bring

Bainbridge up to date with the situation regarding the mysterious letters and the appearance of the man in black at Sir Theobald's funeral. He was like a bloodhound, now, on the scent of his quarry. It was fascinating to see the change that came over him, the sheer energy he derived from the slow unravelling of a case.

"Do you believe that others may be at risk from this Gerber fellow?" asked Bainbridge, when Holmes had finished.

"Indeed I do, Inspector," replied Holmes. "Oswald Maugham would be his next logical victim. He, like Peter Maugham, is a bachelor. He lives alone and is unsuspecting. He also represents a threat – of sorts – to Gerber's inheritance of the Maugham estate. You should dispatch some uniformed men to keep watch on his residence immediately." Holmes glanced over at me, as if bringing me into his little conspiracy. "This evening, Dr. Watson and I, with Oswald Maugham's permission, will lay a trap. We shall spend the evening in wait at his apartment. I do not think it will be long before our killer once again shows his hand."

Bainbridge frowned. "Mr. Holmes, as sound as I judge your intentions to be, I cannot in good conscience allow you to put yourselves in such immediate danger."

Holmes threw his head back and gave a hearty laugh. "I assure you, Inspector, we shall be quite safe."

"Then if you insist upon following this course of action, I shall of course accompany you," countered Bainbridge. "I too wish to bring this matter to a swift conclusion."

"Very good, Inspector!" said Holmes, amiably.

"Is it revenge that motivates Gerber, do you suspect, Holmes?" I said. I'd been pondering for some time on the motivation behind Gerber's letters, but now, to add cold-blooded murder to his list of probable crimes, suggested perhaps an even stronger motivation than his desire to secure Sir Theobald's fortune. "For all of those years of misery, abandoned by his family. I imagine only that could drive Gerber to so comprehensively destroy the Maughams."

Holmes sighed heavily. "Greed, Watson. The green-eyed monster of jealousy and greed has its fingerprints all over this sorry affair."

"And a sorry affair it is, too," agreed Bainbridge. "What with this and the on-going iron men business, I've begun to lose all faith in humanity," he said, quietly.

"Ah yes, the iron men robberies," said Holmes, perking up again. "How goes your investigation, Inspector?"

Bainbridge shook his head. "Not well, Mr. Holmes. They continue to wreak havoc amongst the upper classes, and yet I have very little to go on. They seem to come out of nowhere and disappear again into the night, like the phantoms you accused me of chasing when we met at the morgue."

"Have you spoken with Percival Asquith, the industrialist?" asked Holmes.

"Indeed I have," said Bainbridge, with a satisfied smile. "I interviewed him only yesterday. You believe him to be involved?"

Holmes shrugged. "Of that, I cannot say. I only wondered if there might be some connection?"

Bainbridge nodded. "I'm convinced of it. Asquith represents my main line of enquiry."

"Excellent, Inspector," murmured Holmes. "Most excellent."

Something appeared to catch Bainbridge's attention over Holmes's shoulder. "Ah, now, here's that police surgeon again." He lowered his voice. "The same man who did such a dreadful job at Sir Theobald's house. I suspect he's going to tell me Peter Maugham was clubbed to death, despite the ruddy great knife sticking out of his chest." He laughed conspiratorially. "Until tonight, gentlemen?"

"Until tonight, Inspector," said Holmes. "Watson and I shall make all the necessary arrangements."

Bainbridge shook Holmes by the hand, and went off in search of the police surgeon.

"Who'd have thought it, eh?" I said, laughing.

"Thought what, Watson?"

"That we'd ever happen upon a policeman whom you actually *liked*, Holmes," I said, with a wide grin.

"*Tolerate* is the word, Watson," replied Holmes, smiling. "Tolerate."

"If you say so, Holmes…" I teased, setting off for the door. "Come on, it sounds as if we have some arrangements to make."

CHAPTER FIFTEEN

If my wife had known the situation in which I found myself that night, she would have been struck rigid with anxiety. Far better, I considered, that she was left ignorant of the course of action that would shortly see me engaged in a hot pursuit through the backstreets of the city, on the tail of the enigmatic Mr. Hans Gerber.

Holmes had formulated our plan. He was convinced that Peter Maugham's killer would once again show his hand that very night by making an attempt on the life of Oswald Maugham. Now he, Inspector Bainbridge and I found ourselves in the darkened sitting room of Oswald Maugham's apartment. I could see only by the light that seeped out from between the closed metal shutters of a hurricane lamp. It cast eerie shapes upon the walls and underlit Holmes's face, obscuring much of his expression in shadow.

It was close to midnight and we had been there for nearly three hours, deliberating in hushed tones the wisdom of our plan. Oswald Maugham himself was in his bedchamber, a uniformed officer posted outside his door. Two further men were hidden in the hallway, ready to pounce upon any intruder with their truncheons.

I doubted very much that Oswald had managed to get any sleep. He had been distraught at the news of his cousin's murder, and more distraught still when Holmes had outlined his concerns regarding Oswald's own safety. Consequently, he had readily agreed to allow us to set our trap.

And so there we were, lying in wait. My service revolver was clutched tightly in my fist, cold and hard. All about us the house was silent, save for the creak and sigh of ancient floorboards and the far-off ticking of a clock.

"Well, Dr. Watson, this is a rum sort of affair, is it not?" whispered Bainbridge. He was standing opposite me on the other side of the open doorway. I could barely see him in the dark, other than the outline of his face and the gleam of his weapon, reflecting the thin light.

"Indeed it is, Inspector," I whispered in reply, grinning. "Holmes and I seem to have garnered a great deal of experience lying in wait for criminals during the dead of night. It is not something I ever thought I would make a habit of."

Bainbridge laughed. "And yet still you do, Doctor."

"Well, it wouldn't do to allow Mr. Sherlock Holmes to go and get himself killed, would it, Inspector?" I said, jovially. "What choice do I have? I'd have nothing to write about."

"Watson, you do me a disservice," said Holmes. I could not see his expression, but I guessed he was smiling. "I know how, secretly, you revel in these moments. The thrill of the hunt! Can you feel it? We are near to our quarry, gentlemen. Near indeed!" The excitement was evident in his voice.

Deep in the bowels of the house, I heard the tinkle of broken glass, followed by the sounds of a door being opened.

Holmes turned to us. "Quiet now! He's here!"

My mouth was dry. I kept my back to the wall, preparing myself for the encounter to come.

I could barely believe the hour was upon us, that Holmes had been right in anticipating the villain's movements so precisely – although experience told me I should have trusted his instincts. Here was our chance to bring an end to the entire affair, to capture – red-handed – the mysterious Hans Gerber, and to put him to the question. There was no doubt in my mind as I heard the footsteps in the hallway that Gerber was indeed our man.

Behind me, I could hear Holmes's breath in the near-palpable silence, the fluting of his steady exhalations. On the opposite side of the doorway, I saw Bainbridge raise his cane in the half-light, readying himself to strike the man as he came through the door.

All of a sudden, however, there was a commotion in the hall. I heard a man cry out in surprise and an altercation erupted, accompanied by the grunting of scrabbling men and the dull sounds of fists hitting home. The constables had set upon the intruder before he'd even had chance to walk into our trap. Whether he'd discovered them lying in wait, or they had simply pre-empted our surprise, I did not know.

Whatever the case, I knew that I had to act in order to prevent him from getting away. It had been our intention to lure the intruder into the sitting room and then block the only available exit. With the element of surprise lost, he had the opportunity to flee the way he had come.

I threw myself out into the hallway, followed closely by the others. Too late to make sense of what was happening, and too slow to get out of the way, I took an elbow to my face for my trouble, and fell back, wincing.

The intruder, who was dressed in a black overcoat and clutching a glinting blade, barrelled away down the hall towards the kitchen. Hefting my revolver, I dashed off in pursuit.

"He's getting away!" bellowed Holmes, in frustration.

"Help here!" I heard Bainbridge call loudly from behind me, and realised one of the constables must have been injured in the fight. I pressed on regardless, following the sound of thundering footsteps, the crunch of broken glass underfoot as our quarry fled through the back door and into the garden beyond.

I knew that Holmes would be able to assist the Inspector and, as it had turned out, I had the best chance of stopping Gerber – if, indeed, it was Gerber I was pursuing.

Haring after him, I skidded on the shards of glass and nearly went down, but caught myself on the doorframe, flinging myself out into the garden behind the fleeing man.

I caught sight of him hauling himself up and over the rear wall and braced myself, raising my revolver and squeezing off a shot. It struck the wall, showering the man in a plume of dust and causing him to cry out in surprise, throwing himself down into the alley beyond.

Cursing, I stowed the revolver in my belt and leapt into the flowerbed, pulling myself up onto the wall. I could see the man fleeing along the alley and, never one to give up easily, I dropped down onto the cobbles and followed on behind.

He proved to be a younger, fitter man than I, however, and while I managed to hold him in view, he was gaining ground with every step, charging towards the main thoroughfare at the other end of the alley.

A moment later I burst out of the mouth of the alley and straight into the path of an oncoming hansom. The horses, spooked, reared up and tried to bolt, and I was forced to fling myself down onto the road to avoid a collision.

The hansom slewed on the wet ground, the horses whinnying as they tried to flee in different directions. I jarred my elbow painfully in the fall and had to roll out of the way of the clattering hooves before I found myself trampled. They passed only inches from my head.

The driver called out in colourful language as I scrabbled to my feet, glancing this way and that, searching for my quarry. Alas, it was too late. I'd lost him. He could have disappeared down any of the myriad bustling side streets. All while I'd been rolling around in the filth, trying to avoid being trodden on.

Frustrated, dirty and smarting, I set out to retrace my steps back to Oswald Maugham's residence.

When I returned to the apartment a short while later, I found the place was still in some disarray. Uniformed men were bustling about the place talking in hushed tones. I'd come around the front way and used the doorbell, as I hadn't much liked the prospect of trying to scrabble back over the rear wall, particularly with my elbow still throbbing fiercely from my tumble in the hall.

Oswald Maugham, as I'd suspected, had not slept a wink, and was now ensconced in his sitting room, nursing a stiff drink, a petrified look on his face.

Bainbridge's expression was like thunder, and I knew immediately that he was unhappy with the bungling efforts of his constables. He'd hardly had a chance to berate them, however, as one of them had indeed taken a knife blade to the shoulder, and Bainbridge had been forced to stem the flow of blood with a makeshift tourniquet while he awaited the arrival of the doctor.

Holmes, on the other hand, was in exceedingly high spirits. He was standing in the front bay window, parting the heavy felt drapes with his left hand and staring out at the mist-shrouded street beyond. His lips were curled in a broad smile.

"What are you grinning at, Holmes?" I asked, with a certain

measure of consternation. "It seems to me that this evening's pursuits couldn't have been more of a disaster if we'd tried."

"Oh, quite the contrary, my dear Watson," replied Holmes, brightly. "I now have a much clearer notion of the nature of our killer."

"Oh, right. Do you?" I said, somewhat tired and frustrated. I simply couldn't see how Holmes could be so unconcerned with the fact we'd let the killer get away again, scot-free. We'd come so close to having him in our grasp.

"Quite so, Watson," said Holmes. "Here. I found this by the back door." He made a flourish of handing me the crushed stub of a cigarette.

I took it and gave it a cursory examination. I was in no mood for engaging in his little games, and my elbow was beginning to ache terribly. "The stub of a cigarette…" And then it hit me. "Is it…?"

"It is, Watson," said Holmes, sweeping it out of my grasp and holding it up to the faint light from the window. "Identical in almost every way to the one we found at the home of the late Peter Maugham earlier this very day."

"Then it *was* Gerber," I muttered. This had to be the confirmation we'd been looking for.

Holmes laughed. "While I applaud your enthusiasm, Watson, I fear you have missed one potentially vital clue. There is no way that the man to whom you have just given chase was the same person who murdered Peter Maugham."

"But Holmes!" I protested, bewildered. "Everything points to Gerber. The cigarettes, the motive…"

"The motive? Perhaps," said Holmes, thoughtfully. "Yet the person who killed Peter Maugham was short. This we established from the length of their strides, and also from the relative height of the wounds inflicted upon the victim. The man you have just pursued, as well you saw, was far taller."

"Good heavens, Holmes!" I exclaimed. "You're right!" I frowned, uncertain now. "But what of Gerber?"

Holmes raised a single eyebrow. "That is quite the question, Watson. What of Gerber indeed..."

CHAPTER SIXTEEN

Annabel Maugham was in a dreadful state when Holmes and I called on her the following morning. Her brother was out on undisclosed business, and while she was alone she had received another threatening letter from the notorious Mr. Hans Gerber.

It appeared that – somehow – the odious wretch knew exactly when to time the delivery of his missives to achieve the most devastating effect. It seemed clear to me that he was surreptitiously observing his cousins, and I mentioned as much to Holmes on the journey over. Holmes, of course, had already considered this notion, and waved his hand nonchalantly in the back of the brougham. "Of course, Watson," he said, imperiously. "That much is obvious. Yet I cannot see how it might assist us in bringing him to justice."

"Well, for a start, we might ourselves observe the households in question, and if Gerber puts in an appearance we can swoop in, restrain him and take him into custody," I ventured, perplexed that Holmes had missed such an obvious plan.

Holmes shook his head. "A clever man, Watson, would use

agents to achieve such ends. We would not know for whom we were waiting, meaning we would undoubtedly find ourselves challenging every caller to the house, be they maid, delivery man, salesman or relative. Even then, the agents will only be briefed with what information is pertinent to them achieving their goal and getting paid. The information they could give us would be largely useless." He took a long draw from his pipe, and exhaled a cloud of pungent smoke into the confines of the cab. I coughed and spluttered pointedly, and he smiled. "I believe our time would be much better spent pursuing other avenues of our investigation, such as those we are already set upon."

I nodded, seeing the logic in Holmes's argument, but not wishing to give him the satisfaction of admitting defeat. He was, of course, correct – I saw the sense in what he said – but truthfully his patronising tone and easy dismissal had somewhat grated upon me that morning, and I preferred to sit and brood. I was tired and fractious following our exploits at Oswald Maugham's apartment and did not wish to sour things further with brittle words, and so we sat in silence until our arrival at the home of Joseph and Annabel Maugham.

Upon arrival we discovered that – distressed by the contents of the new letter, and unsure what else to do – Miss Maugham had sent directly for Tobias Edwards, who had immediately hurried across town to sit with her. It was he who showed us in.

He looked haggard and put-upon. He had dark rings beneath his eyes and his complexion was decidedly pale. Clearly he, too, was desperately concerned over the Gerber matter, and it was a simple matter to deduce that he wasn't sleeping. I made a mental note to offer him any medical assistance he might require before the morning's interview was over.

He beckoned us into the hall, but hesitated there for a moment, speaking in a sepulchral whisper. "I should warn you,

Mr. Holmes, that Miss Maugham is in no condition to receive visitors. I imagine, however, that despite this she would benefit greatly from your support." His eyes searched Holmes's face, looking for comprehension.

Holmes smiled warmly. "I understand, Mr. Edwards," he said.

Edwards nodded thankfully and led us into the sparsely furnished sitting room, where previously we had briefly interviewed Miss Maugham and her brother.

She was standing by the hearth, clutching a scrap of paper in her hands, and she rushed over to Holmes when we walked in, her expression imploring. It was clear she'd been crying. "Oh, Mr. Holmes! Thank goodness you're here! I fear I am beside myself. I do not know what to do. Mr. Edwards here has tried but can offer little consolation. It seems Mr. Gerber is set upon destroying this family."

"You have received another letter, I see, Miss Maugham," I said.

"Indeed I have, Dr. Watson, this very morning. Joseph left early, with business to attend to, and after taking breakfast I came to the door to collect the post and found this upon the mat." She brandished the crumpled letter before her as if it were a dirty rag.

"It seems this Gerber fellow has nerves of steel. After what he's done… to continue in such a fashion!" I said, disapprovingly.

"May I see the contents of the letter, Miss Maugham?" asked Holmes.

"Yes," she replied, handing it to him and stepping back to warm herself before the spitting fire, "of course." She appeared to regain her composure somewhat, although I noticed she continued to wring her hands anxiously behind her back. I resolved that, whenever we caught the vagabond who had caused this woman such grave distress, I would make sure that he paid dearly for his crimes.

"Thank you," said Holmes, unfolding the crumpled note and smoothing out the creases. "I'll read it aloud, if I may?" He glanced up at Miss Maugham, and she gave a curt nod of approval.

Holmes cleared his throat:

My dear Miss Maugham,

May I offer my sincerest condolences upon the death of your cousin, Peter. I am sure that the circumstances must weigh very heavily upon your conscience. For him to die in such a fashion seems hardly befitting for a man of his station.

Allow me to assure you that, as the day approaches when I shall assume responsibility for this family's affairs, I will make it my business to ensure that you, Oswald and your brother receive all that you deserve.

Regards

Mr. Hans Gerber

Holmes finished reading and looked up, appraising our reactions.

"Good grief!" I said, unsure how to articulate my disgust. "He writes only to gloat of his own handiwork. 'On your conscience' indeed! The sheer gall of the man! He knows no bounds! This letter constitutes a very real threat to Miss Maugham's life, Holmes."

"Perhaps so. These are the words of a very bitter man, Watson." Holmes folded the note again, handing it to Tobias Edwards, who was hovering at his elbow, following proceedings with a keen interest. Not for the first time, I wondered if this interest in Miss Maugham's affairs was something more than professional. I suspected it was – he had already gone far beyond the remit of a family solicitor in attending her at her home. She was, after all, a striking woman.

"My brother Joseph cannot hear of this," she said, stifling a sob. "It would drive him to distraction, and he has such a violent temper. I don't know what he might do…" she trailed off, her hands to her mouth.

Edwards went to comfort her, placing a hand on her arm. "There, there, Miss Maugham. All will be well."

It was clear to me from Annabel Maugham's pale aspect that she was fearful for her safety. Not only at the hands of Mr. Hans Gerber, but perhaps also at those of her tempestuous brother. She shook as she spoke of him, but seemed to take some measure of comfort, at least, from the presence of Edwards.

I had met Joseph Maugham only briefly, but he'd seemed to me like a brute of a man, and it had been clear at the time that he and his sister had concluded an argument only moments before Holmes and I arrived. Indeed, he'd been quarrelsome during the interview itself. I wondered how long she'd been suffering at the hands of this man; what power he had over her. Perhaps it was related to their financial arrangements; she'd risk ruin if she even considered setting herself up as a woman of independent means without her brother's support. Or perhaps there was more to it than that. Familial ties, I knew, ran deep, even when one party showed nothing but utter contempt for the other.

For now, however, she was safe. Uniformed constables had been placed on watch outside the house, and Holmes had spoken with them prior to entering – despite his earlier assertion that there was nothing to be gained from watching the comings and goings around the premises.

They had seen nothing to raise suspicion. Joseph Maugham had returned to the house late the previous evening, smelling of cheap gin, and had left early that morning, just as Miss Maugham had described. They were not aware of his destination, any more than Miss Maugham herself appeared to be.

No one else, other than the postman, had been near the

property, and Annabel herself had not left the house.

She looked over at us now, the concern evident on her face. "What of poor Oswald? I understand there was an incident at his apartment last night?"

Holmes nodded. "I fear, Miss Maugham, that an attempt would indeed have been made on his life, had Dr. Watson not acted as swiftly and commendably as he did to prevent it."

I couldn't help but smile at Holmes's unusual praise. It was reassuring to know that my efforts were appreciated.

"Is it too much to hope that you managed to detain the culprit?" she pressed, anxiously.

"I'm afraid not, Miss Maugham. He is a wily devil, and although I gave chase, I fear I lost him," I said, with a shrug.

"Do you think he might come here?" she asked, clutching Edwards's forearm.

"I think it very likely he might try, Miss Maugham," said Holmes. "For that reason, and that reason alone," at this juncture he offered me a sly, knowing look, "the two police constables posted outside of your home will remain here indefinitely. At the very least until this situation is brought to a satisfactory resolution."

"Satisfactory?" replied Miss Maugham, with bitterness in her tone. "Satisfactory for whom, Mr. Holmes? Peter is dead. Uncle Theobald's will is missing. Joseph is incensed beyond reason and soon I shall be destitute. I see very little satisfaction to be derived from this situation." Clearly, the pressure was becoming unbearable.

"Now really, Miss Maugham," said Edwards, in a conciliatory fashion. "It's not as bad as all that. You must trust in Mr. Holmes. He will find a way out of this mess, for all of us. I know he will." He paused, glancing up at Holmes, whose expression remained rigid and unreadable. "Now, alas, I must take my leave," he continued. "There is much to be done. I shall call again in a day or two, to see if I might be of further assistance." He lowered his voice. "And you must feel free to send for me at any time, if there is anything you need," he said, softly, to Miss Maugham.

"Thank you, Mr. Edwards," she replied. "I'm not at all sure what this family would do without you."

"It's nothing," he said, smiling.

"Your compassion does you credit, Mr. Edwards," I said. It had occurred to me, as I'd watched the two of them interacting, that perhaps Edwards represented a means of escape to Miss Maugham, a way to free herself from the curse of her unruly brother.

"It is only right that I be at the side of this family in their hour of need, Dr. Watson," he said, stoically. He offered me his hand, and I took it and shook it firmly. "Good day to you. Mr. Holmes, you know where to find me if there's anything I can do."

"Quite so, Mr. Edwards," replied Holmes.

"Good day, Mr. Edwards," said Miss Maugham, quietly, as he left.

Holmes cleared his throat, pointedly. "Miss Maugham. We shall leave you now in the capable hands of the police. Please, do not leave the house unless absolutely necessary. Take all due precautions and inform the constables of your whereabouts at all times. Follow these instructions and all will be well."

"And Mr. Gerber?" she said.

"The net is closing on Mr. Hans Gerber," replied Holmes, cryptically. "Soon, all will be revealed…"

CHAPTER SEVENTEEN

FROM THE TESTIMONY OF
INSPECTOR CHARLES BAINBRIDGE

I was strolling home through Holborn when it happened.

It was late – after eleven – and I was wrapped up against the frigid wind, my collar turned up, my hat pulled down low over my brow. Perhaps I'd have heard them coming if I hadn't been so intent on getting home, and so muffled against the inclement weather.

I'd passed a pleasant evening at my club in the company of Inspector Lestrade, lamenting over the lack of progress in our respective investigations. He was engaged in a missing persons enquiry and suspected that the "victim" – in this case a high-profile City banker – was in fact a bigamist who had fled to Malta with his second wife, abandoning his first wife and child to fend for themselves. Of course, it was proving nigh on impossible to trace the fellow, and despite Lestrade's suspicions, he had no conclusive evidence to support them.

For my part, I was still concerned with juggling the matter of Sir Theobald Maugham's suspicious death with the increasingly concerning rash of iron men robberies. Lord Roth, of course, was pushing for progress in the latter case, insisting I bring about a swift resolution to the Maugham matter in order that I might divert all my resources to the iron men case.

I, however, felt Roth's assertion that Sir Theobald's fall was a clear example of accidental death was blatantly misguided, particularly in light of the murder of Peter Maugham, and had already made the decision to ignore this directive, given that I knew it was born out of a desire to brush the matter under the carpet so that Roth might save face. I intended to continue with the investigation, working alongside Holmes and Dr. Watson. I also understood that I would have to do so in a manner that – if not surreptitious – did not draw the attention of Roth or his loose-lipped cronies.

I mused on this as I traipsed home through the cold streets, mulling over my options for the following day.

It was then that the automatons came at me as if from nowhere; as if the night had somehow just given them up, spitting them forth from the very depths of hell itself.

There were two of the things, propelling themselves along with a measured, lumbering gait. They matched perfectly the descriptions recounted to me by the victims of their crimes, resembling nothing so much as animated suits of armour. Steam curled above their heads from twin exhaust shunts that jutted from their shoulders, and they wore much of their workings on their exterior, encrusted over their armour plating. Complex arrays of pistons and cogs clustered around each major joint, sighing and whirring with every juddering movement. Their eyes were burning red coals, and although their expressions were fixed and cold, I could sense their malevolent intent. It was clear they meant to kill me.

I turned to flee, thinking that perhaps I could outrun them, but to my horror I discovered that a further two machines were closing in behind me. They had picked their timing perfectly: I was hemmed in, with nowhere to run.

I hefted my cane, gripping it in both hands, although I doubted it would do me much good against the metal monsters. I would give it my damn best shot, however. I would go down fighting.

Despite my burgeoning terror, I couldn't help but wonder at the marvellous engineering these iron men represented. They were walking miracles – thinking, intelligent machines, able to follow the most complex of instructions, to employ subtle strategies as well as absolute brute strength. Everything that made them dangerous made them utterly magnificent, too, and I realised now why Percival Asquith had been so animated when he'd described them to me earlier that day. They were a remarkable achievement, despite the nefarious use to which they had now been committed. I wondered for a moment if they were not truly machines at all, but demons trapped within metal skeletons, given physical form to walk amongst the living.

As the iron men closed in on me from all directions, I found myself backing up against a derelict building, brandishing my cane before me. In panic I tried the narrow door, but it was locked, bolted from the inside. I put my shoulder to it, but it would not give. I could not fathom any other means of escape, but I was damned if this was going to be my final hour.

The first of the automatons lurched within striking distance and I swung my cane, throwing all of my weight behind it. It struck the side of the machine's head and the force of the blow caused it to step sideways in order to maintain its balance. The pain in my wrists, however, was excruciating, as the mahogany rebounded from the metal plating, sending painful tremors along my forearms.

The iron man, however, seemed hardly to notice my attack, and showed no sign of being dazed by my blow. It thrust out its knife-like metal claws and grasped for my face. Desperately, I twisted away and it caught my coat, shredding the fabric as it attempted to reel me closer.

Another of them came at me from the opposite direction, this time catching my upper arm, ripping through my coat, jacket and shirt to gouge furrows in the soft flesh. I howled in pain, dropping my cane. I kicked at the thing, but it was a futile gesture, serving only to highlight my weakness in the face of these powerful machines.

The remaining two iron men had now joined their brethren to complete the circle, and the four of them peered at me impassively as I cowered, awaiting my fate. Warm blood was trickling down my arm, and while I knew the injury was not severe, the pain was almost enough to make me swoon. I fought to stay alert, to fight down the pain and focus on how the hell I was going to get away.

The first of the iron men stepped forward again, slowly and deliberately pulling back its arm and forming a fist. I tried to anticipate its timing, and as it thrashed out, I dropped to my haunches, the fist passing harmlessly above my head, smashing through the door. Splinters of wood showered down onto my neck and shoulders. I realised I'd lost my hat in the scramble to get out of the way.

Wordlessly, the iron man struggled to free its hand. In doing so it inadvertently wrenched away another shower of wooden fragments, and glancing up, I realised with a glimmer of hope that the impact had exposed the metal bolt that barred the door.

The iron man stepped back, regarding its hand inquisitively, and I saw my chance. I sprang to my feet, reaching through the door for the bolt. My fingers clutched at the cold metal and the bolt slid free. I fell against the door, which heaved open, and I tumbled into the interior of the abandoned building, cracking my knee against a broken table and going down hard.

I scrabbled immediately to my feet, grimacing as lancing pain shot through my left arm. Through the doorway, I could see only the bulky silhouettes of the iron men, their glowing red eyes hovering in the gloom.

One of them stepped forward, ducking its head beneath the lintel, but its shoulders struck the edges of the doorframe. It twisted and turned for a moment, struggling to force its way through, but its broad shoulders simply bashed against the wood and surrounding brickwork, grinding noisily. The opening, it seemed, was too narrow for it.

I watched, breathless, as it tried again, this time adjusting its poise and rotating its shoulders to make itself smaller. Once again, however, it struck the edges of the frame, unable to force its bulk through the doorway. It glowered at me for a moment, its claws outstretched as it strained to reach me, and then withdrew.

Its footsteps echoed noisily as it stomped away.

I allowed myself to breathe a cautious sigh of relief. Had they gone? I peered out into the gloom, but could discern nothing but the empty street beyond. I dared not approach the opening in case the machines were still outside, hoping that I'd think they'd retreated and attempt to flee.

I glanced around, attempting to get the measure of my surroundings. The building was clearly in a state of disrepair, and was in the process of being renovated. There was a musty reek of damp and disuse. A pile of bricks sat in the middle of the floor, buckets and rags had been discarded haphazardly all about the place, as if the men had simply walked away from their work upon the chiming of the clock.

The place was cavernous, and walls had evidently been demolished to open up the space. Behind me, a rickety-looking staircase led to an upper floor. If I could find an alternative exit from the building, I decided, there was still a chance I could get away.

I turned at the sound of a noise from outside, just in time to see one of the iron men collide with the doorframe. The entire building seemed to shake with the impact, and to my horror, the bricks around the door exploded, showering me with dust and debris.

The metal monster was now jammed in the frame, embedded part way into the wall. Its metal talons grasped at the edges of the opening, tearing away handfuls of the ruined brickwork.

With a grating screech it heaved itself through into the room, its metal feet crunching on the loose fragments. Over its shoulder I saw another of them waiting to force its way in, and I knew then that they would not stop until I was dead. They were unstoppable.

I turned and fled, my heart pounding, looking for a window or another doorway through which I might effect an escape. Aghast, I realised that all the exits had been boarded up by the workmen, and the only option left open to me was to take the stairs to the upper floor.

I reached the bottom step only inches ahead of an iron man and took them two at a time, hoping to outpace it. It was fast, however, faster than its bulk might suggest, and I barely had time to glance down through the banisters to see the others hauling themselves into the building and following on behind.

I slipped on the landing carpet, almost going over, but managed to use the handrail to save myself, and I swung round onto the upper floor, desperately searching for somewhere to take cover. I knew that nothing I might do, no weapon I might find in this house would have any effect on the machines, but still, in my desperation, I held out hope.

The upper floor was as desolate and abandoned as the ground floor. The empty bedrooms would offer me no salvation, and a drop from the windows at this height would ensure only two broken legs, if not worse.

The stairs had seemed to slow the iron men fractionally, and so I pressed my advantage and hurtled up a second flight, heading towards the attic, and from there, the roof. I had no notion of what I might do when I got there, but at that point I was desperate and buying myself even a few more seconds felt like a victory.

The attic was empty and my entrance stirred whirling pools of ancient dust, causing me to hack and cough and cover my mouth in the crook of my elbow as I staggered towards the roof door.

I didn't even stop to try the handle, but forced the door with my shoulder, bursting out into the frigid night. The roof of the small building was a square, gravelled terrace, overlooking the street below. A low stone lintel ran around the perimeter of the roof, but otherwise it was featureless. A sudden gust of cold wind threatened to knock me from my feet. The view across the neighbouring rooftops would have been quite breathtaking, if the circumstances had been different; a thin fog was beginning to descend, softening the moonlight and giving everything a hazy, diffuse appearance. For a moment it felt as if I was alone in an empty city, the only sound the whistling of the wind, drowning out everything else.

I heard movement behind me and ran across the roof to the opposite edge, glancing down at the street below. From three stories up the slick cobbles surely represented certain death. The nearest building was at least ten feet away, a squat, two-storey office building with a flat roof. I didn't like the odds of being able to make the jump, especially without a run-up.

Behind me, the four automatons emerged from the doorway, fanning out across the roof. I believe the thing that terrified me most about them was the lack of even the slightest emotion on their blank, metal faces. I had faced killers before, brawled with men intent on my murder, had even been shot, stabbed and left for dead during my time as a police constable, but never had I been so afraid as I was when faced with the sheer, cold calm of those metal faces. Nevertheless, I stood my ground as the machines once again drew their circle around me, closing in.

I stepped back, onto the stone lintel, and felt the wind at my back. I could hardly breathe for fear, and my mouth was dry, filled with the metallic tang of adrenaline. I was certain I was going to die.

The iron men came at me, their talons raised.

I was out of options. I could go down fighting, or I could jump. Either seemed like utter madness, but I did not dwell on my decision. With a deep breath I dropped into a crouch, and then, forcing as much power into my legs as I could muster, uncoiled like a spring, twisting in the air, stretching out my arms and praying for all I was worth as I tumbled through the air.

In the event I overshot and stumbled as I landed on the rooftop of the building opposite, pitching forward and slamming down upon my damaged arm. Crying out in pain, I broke into a roll to slow my momentum, and then, seconds later, came to rest on the damp, dirty gravel.

I could barely believe that I was still alive, but I wasn't taking anything for granted. I turned, climbing to my feet and looking back to the iron men, who remained on the other rooftop, their red eyes burning in the darkness. It didn't appear as if they were prepared to risk the jump.

Smarting, but with fresh hope blossoming in my chest, I glanced around, catching sight of a cast-iron stairwell fixed to the side of the building: a fire escape. I ran for it, jumping onto the platform and practically sliding down the steps to the alley below, where I landed with a thump on the cobbles.

Panting, bruised and bleeding, I didn't look back to see if the iron men were following me. I ran out into the thoroughfare, frantically waving down the first cab that I saw, and gave instructions to be taken directly to Scotland Yard.

CHAPTER EIGHTEEN

The next morning I woke to a quiet, empty house. I rose, saw to my ablutions, and then treated myself to a large breakfast of grilled kidneys, tomatoes and toast. For a good while I sat at the breakfast table reading the previous day's newspaper, and contemplating the day ahead.

I had resolved to spend the day at my surgery, seeing to a number of urgent matters. My patients, thankfully, were largely understanding of my absences. Many of them had read the published accounts of my adventures with Holmes, and understood that my infrequent periods away from the surgery typically denoted a new mystery in the works. Often, upon my return, they would question me for details – which I would not, of course, provide – or speculate wildly on the nature of the case.

Nevertheless, I was deeply conscious of the fact that my duty as a physician was to their health, and not to their entertainment, and I made every effort to attend to them whenever I could.

My mind, however, kept on wandering back to the events of the previous day – particularly the stricken look on the face of

Miss Annabel Maugham. I wondered what sort of monster Gerber must be, to inflict so much anxiety on an innocent, grieving woman. In truth, I knew the answer all too well, for I had met many of his type over the years: those so shaped by bitterness, so caught up in their need for revenge and their desire for personal gain that they will stop at nothing – not even the murder of those they purport to love – to achieve their aims.

The thought gave me pause. It was a brutal world that gave rise to such villains, and I was grateful for men like Holmes and Bainbridge who were prepared to stand up for what was right. Idly, I wondered how Bainbridge's investigation into the iron men was coming on. He'd seemed most concerned with the lack of progress during our last encounter, and I could only imagine the sheer amount of pressure he must have been under to obtain a swift result.

I had just finished my second coffee when I heard the letterbox clatter down the hall. I glanced at the clock on the mantel, frowning. It was too late for the first post, and yet too early for the second. Someone, then, had dropped a missive through the door.

I pushed my chair back and stood, fully suspecting it to be the work of Holmes, sending yet another urchin around to summon me to Baker Street. Well, today he'd have to wait, at least until later that afternoon, when any urgent matters at the surgery had been properly attended to.

I strolled down the hall in no particular hurry, eyeing the cream-coloured envelope lying on the mat. Groaning, I stooped and retrieved it, turning it over to examine what was written on the front. It read simply: DR. WATSON in an unfamiliar hand. So, it wasn't from Holmes after all.

Intrigued, I tore the envelope open, and withdrew the thin slip of paper from within. It was poor-quality notepaper, wafer-thin and near-transparent, and obviously not the work of my friend. I unfolded it and began to read:

Dear Dr. Watson,

Allow me to begin by offering my sincerest apologies. It was most rude of me to cut out on you at the cemetery, but I fear a conversation at that point in the proceedings would not have ended satisfactorily for either of us. I do hope, however, that we will meet someday soon, once this business is over. I have long been an admirer of your little fictions.

My name, of course, is Mr. Hans Gerber, and I write today to request that you desist from your dirty little investigations into my family's private affairs. Your continued interference cannot end well. You are an intelligent man and I am sure you understand me. These are private matters that do not concern you or your impertinent friend, Mr. Holmes, and you will no longer be party to them, one way or another.

I bid you a good day, Dr. Watson, and continued good health.

Yours,
Mr. Hans Gerber

"Little fictions!" I exclaimed, incensed. "Dirty little investigations!"

I tossed the letter on the floor in abject disgust. I felt my face flush in anger. How dare he! To speak of impertinence, to threaten me in such a manner… It was all I could do to remain calm.

Gerber would not, of course, dissuade me from our investigation by such cowardly means. If anything, his note would strengthen my resolve to get the man safely behind bars.

I left the scrap of paper where it lay on the tiles, and started out towards the breakfast room. I'd traversed about half the length of the hallway when it suddenly struck me: the note had not come by the post, but had been delivered by hand, either by Gerber himself or by an agent in his employ. This meant two things. Firstly, that Gerber knew where I lived, and secondly, that he might still be in the vicinity.

My blood up, I reversed my trajectory and hurried to the front door. I flung it open and stepped out onto the pavement, glancing from left to right for any sign of the odious wretch.

Sure enough, I spied him only a moment later, standing beside a lamp post at the far end of my street. He was dressed in a similar fashion to when I'd seen him at Sir Theobald's funeral, with a wide-brimmed hat obscuring his face, and a black overcoat draped over his shoulders. There was no mistaking it. It had to be Gerber.

As if to underline the point, when he saw me he reached up and touched the brim of his hat, slightly inclining his head in acknowledgement. He'd clearly been loitering there since posting the note through my door, waiting to see my reaction. The only possible reason was to gloat.

I saw red. I was incensed by the audacity of the man. How dare he come here, to my home, and threaten me in such a manner? Not only that, but to stand there revelling in my confusion and rage.

My anger consumed me, leeching away all sense. I barely knew what I was doing. I slammed the door shut behind me, and took off along the street towards him. This scoundrel deserved to be brought before a magistrate and I was not about to let the chance to apprehend him pass me by for a second time.

I was still dressed only in my shirtsleeves and trousers, but barely felt the cold as I marched past a clutch of women out for an early morning stroll. They stared at me, wide-eyed, no doubt shocked by the wild look in my eyes and the fixed expression of determination in the set of my jaw.

Gerber, of course, had seen me coming, and I watched him turn and slip away around the corner, disappearing from view, just as he had at the cemetery. I broke into a run, huffing noisily as I attempted to gain ground. My recently consumed breakfast sat ill in my stomach as I ran.

I reached the lamp post where I had last seen him and flung myself around the corner, almost barrelling into an old man, who was shuffling along the street, his back severely stooped. He waved his cane at me and cursed as I danced around him, searching for any sign of Gerber.

As before, however, he had gone – lost amongst the milling crowds of pedestrians, the stream of horse and carriages, the hansom cabs. He might have entered any of the numerous buildings, or ducked down an alleyway between two properties, scrambling out of sight. Perhaps he'd even bolted at speed along the street and was off somewhere, still running.

"The damn coward!" I exclaimed, drawing interest from any number of passers-by, who turned to glare at me as if I were a madman. I glowered back at them, my heart still racing.

Once again, I had lost him. I had missed another opportunity to bring the whole business to an early conclusion, and I cursed myself for letting the chance pass me by.

My shoulders sagged in defeat, and I turned and slowly walked back towards my home, brooding and angry. I stopped only to apologise to the old man whom I had nearly sent flying a few moments earlier, but he seemed disinterested in anything I had to say, and turned his back on me hurriedly, shuffling off in the opposite direction.

The letter was still waiting for me in the hallway when I opened the door, and I bent to retrieve it. I fought the urge to screw it into a ball and throw it into the fire, instead folding it and returning it to the envelope. It might, I realised, prove to be valuable evidence, and so I slipped it into my pocket for safekeeping.

For a few moments I considered taking a cab directly to Baker Street, to show the letter to Holmes and relate my experience. In the end, however, I decided not to allow the morning's events to upset my day. I had resolved to see to my patients, and see to my patients I would. Gerber's note had not changed a thing. There was no new information here for Holmes, nothing that might alter the direction of his investigation or help to bring the elusive Gerber to justice. Nor would I be dissuaded from my part in proceedings. Indeed, more than ever, I looked forward to a time when I might have an opportunity to pose some questions to the man, and then the satisfaction of seeing him dragged away and tossed into one of Bainbridge's holding cells. Gerber's tactics might work to inspire fear in the hearts of innocent women such as Annabel Maugham, but I was made of sterner stuff.

I returned to the breakfast room, where I had abandoned the detritus of my meal. There was still some lukewarm coffee in the pot and I poured myself another cup, downing it quickly. My hand was trembling – not with fear, but with barely repressed rage. I forced myself to calm down, breathing slowly, and then, with a quick stop before the hall mirror to make myself presentable, I snatched up my jacket and set out for my surgery.

Gerber and Holmes would have to wait. Today, first and foremost, I would assume the mantle of my profession, and live up to my title as Dr. John Watson.

CHAPTER NINETEEN

I barely saw anything of Holmes during the course of the following two days. I called at Baker Street early both mornings, only to be told by Mrs. Hudson that he had already left for the day and that she had very little idea of when – or if – he was expected back. This was typical of Holmes's behaviour during his more manic episodes, and, I assumed, indicative of his engagement with the case. I'd seen him like this on any number of occasions, and was well aware of his tendency to exclude all else – such as the matter of his own whereabouts or need to eat – in his pursuit of the solution to a puzzle.

For my part, I wished to discuss with him the note I'd received from Gerber, but his business must have been pressing indeed, for despite my leaving a message with Mrs. Hudson, I heard nothing from him in return.

Left to my own devices I returned to my patients, who I had been badly neglecting while gadding about with Holmes. The days passed quickly and quietly, although I admit I found it difficult to focus on anything but the Gerber matter, and not for the first time

I found myself wondering how this errant German could have evaded the usually so indefatigable Holmes for so long.

Gerber remained at large, and he continued to prosecute his campaign of terror against the Maughams, all the while staying – frustratingly – one step ahead of Holmes and the police. As well as myself, both the Maughams and Tobias Edwards received further letters, and a number of sightings were reported of men matching Gerber's description. Inspector Bainbridge arranged for constables to be posted outside the homes of each of the surviving cousins, round the clock. So far as I knew, no further attempts had been made on the life of Oswald Maugham, but it felt to me as if everyone involved with the matter was holding their breath, waiting for Gerber to strike.

Inspector Bainbridge relayed this information when, frustrated by my inability to speak with Holmes, I took my own note from Gerber to his office at the Yard. He considered Gerber's threatening remarks to be more of a deterrent than a reflection of the man's actual intent; being on the periphery of the investigation, it was perhaps unlikely that I should be made a target above, say, Holmes himself. Nevertheless, Bainbridge offered to provide a constable from his already stretched force to take up residence outside my house, and I agreed that if the affair was not concluded by the time my wife had arrived home from her mother's, then I should gratefully take up his offer. It was one thing to willingly put *myself* at risk in the pursuit of the villain, but quite another to jeopardise the safety of my family.

Still, as anticipated, nothing came of Gerber's threatening missive, and so I pushed it to the back of my mind and pressed on with my work. There was little else for me to do, and so I turned my attentions once more to boils, infections, swollen ankles and gout. The life of a General Practitioner is not, alas, a glamorous one.

When word finally came it was in the form of a short note, delivered to my surgery by a street urchin at around noon on the third day. It was written in Holmes's characteristic scrawl and read simply:

Watson
Be at Baker Street tonight, seven o'clock prompt.

Holmes

Frustrated once again by his opacity, but nevertheless curious to discover what he'd been up to in the time since our last meeting, I made hasty plans to do as he requested. My wife was still absent, but was due to return in two days. It was looking increasingly unlikely that the case would be resolved before her homecoming – a fact that gave me no small cause for concern.

I arrived at Baker Street a little before seven, only to find Holmes had still not returned. The unflappable Mrs. Hudson ushered me in, however, and I was soon ensconced by the fire with a brandy and a copy of the evening newspaper.

The headlines were, as they had been for days, dominated by news of further "iron men" burglaries. I felt for Inspector Bainbridge, who – when I had visited him two days earlier – had seemed to be buckling a little under the sheer weight of the responsibility. I wished again that Holmes had been more prepared to consider assisting Bainbridge with his investigation, and decided to redouble my efforts in persuading him to help.

The news was otherwise dominated by the usual political machinations and financial affairs, but one particular item caught my attention. It was a brief report of a rich foreigner, Count Laszlo Ferenczy of Hungary, who had come to London bearing a magnificent jewel. The gem had been christened the Moon Star, and it purported to be a diamond of previously unseen proportions. The Count was displaying it in the house he had taken in Pimlico, and inviting interested parties to send their cards in advance if they wished to arrange a viewing. I gathered that the reason for the Count's visit to London was that he wished to find a buyer for the stone.

I couldn't help thinking that the man was a fool to show such a complete disregard for the current situation in the capital, and the instructions issued by the police for people to ensure their valuables were well concealed or securely deposited at a bank. Granted, the man was a foreigner recently arrived in the city, but even so, he must have been aware of the on-going threat posed by the iron men. It was all the newspapers were talking about. By advertising his possession of the stone in such a way – not to mention its present location – he was simply asking for trouble, offering himself up as a prime target for theft.

I heard the clock chime and realised it was seven o'clock. Holmes's instruction to be prompt, it seemed, had been somewhat in vain. I was surprised a few moments later, however, to find Mrs. Hudson showing up another caller – a distraught Miss Annabel Maugham – who had apparently come to the door demanding to see Holmes. In his stead, I showed her to a seat and poured her a stiff brandy for her nerves.

"There you are, my dear. That should help," I said, as I handed her the drink.

"Oh, thank you, Dr. Watson," she said, the relief evident in her voice. She was perched on the very edge of her seat, and was toying nervously with the hem of her jacket with her left hand. Her face was flushed and, judging by the redness around her eyes, she'd been recently crying. She was clearly shaken, and as she took a series of steady gulps from her brandy glass, I began to suspect the worst.

"Gerber?" I asked, wondering if she had, in fact, been

subjected to an attack at the hands of the mysterious German. "Do I take it that there's been a… new development of some sort?"

She nodded quickly, lowering her glass. "Yes. Indeed there has. I had hoped to speak with Mr. Holmes…" She looked at me imploringly, as if hoping that I would somehow be able to conjure him up.

"I'm afraid Holmes has not yet returned, but he'll be along shortly. In the meanwhile, would you care to outline the situation for me?" I said, softly, in an effort to reassure her. "I would offer what services I can."

She was silent for a moment, as if weighing her options, and then made her decision. "Thank you, Dr. Watson. It's my brother. I… I fear for his life." She looked as if she were on the verge of breaking into tears again.

"His life?" I said, surprised. "Does he not remain under the protection of the police?"

She shook her head. "Alas, Joseph pays little heed to the constables posted outside our home. He goes about his business as he wishes, despite any concerns I may have for his safety." She took a deep breath to steady her nerves. "He is a foolhardy man, Dr. Watson. As much as I am fearful of his changeable moods, he is, nevertheless, my brother, and I wish for him to be safe."

"Of course," I said, wishing I had Holmes's eye for understanding the complexities of our interview. It was all I could do to offer her some reassurance and attempt to understand the nature of her sudden fear. By now, Holmes would have ascertained the finer details of her journey here, the reason for her visit and a host of other pertinent facts. Most probably, he would have even discerned what she had eaten for luncheon from the crumbs upon her sleeve. I, on the other hand, was left to stumble through with a series of questions. "Now, what is it that gives you reason to fear for his life, Miss Maugham? A new threat from Gerber?"

"Precisely that," she said. "Joseph received a letter in the second post. Upon reading it he flew into a blind rage. He smashed his fist into a mirror and stormed out of the house, announcing that he was going to 'meet Gerber and put an end to everything tonight.'"

"To meet Gerber!" I exclaimed. My mind was racing.

"You see, Dr. Watson, why I have cause for concern?" prompted Miss Maugham, with a sad smile.

"Indeed so," I replied. Was this our chance to bring the matter to a head? Could we intercept this meeting and finally bring Gerber to justice? "Do you have the letter?" I ventured.

"No," she replied. "Joseph took it with him."

"Then did he give you any indication of where he was to meet Gerber?" I asked, trying to keep the exasperation from my voice. It was hardly the fault of this poor woman that her brute of a brother was too hot-headed to consider his own actions.

She shook her head. "He did not."

"If only he'd come to us!" I said, banging the heel of my hand against the arm of the chair in frustration. I could not see how we could help Miss Maugham secure her brother's safety, and more, how we could seize this opportunity to finally learn the truth about Gerber.

"No matter, Watson! I have located Gerber's hideaway." I turned at the sound of Holmes's voice to see him framed in the doorway, still wrapped in his winter overcoat. He was wearing a fiendish grin as he regarded us from beneath the brim of his hat.

"Holmes! You're back!" I said, with a measure of relief.

"How astute of you to notice, my dear Watson. And back in quite the nick of time, it seems." He took off his hat and cast it aside, with no regard for the location of the hat stand. It landed on the table amidst a heap of books. "Miss Maugham," he went on, "did your brother state at what time he was due to meet with Mr. Gerber?"

"Only that the meeting was to take place this evening," she replied.

"Then we have little time to waste. I shall begin preparations immediately. Watson, show Miss Maugham to her cab, and then send for Inspector Bainbridge. Tonight we shall have our man!" Holmes ended this remarkable address by rushing directly to his bedroom, slamming the door behind him.

I glanced at Miss Maugham, quite unsure what to say. I was just about to speak when the strains of a violin – Holmes's violin – came drifting through from his chamber. I shrugged and cleared my throat, embarrassed. "I do apologise if Holmes seems a little… abrupt. Such is his way when a case is upon him."

"Think nothing of it, Doctor," countered Miss Maugham. "I am only pleased to hear that Mr. Holmes's enquiries have met with some degree of success."

I smiled, grateful for her understanding. "Have no doubt, Miss Maugham. Holmes will see this matter through to its conclusion." I stood. "Now, if you'll excuse me, I must make ready for this evening's outing and send for the police."

"Quite so," she replied, rising from her seat.

I walked her towards the door. "Will you be safe, Miss Maugham?"

"My concern is for Joseph, Dr. Watson," she said. "But you can rest assured that I have taken the necessary precautions. One of the constables is waiting for me downstairs in a hansom, and Mr. Edwards has agreed to call this evening."

"Very good. Then I bid you farewell," I said, holding open the door.

"Good evening, Dr. Watson. And good hunting."

I stood for a moment after she'd gone, listening to the sounds of her footsteps on the stairs and the violent chopping of Holmes's violin, and pondered what the night ahead might bring.

Then, without further ado, I collected my coat and hat and set out with the intention of getting word to Inspector Bainbridge.

CHAPTER TWENTY

It was dark when we finally left Baker Street.

The evening was cold and clear, the sky a canopy of rich, dark blue, pinpricked with stars. London was retiring for the night – or at least, the more salubrious inhabitants were – and the streets around Baker Street seemed filled with the bustle of people making their way home from a hard day's work, as we rumbled through the city, speeding towards our destination.

Inspector Bainbridge had joined us in the back of our hansom, and two uniformed constables followed behind in a second cab. He sat now beside Holmes, staring contemplatively out of the window.

I was carrying my service revolver in anticipation of the encounter to come, and was wrapped up against the brisk weather in a short, heavy cape. Holmes was dressed in a similar fashion, a hat pulled low over his brow. I watched him as we bounced over the cobbled roads, his forehead creased in a deep furrow. His eyes were closed, his long, thin fingers forming a steeple beneath his chin. He was brooding, and I knew better than to disturb him while he was lost in such deep thought.

Bainbridge, on the other hand, was alert and ready for action. I could see from the manner in which he clutched his cane, his knuckles whitening around the shaft, that he was eager to draw a line beneath the whole, sorry business.

Gerber, it seemed, was finally within our reach. Holmes would deliver him to us that very evening.

We sat in considered silence, each of us preparing in our own way for whatever the evening might bring. I thought again of my wife, and how much I missed her company when she was away. All of this gallivanting about with Holmes was invigorating, of course – enjoyable, even – but in my book, there was nothing so comforting as being able to return to a warm home, where an even warmer reception would await me. I looked ahead to this whole Gerber affair being over, and my wife returning from her trip.

Presently, I heard the driver call out to the horses, and the cab began to slow. I had no idea where we were; Holmes had refrained from giving us the address, and the fleeting glimpses of the city I'd managed to catch through the windows had offered little in the way of clues – we might be anywhere amongst the numerous slum districts of the capital.

Within moments the cab had come to a halt. Holmes's eyes flicked open, and he looked across at me, his eyes hard. He leaned over and opened the door, and beckoned silently for Bainbridge and I to exit the hansom.

We spilled out into the cold night to find ourselves in a quiet, empty street. The other cab was drawing to a halt behind us, the horses whinnying and stamping their hooves. Sweat lathered their flanks, and steam billowed from their nostrils like the smoky exhalations of dragons.

Once the five of us had assembled, Holmes sent the drivers on their way and led us on in silence, across a small square, past a church with a tumbledown spire, and down another side street that smelled of rotten vegetables, and worse. This, I realised, was the Whitechapel district, home to all manner of unsavoury denizens.

I clutched the handle of my revolver in my pocket as we walked, wary of being set upon by those who wouldn't take kindly to our presence, or others who might see an opportunity to enrich themselves with the contents of our wallets.

Nearly ten minutes later, we came upon the rundown shell of a terraced house, and Holmes stopped to indicate we had reached our destination. It was a rum sort of place, with boarded-up windows and detritus strewn across the front garden: a damaged bicycle wheel, the remains of a wooden box, scraps of threadbare carpet. The neighbouring buildings were just as grim but at least they showed signs of human habitation – a flicker of light in an upstairs window, the sound of hushed voices within.

Holmes mounted the first step up to the front door, and Bainbridge caught his arm. "This is it? *This* is where you found Hans Gerber?" He appeared somewhat baffled that our villain might be found in such an impoverished place. I'll admit, it did seem rather at odds to even the circumstances in which Oswald Maugham eked out his existence, let alone the faded grandeur of Sir Theobald Maugham's house.

Holmes nodded. He gave a tight-lipped smile. "Quite so, Inspector. I have no doubt that inside we will find the man we are looking for, along with evidence of his crimes."

Bainbridge released Holmes's arm. "Very well. Lead on, Mr. Holmes."

I hurried to the foot of the short set of stone steps. "Surely you're not simply going to knock, Holmes?" I hissed, trying to keep my voice down, despite the urgency. I did not want to alert anyone inside to our presence, lest they deem it a warning and take the opportunity to escape.

Holmes, however, appeared to have no such hesitation. I

watched, surprised, as he bunched his gloved hand into a fist and used his knuckles to shatter a small glass pane in the door. The fragments tinkled as they struck the ground. "Indeed not, Watson," he said, as he reached in and unlatched the door from the inside. Then, standing back, he gave the door a quick, sharp shove, and it yawned open, revealing the cavernous darkness within.

"I warn you, gentlemen," said Holmes, addressing the assembled men. "This is no trifling matter. The man we are dealing with will prove a formidable opponent if engaged in hand-to-hand combat. Arm yourselves if you have the means. He will not come quietly."

I followed Holmes into that stinking pit of a house expecting Gerber to leap out on us at any moment. The building was in a terrible state of disrepair, although signs of habitation were everywhere – abandoned food wrappings, the stubs of burned-out candles, evidence of a recent fire in the grate. There were also signs of damp, and of rodents, and I felt the hairs on the back of my neck bristle at the thought of rats scuttling beneath our feet.

Holmes led us deeper into the house by way of candlelight, producing a book of matches and taking up one of the half-used stubs. It soon became apparent, however, that Gerber was not there. As Holmes had predicted, though, there was clear evidence that he *had* been, and recently, too. In the kitchen a black coat had been thrown over the back of a chair, stained in great splashes of rust-coloured blood. A packet of cigarettes rested on the rickety table, along with a box of matches. Holmes held the former aloft when he saw me looking.

"The same German brand as was found at the scene of Peter Maugham's murder, Watson," he said, "as well as in the grounds of Oswald Maugham's apartment, following the intrusion."

"And no doubt this is the coat Gerber was wearing when he murdered Peter Maugham, too," I said.

"Yes," said Bainbridge, understandably impatient. "But where is he?"

"Patience, Inspector," replied Holmes, quietly. "Our quarry will be along soon. He's expecting a visitor."

"What are you playing at here, Holmes?" I asked. Cold, tired and more than a little jumpy, I had little time for Holmes's cryptic games. We had willingly put our lives at risk to accompany him here in pursuit of Gerber. I fully intended to get the full story.

In the event, however, Holmes wasn't given a chance to answer my question before the sound of a creaking floorboard in the hallway caused us all to lapse into a hasty, attentive silence.

Someone else was in the house.

I slid my revolver carefully from my pocket and thumbed the safety catch.

Holmes handed the candle to Bainbridge and withdrew a small silver pistol from his coat pocket. He crept silently towards the kitchen door, glancing back at me just the once before reaching out, tentatively, and then grasping the handle and throwing open the door.

For a moment nothing happened. Then, with a ferocious roar, a shadowy figure from the hallway launched itself at Holmes, sending them both sprawling to the ground.

They landed with a heavy thump, the newcomer cursing defiantly as they struggled. In the gloom and chaos I could tell only that the figure was that of a man, dressed in a long black overcoat.

I saw Holmes's pistol skitter across the tiles and rushed forward, but the man, realising his error – that Holmes was not the man he had come to meet and murder, and doubly, that he was not alone – leapt up from the floor and turned to bolt.

By now the constables were shouting and scrabbling for the door, as I hefted my revolver, took aim, and squeezed off a shot.

The report of the gun was deafening in the confined space of the kitchen, but my aim was true and the bullet caught the fleeing man in the upper arm, causing him to stagger and howl in pain, but failing to bring him down. Before I had time to take a second shot, however, the policemen were in the hallway, giving chase and blocking my line of sight.

"Get after him!" bellowed Bainbridge from the kitchen door.

I heard the front door burst open and Holmes's assailant, hotly pursued by the two uniformed men, hurtled out into the night. I decided, this time, to allow the younger men amongst us to do the running.

I dropped my revolver on the table and turned to assist Holmes. I stooped low, caught him by the arm and hauled him to his feet. To my consternation, I realised he was laughing.

"What the devil is so amusing, Holmes?" I asked, wondering if he'd received a blow to the head in the fall.

"Good God, man," said Bainbridge. "He could have killed you!"

"Fear not, gentlemen," replied Holmes, still laughing. "The final part of the puzzle has now fallen into place. We will not lose our man. Call your men off, Inspector. I know where he is headed."

In the thin light of the candle I could see Bainbridge's concerned expression. He, as I, did clearly not enjoy feeling so many steps behind Holmes in his understanding of the situation.

"How could you possibly know that, Holmes?" I said, frustrated. "It's taken you days to find this place. Now Gerber is loose again, and worse, he knows that we're on to him. He'll go to ground. We'll never find him if he heads into the slums."

Holmes shook his head. "He will not. Whatever he would wish us to believe, that man was *not* Mr. Hans Gerber."

"You astound me, Holmes!" I cried. "I cannot fathom what you're talking about. *Not Gerber*?" I sighed heavily. "Who was he, then? And what of Gerber?"

Holmes gave a deep and hearty rumble of a laugh. "My dear Watson," he said, in the tone a schoolmaster might reserve for his slowest pupil. "I *had* thought you might have worked it out by now. You know my methods. I am – or rather, I have *been* – Mr. Hans Gerber all along."

Bainbridge looked as if he were about to walk out in exasperation. His face had reddened, and he was staring at Holmes with such a look of incomprehension that my friend might have been a foreigner attempting to communicate with us in an entirely different language. "*You're* Hans Gerber?" he finally managed to say. "Forgive me, Mr. Holmes, but you have me at a loss. Are you asking me to arrest you?"

Holmes chuckled amiably. "Not at all, Inspector. Hans Gerber – who was, indeed, a disenfranchised nephew of Sir Theobald – was reported dead six years ago, killed in action on military campaign in Afghanistan. I correctly assumed that none of the surviving Maughams would be aware of their cousin's death – given their relationship with that part of their family – and therefore I decided to act in his name in an effort to provoke Sir Theobald's murderers."

"So it was you at the funeral, you behind the letters? You who called on Annabel Maugham while her brother was in town?" I said, shocked by this revelation.

"Indeed, Watson," replied Holmes.

"But think of all the needless concern! Think on how harrowing those letters have proved for the innocent parties. Was it really necessary, Holmes?" I asked.

"I believe it was, Watson. It was the only way to encourage Sir Theobald's murderers to show their hand," he replied.

"And why me? Why was it necessary for Gerber to threaten me in such a way?" I prompted, with some consternation.

"For that I can only apologise, Watson, and hope that you will forgive me." Holmes put a hand on my shoulder. "It was, however, a necessary precaution. I had to ensure that the interested parties believed Gerber to be real. If you received a letter – and your concern was genuine – then it could only work to strengthen the illusion, to add veracity to my little scheme."

"Well, I hope it was worth it, Holmes," I muttered, but in truth I had already forgiven him. It was not the first time he'd been forced to deceive me in order to lure an unsuspecting villain into a trap, and I doubted it would be the last.

Bainbridge, who'd been listening to this exchange intently, suddenly started, struck by a question that I had not yet thought to ask. "Hold on, Mr. Holmes! If you're Hans Gerber… then who *is* the killer?"

"*Killers*, Inspector," said Holmes, emphasising the plural. "There is more than one party responsible for this sordid affair."

"Then who was that man who just attacked you?" Bainbridge pressed.

"That, Inspector, was Mr. Joseph Maugham."

"Joseph Maugham!" I exclaimed. "But…" I was unable to find the correct words to form my question.

"Quite so," said Holmes. "The fortuitous bullet wound caused by your excellent shot, Watson, will be enough to prove it." He paused, as if weighing his next words. "This whole encounter was a carefully laid trap. I've been following his movements for days, tracking him across London. When I discovered his hideaway, here in this derelict house, I knew I only needed enough evidence to prove my theory. I wrote to Joseph Maugham as Gerber, telling him I knew his secret and demanding that he meet with me tonight, here at his secret bolthole in Whitechapel. He believes Gerber to be real, and to have a very real claim upon Sir Theobald's money."

"So he came here tonight to kill that phantom!" I said. "To kill *you*!"

"Precisely, Watson! And now, when he shakes the constables, as he surely will, he will head home to his sister, thinking he is safe, thinking that we'll assume it was Gerber we met in that house!" Holmes sounded damned pleased with himself, but I had to hand it to him – he'd woven a complex web of his own in order to entrap our villain.

"Holmes, you're a sly old dog," I said, ruefully. "But don't think for one minute that I'm not furious with you for keeping me in the dark once again."

"Come now, Watson," he replied, in a conciliatory tone. "You know my methods well enough by now."

"Indeed I do, Holmes," I said, laughing. "Indeed I do."

"Well, that's enough prattle for now, gentlemen," pronounced Bainbridge, heading for the door. "We must get after him!"

"Indeed we must!" agreed Holmes, elatedly. "Lead on, Inspector!"

And with that, we bustled out into the frigid night in search of a hansom, and Mr. Joseph Maugham.

CHAPTER TWENTY-ONE

From the Testimony of Miss Annabel Maugham

I was feeling somewhat out of sorts when Mr. Edwards called upon me that evening. Or rather, to put it a little more bluntly, I was consumed by anxiety over my situation. I'd been pacing the house for hours, alone and restless, unable to see a way out of my present crisis.

Matters were becoming desperate. As things stood, I would lose everything within a matter of days. Uncle Theobald's fortune and estate would pass into the hands of the despicable Hans Gerber, who continued to evade Scotland Yard, and I would be left destitute and alone, my allowance cancelled, my inheritance gone.

I knew that Joseph would not leave me to fend for myself – he might be a brute with a fearful lack of self-control, but he was not cold-hearted, and I knew that he cared for me. Nevertheless, the thought offered little comfort, for Joseph, too, had lived his entire life on the generosity of my late uncle, and so far as I knew, whatever mysterious "business" he pursued generated no real income or means of securing our future. Our only hope lay in the recovery of the will and the capture and subsequent prosecution of Hans Gerber for the murder of my poor cousin, Peter.

Time, however, was running out.

Mr. Edwards knew all of this, of course, and tried his best to offer what comfort he could. I could tell from the look on his face when I went to the door that he knew I'd been weeping. He, too, looked harassed and anxious – as if affected almost as deeply as I by the events unfolding around my family – but his demeanour remained as calm and reassuring as ever as I led him through to the sitting room and bade him take a seat. It was a chill night, and I set about building a fire. Mr. Edwards, ever anxious to assist, took it upon himself to organise a pot of tea, and by the time he returned from the kitchen with a rattling tray, the fire was stoked and burning fiercely.

He sat, pouring out the tea in silence.

"Well, Mr. Edwards, what news do you bring?" I asked, finally, unable to restrain myself any longer. "Have there been any developments?"

He looked sheepish as he passed me my teacup and saucer. "I fear, Miss Maugham, that I bring only news of the worst sort. The matter of your uncle's estate will go before a magistrate this coming Wednesday, and a decision will be made. The beneficiaries will be named."

"Mr. Edwards, I must insist that you try to hold them off for a little longer," I said, imploring him to help. "We cannot allow anyone to act hastily. I'm sure it's only a matter of time before the will is uncovered and everything is made clear. Mr. Holmes is still on the case, after all… I know you've been a great friend to this family, and a true comfort to me –" I placed my hand upon his as I talked, squeezing it gently "– and you must understand that a little more time would make all the difference to my situation. It cannot truly be necessary that they settle the matter so soon after my uncle's death?"

Mr. Edwards looked pained. He withdrew his hand, rubbing nervously at his chin. "Miss Maugham, you speak nothing but the truth. I *do* appreciate the difficult situation in which you find yourself, but I fear the matter is no longer in my hands. Without the will, there is very little anyone can do. The magistrate will settle the case, and that'll be the end of it."

I stood, turning away so as not to display my frustration. I could not, however, prevent it from seeping into my voice. "And so Mr. Hans Gerber, wretch that he is, shall inherit my fortune. He walks free from prosecution, despite his murderous crimes, whilst I, innocent, shall be cast down into penury. I shall be rendered homeless, Mr. Edwards. Destitute."

"Now, now, Miss Maugham!" exclaimed Mr. Edwards, scandalised by my outburst. "It will not come to that. I would never allow it to come to *that*."

"But Mr. Edwards, as you so ably put it, the matter is no longer in your hands," I replied, a little too sharply.

"My dear Miss Maugham –" he began in response, exasperated, but stopped short at a loud crashing sound in the hallway. He jumped to his feet in alarm. Moments later, the sitting room door banged open and my brother Joseph staggered in, clutching his shoulder.

His hands were covered in blood and his expression was a twisted grimace of pain. He was bleeding profusely from a wound in his upper arm, and swayed unsteadily on his feet.

"Joseph! I… I…" I stammered, rushing to his side.

"Good God, what happened to you, man?" exclaimed Mr. Edwards. "I'll send for the police immediately." He started towards the door.

"No!" bellowed Joseph, stopping Mr. Edwards in his tracks. His breath was ragged and whistling through his gritted teeth. "No police!" He staggered across the room, slumping into an armchair, his head hanging.

"Really, Mr. Maugham. You're in a bad way. We should send for help. A doctor at the very least," pressed Mr. Edwards, hovering indecisively in the doorway.

"We send for no one," barked Joseph in reply, pulling off his coat and tossing it on the floor. Every movement caused him to wince in pain. I could see now that there was a wound in his shoulder, and the bloodstain was spreading like a blooming flower upon his shirt.

"Here, let me take a look," I said, quietly, moving to unbutton the front of his shirt. I tried to remain calm, but my only thought was that Hans Gerber must have been responsible for this. But what of Gerber himself? What had Joseph done?

Joseph slapped me away angrily with his good hand, leaving a sticky crimson smear on my dress. "Get off me, woman! It's superficial. I'll be fine. Fetch me some hot water and linen."

"Very well…" I said, unsure. While I readily admit that I am no expert in such matters, the wound looked anything but superficial to me. "But tell me, Joseph, is this the work of Hans Gerber?"

"It's none of your business *what* it is," he replied, bitterly.

"Come now, Mr. Maugham," said Mr. Edwards, "I hardly think that's the tone with which to speak to your sister."

"And I think you should mind your own damn affairs, Mr. Edwards," spat Joseph, angrily. I stepped back, giving him space. I knew that if it wasn't for Joseph's injury, Mr. Edwards' comments would have precipitated a brawl. Joseph was not one to take such criticism lightly.

"Mr. Edwards, I think it best that –" There was another crash from the hallway, cutting me off. Voices echoed down the passageway.

Joseph leapt from his chair, panic-stricken. "My God! They're here! They must have followed me!" He hobbled towards the conservatory, still clutching his shoulder. "Hold them off. Do anything, Annabel. Stall them until I can get away." His pleas, however, came too late. I looked round to see Mr. Holmes, Dr. Watson and a small army of policemen burst into the sitting room, panting for breath.

"Stay right where you are, Mr. Maugham!" bellowed Inspector Bainbridge, levelling his revolver at my brother. "It's over."

CHAPTER TWENTY-TWO

We couldn't have been more than a few minutes behind Joseph Maugham when Bainbridge put his shoulder to the door and forced our entry into the man's home.

I was breathless and my nerves were somewhat frayed following our encounter in Whitechapel, but my dander was up and I was ready to do what was necessary. I had never been one to shy away from a fight, so long as the cause was just and the odds weren't too unbalanced.

The door gave way on the second attempt, splintering the frame and wrenching the lock from its housing. It swung open, banging noisily against the wall, immediately eliciting cries of alarm from within. We rushed forward, Bainbridge, Holmes and I, followed closely by a gaggle of uniformed men. Bainbridge evidently had blood in his sights, and Holmes was wearing a satisfied smile. Experience told me this meant he believed the end of the matter to be in sight.

I found myself hoping that his assertion about the culprit was correct; I rarely had cause to doubt Holmes's convictions, but if we found Joseph Maugham innocent of the crimes which had been lain at his door, then we had just barged uninvited into the home of two grieving siblings. In truth, my thoughts were for his sister, who I knew would be devastated by either possible outcome.

The scene in the sitting room, however, was enough to render my concerns immediately irrelevant. Joseph Maugham, bleeding profusely from a gunshot wound in his shoulder, was hobbling towards the conservatory in an effort to escape, while a stunned Miss Annabel Maugham stood in the centre of the room, clearly torn over whether to assist him, or whether to wait for the policemen who had just burst in. Mr. Tobias Edwards was perched on the edge of the sofa, baffled and wide-eyed.

"Stay right where you are, Mr. Maugham!" bellowed Bainbridge, panting for breath. "It's over."

"Inspector Bainbridge?" exclaimed Miss Maugham, as if searching for an explanation to the extraordinary events unfolding before her. "Mr. Holmes? Dr. Watson?" She looked at me, her eyes pleading, and I found my heart going out to the woman. Clearly, she was at a loss.

"Inspector, have your men restrain Mr. Maugham," said Holmes, his voice level. Bainbridge nodded and indicated for two of his constables to pin Maugham's arms by his sides. He grimaced and gave a half-hearted attempt to struggle free, but he was clearly spent. I fancied I could almost see the fight leave him as his shoulders slumped and he allowed himself to be led to a chair, where he sat, the two policemen on either side of him, each with a hand on one of his shoulders. Dark blood was still seeping through the front of his ruined shirt, and so I fished around in my pocket for a handkerchief, folded it and handed it to him. "Press this to the wound," I said. "It'll staunch the flow." I turned to Bainbridge. "And send for a carriage; this man needs to go to hospital."

"Harris?" said Bainbridge, calling to one of the constables.

"Yes, sir?"

"Do as the doctor says," muttered Bainbridge. "Wouldn't do to let the man die. At least until he's finished answering our questions."

"Yes, sir," echoed Harris, disappearing into the hall.

Satisfied, Holmes glanced at Annabel Maugham. "Miss Maugham, must I ask the police to restrain you, also?"

Miss Maugham looked utterly confused by the question. "Restrain me?"

"Now look here, Holmes –" I started, but he silenced me by raising a single finger. He didn't once remove his gaze from Miss Maugham's face.

"Come now, Miss Maugham," he said, his tone reasonable, but firm. "I think the time has passed for your protestations of innocence. The truth of the matter is plain to see."

"It is?" she replied, quietly. "I admit, I am at a loss as to what 'truth' you refer to, Mr. Holmes."

Holmes's expression hardened. "That you orchestrated the death of your uncle so that you and your cousins might inherit his fortune."

"Dear God!" I exclaimed. This was not a revelation I had anticipated.

Bainbridge looked as surprised as I was. "You mean to say that Miss Maugham and her brother are responsible for the death of their uncle?"

"I mean to say," said Holmes, "that Miss Maugham and her brother, along with their cousins Oswald and Peter Maugham, were jointly responsible for his murder."

"All four of them?" I whispered, astounded. I looked to Miss Maugham, whose expression was largely unreadable. She refused to meet my eyes. I simply could not believe that this woman, who to me had appeared so innocent, so fragile, could be responsible for such a terrible crime. "Are you certain, Holmes?"

"I am correct, am I not, Miss Maugham?" ventured Holmes.

There was a moment of silence as we collectively held our breaths, waiting for Miss Maugham to speak. When she did not, Holmes shrugged and continued. "I suspect it had been going on for some time. All four of the cousins were aware of the contents of Sir Theobald's will, and all were entirely dependent upon his generosity."

At this, Joseph Maugham issued a long groan of pain, and hunched forward in his chair, gripping his shoulder. I went to him, adjusting the compress. He glowered at me, his teeth gritted, but said nothing.

Holmes folded his hands behind his back, and began pacing back and forth before the hearth. "It is clear to me that Sir Theobald was growing rather more eccentric in his dotage, but showed no signs of passing on. He was in rude health, free from rheumatism, arthritis and the many other ailments that typically plague men of his age. He was in no hurry to quit this world, and it was this dogged will to survive that eventually became his undoing."

Holmes stopped pacing for a moment before Miss Maugham, and then resumed. "Greed and desperation are at the root of this business, the motives responsible for the fiendish plot that led the four cousins to form a murderous cabal." Holmes was in full flow now, giving forth his summation of the plot that he had been so intent on unravelling for the last few days. "Oswald Maugham provided the chemical compound used to drug Sir Theobald, slipping it into his drinks during the course of that fateful evening, even getting up to provide a further dose when he heard his uncle stir in the night, smashing his water glass on the floorboards. That much was evident after only a cursory examination of Oswald's apartment and discussing with him the depth of his admiration for the chemical sciences."

"But what of the others?" interrupted Bainbridge, and Holmes shot him an impatient look.

"Peter and Joseph were responsible for the act itself, tossing their unconscious benefactor down the stairs in the middle of the night, leaving him there so that he could be 'discovered' the following morning by the housemaid." He turned and pointed accusingly at Miss Maugham. "Annabel, I can only postulate, was the mastermind behind the plan and took it upon herself to handle the police the following morning. Forgive me, Inspector, but a woman in distress may prove to be a great distraction at the scene of a crime."

"Good God!" exclaimed Bainbridge, echoing my earlier sentiment. He, too, had been taken in by this woman.

Annabel Maugham swallowed, and finally raised her head to meet Holmes's gaze. "I had no hand in the matter, Mr. Holmes. I am innocent of any charge you might lay against me for my uncle's death."

"Liar!" barked Joseph, suddenly, with bile. He bucked in his chair, trying to get up, and the two constables were forced to restrain him again.

"I took no part in his murder," stated Miss Maugham, affecting innocence.

"Not directly, perhaps. Yet the same cannot be said of your cousin Peter's death, can it, Miss Maugham?" asked Holmes, allowing the briefest flash of anger to reveal itself in his tone.

It suddenly struck me what he was getting at. "The shorter man who attacked Peter Maugham!" I exclaimed. "It wasn't a man at all!"

"No," confirmed Holmes, with an approving nod in my direction. "It was a woman. *This* woman, to be precise. Wearing her brother's boots and coat in an effort to cover her tracks. The same woman who bought a very particular brand of German cigarettes from a tobacconist's shop on Oxford Street, and then left one of the butts at the scene in an attempt to make us believe that the mysterious Hans Gerber was the real perpetrator."

"But why?" asked Bainbridge, furrowing his brow. "Why kill Peter?" He glanced at Miss Maugham, but she remained tight-lipped. The look she was giving Holmes, however, was fierce enough to burn right through him.

"Because he came to us, Inspector," explained Holmes. "When the will went missing, the cousins all accused one another of stealing it, falling out with each other and disagreeing on how to proceed. They all thought the others were double-crossing them. In Peter's case, he probably was. I imagine he thought he'd be able to frame his cousins for his uncle's murder and walk away with the entire inheritance himself."

"He always was a devious fool," added Miss Maugham.

"His murder served a dual purpose, you see. On one hand, it reduced the number of claimants to the inheritance and prevented him from pointing the finger of suspicion at his cousins. On the other, it provided Miss Maugham with the perfect opportunity to discredit Hans Gerber, from whom she had only just received a visit. Gerber posed a very real threat, for without the will, he was in line to inherit everything." Holmes had again resumed his pacing.

I saw that Joseph Maugham was struggling to maintain consciousness and crossed to him, adjusting his posture and resting his head upon the back of the chair. His eyelids fluttered lightly, but it was clear that he was weakened by blood loss. I lifted his fingers from my blood-soaked handkerchief and assumed responsibility for applying pressure to the wound. He was not at risk of bleeding to death; the bullet had missed any vital organs or arteries, and a good surgeon would be able to remove any fragments and cauterise the wound.

Over my shoulder, Bainbridge was still questioning Holmes. "Then why make an attempt on Oswald's life?" he asked. "He was not party to Peter's plans."

"That was Joseph," said Holmes, "no doubt driven by his sister's greed, as well as the need to cover their tracks. Oswald must have suspected the truth about Peter's death. Only he could identify the likely suspects, because he understood their motives. And, of course, he was party to the truth about Sir Theobald's fall. Just like Peter, removing Oswald could only benefit Annabel and Joseph, provided they could pin the crime on Hans Gerber."

Holmes put a hand on Bainbridge's shoulder. "You must send some of your men to arrest Oswald Maugham, Inspector. He is every bit as guilty as these two sorry specimens."

"Very well," said Bainbridge, sighing. "It's a rum affair, this, Mr. Holmes."

"But what of Hans Gerber?" blurted Tobias Edwards, and I admit, at that point in proceedings I had almost forgotten he was there. He'd remained silent and observant while events carried on around him, but now everyone turned to look at him, weighing his question. His was still sitting on the edge of the sofa, his hands clasped upon his knees. He glanced from Miss Maugham to Holmes, waiting for Holmes's response.

"Ah, yes," said Holmes, laughing. "Hans Gerber. I fear that I may not have represented you at all well during the course of this endeavour, Mr. Edwards. Nevertheless, I hope you will forgive me for temporarily liberating your name. Your real name, that is."

Edwards looked for a moment as if Holmes had just slapped him across the face. His eyes went wide and he emitted a startled, strangled noise as he fought panic. He glanced at the door, but two of the uniformed men stepped further into the room, blocking the exit. "I… well…" he started, his face reddening. He looked hopefully up at Holmes, and then sighed wearily. His shoulders fell. "You have me, Mr. Holmes. I should never have been in doubt that you would."

I twisted around, still keeping my hand pressed against the wound in Joseph Maugham's shoulder. "You mean to say that Hans Gerber didn't die in Afghanistan, Holmes? That Mr. Edwards is, in fact, the real Hans Gerber?" I could barely credit it. The web of lies and betrayals weaved by the Maugham family was more complex than I could ever have imagined.

"This is too much, Mr. Holmes!" declared Bainbridge, throwing his hands up in dismay. "Too much!"

"I fear it is all true, Dr. Watson," said Edwards, tremulously. "I am, indeed, Hans Gerber."

"You?" exclaimed Miss Maugham, angrily. "You're Hans Gerber?"

I felt Joseph start up out of his chair, and turned to see his eyes had opened and he was straining against the constables' grip. I added my weight to theirs, forcing him back into his seat. "Let me free!" he burbled, flecks of spittle on his lips. "I'll kill him!"

"Hold him!" called Bainbridge, and another of the policemen came to take my place, pinning him down. I stood, stretching my aching legs, and fished another handkerchief from my pocket to wipe the sticky blood from my fingers.

Edwards barely seemed to know whom to address. In the end, he settled on Holmes. "I admit, Mr. Holmes, that I feared I might never be able to come forward once you had begun your campaign against the Maughams. Of course, I had no notion that you were my impersonator, but I knew that whoever was, they could not be the real Hans Gerber. I could say nothing, however, lest I inadvertently incriminate myself." He paused, as if appraising Holmes respectfully. "But tell me – how did you work it out?"

Holmes grinned. "Elementary, Mr. Edwards. The painting on the wall in your office shows a man standing before the banks of the Rhine. The likeness in the eyes is uncanny. I took him to be your father at once. A German. Your injured hand, although possibly the result of a childhood mishap, was more likely caused by a misfiring weapon, the sort of injury one might expect to be sustained by a military man." Holmes was on a roll, now, describing his method. The sheer simplicity of his deductions never ceased to amaze me.

"That leaves only the motive and the opportunity to destroy the will," he went on, "which you burned in the grate of Sir Theobald's study upon the morning of his death. No one else had cause or opportunity to do it, Mr. Edwards. Together, these three simple facts allowed me to deduce that Hans Gerber had not, contrary to the newspaper reports of the time, died in Afghanistan, but was alive and well and living under an assumed name in London.

"Add to that the realisation that Hans Gerber, despite the Germanic name bestowed upon him by his father, was born in England to an English mother, and it was no leap at all to assume that Hans Gerber would sound very much like an Englishman, with an English taste in tobacco. A fact that both Annabel and Joseph Maugham missed when they planted evidence at the scenes of both their crimes, supposedly incriminating Gerber, but in fact suggesting quite the opposite," he finished, with a flourish.

"Quite remarkable, Mr. Holmes," said Edwards, with the hint of a smile.

"But why, Mr. Edwards?" I asked. "Why adopt a new name and allow everyone to consider you dead?"

"I wanted a new life, Dr. Watson," replied Edwards. "A better life. I'd lived in squalor for so many years, watched my mother die of cholera. When I was injured during the war and invalided back to England, unable to fire a weapon because of my lost fingers, I adopted the name of a dead friend whom I knew to have no surviving family back home. It felt like a new beginning." He rubbed his hands over his face, sighing.

"It was not a difficult pretence, and soon I had managed to find a position with a firm of solicitors. It took me three years before I was finally able to meet Sir Theobald – my uncle – and to earn his confidence and respect."

At this Miss Maugham scoffed bitterly, and Edwards looked momentarily pained, but continued regardless. "In those early months of our acquaintance I had dreams of reuniting the family. I saw it as a chance to make reparations and heal the rift that had caused my mother to be so devastatingly cut out. I was soon to discover, however, when drawing up Sir Theobald's will, that reparations were far from his mind. He made no provision for his sister's family in the settlement of his estate, and refused to even acknowledge their existence when pressed. I was disgusted, of course, but there was very little I could do."

"Until, that was, you were called to the house upon the morning of his death in order to begin the appropriate legal proceedings," said Holmes.

"Quite so," agreed Edwards. "It was while fetching the document that I had the idea. I'd seen the way my cousins had treated the old man – with little more respect than for a lame dog – and felt no remorse for them or their lost incomes as I set the document alight in the grate. Little did I realise, of course, that Sir Theobald had been murdered, nor that someone would shortly come along and impersonate me, drawing attention to my name, even incriminating me for murder. All of this meant, of course, that I could not come forward to claim my inheritance. Until now."

There was a brief commotion in the hall and I saw Harris appear in the doorway, indicating that the carriage had arrived.

"I take it, then, that you did indeed have a second copy of the will at your offices, but that, too, met its end in the grate?" I prompted, keen to understand just how far this man had gone to seek revenge upon his benighted family before the opportunity to question him was lost.

"Precisely so, Doctor," confirmed Edwards. He knew the game was up, that the whole affair was at its end, and that his only recourse was to go quietly with the police. I respected him for that, at least.

"How dare you! How dare you do this to us!" shrieked Miss Maugham, wringing her hands in frustration. I thought for a moment that she would rush forward and attempt to strike Edwards, but she managed to regain her composure and remained where she stood, flushed with anger and glowering at the duplicitous solicitor. I was astounded by the change that had come over her, now that she had allowed her innocent facade to slip. She was not the woman I had thought she was, and I was somewhat ashamed of myself for having been taken in by her. Bainbridge, it seemed, was not the only one of us to make dangerous allowances for a woman in distress.

Edwards smiled sadly. "I do this safe in the knowledge, Annabel, that neither you nor your cousins are any more worthy than I."

At this, Holmes threw back his head and issued a long, heartfelt laugh.

"Take them away, Harris," said Bainbridge, shaking his head. "All of them."

I watched as the constables assisted the ailing Joseph Maugham to his feet and guided him out towards the waiting carriage. Tobias Edwards and Annabel Maugham were escorted out next, in silence, and a moment later, Holmes, Bainbridge and I were the only people left standing in the Maughams' sitting room.

"I can barely warrant it, Holmes," I said.

"Greed can cause people to do terrible things, Watson," replied Holmes.

"I'm only pleased that it's over," I said, relieved.

"Indeed," added Bainbridge. "Your assistance has been most appreciated, Mr. Holmes. I fear I should never have got to the bottom of it without you."

I saw the curl of a smile form on Holmes's lips, but he remained silent.

"It's a relief to know the matter is resolved," continued Bainbridge. "I only wish I could say the same about this blasted iron men business." He gave a weary sigh. "What is it they say? 'No rest for the wicked'? I must have done something dreadful in a previous life." He chuckled, but the laughter didn't extend to his eyes. "Well, gentlemen. A good night to you. And thank you once again." He started towards the door.

Holmes reached out a hand and caught Bainbridge by the shoulder. His smile broke into a grin. "Didn't I read, Inspector, that Count Ferenczy would be exhibiting the Moon Star at his rented house in Pimlico tomorrow night, to a party of prospective buyers?"

"Yes, but..." Bainbridge started, frowning, but trailed off. "Of course!" he exclaimed a moment later, revelation lighting up his face. "You're right. They'll be there, won't they? Whoever's issuing their orders will be unable to resist such a grand prize. They'll come for the diamond."

Holmes laughed. "Quite so, Inspector."

Bainbridge looked thoughtful. "Then I shall lay a trap," he said, decisively. "I shall bring an end to their campaign of terror."

I stepped forward. "I shall gladly assist you, Inspector," I said. I turned to Holmes, expecting him to pledge a similar offer of support. "Holmes?"

"I fear I have a prior engagement," replied Holmes, levelly. "Although I wish you every success, Inspector," he added.

Bainbridge nodded in acknowledgement, while I stared at

Holmes, utterly flabbergasted. Never before in all the long years of our friendship had I seen him turn away a good man so in need of his assistance.

"Well, thank you once again, Mr. Holmes," said Bainbridge, heading for the door. "Dr. Watson – I shall be in touch with arrangements for tomorrow evening. Goodnight, gentlemen."

"Goodnight, Inspector," I called after him. I turned to Holmes. "Badly done," I said, in an admonishing tone. "Badly done, Holmes." And with that, I took my leave.

CHAPTER TWENTY-THREE

It was a chill night, and I'd turned up the collar of my coat to stave off the penetrating cold. Frozen fog had descended over Pimlico and, even at this twilit hour, the pavements had already begun to succumb to a layer of hoary frost. My breath plumed before me and I found myself wishing for the second time that evening that I'd thought to bring along my hip flask. A nip of warming brandy would have been most welcome indeed.

Beside me, Inspector Bainbridge seemed twitchy and on edge. It was understandable, I supposed – if this operation did not go according to plan, many lives would be at stake. I'd seen men like this before, out in Afghanistan on the eve of battle, and I recognised the haunted look in his eyes, the burden of responsibility. It was a sign of his character that he cared so deeply about his fellow men.

Around us, hidden in the formal gardens of the square, were uniformed policemen, each of them wrapped in thick, woollen overcoats and bearing pistols. It was approaching half-past eight and we'd been in situ for over an hour, observing the grand townhouse that had been let by Count Ferenczy. There was a growing numbness in my legs, which felt as if they were slowly transforming into solid blocks of ice. I stamped my feet in the muddy loam in an effort to get the blood circulating. I hoped that this endeavour would not be in vain, and that we should not find ourselves suffering from hyperthermia for nought.

I was still furious with Holmes for his decision not to accompany us that evening. To my mind, it showed an utter disregard for the efforts of Inspector Bainbridge and his men. Worse, I fully suspected his "prior engagement" was nothing more than an excuse to lose himself to the vagaries of his addiction. At times, the man could be most infuriating. His expertise might have proved invaluable.

Presently, two figures emerged at the other end of the street. From my vantage point I found it difficult to discern the exact nature of the newcomers, although from their size and gait I knew them to be human and not the automata for whom we laid in wait.

Sure enough, as the two figures drew closer I caught a glimpse of their faces in the thin glow of a street lamp: two men, smartly dressed in overcoats and top hats. They paused for a moment by the curb and one of them withdrew a cream-coloured notecard from inside the breast pocket of his jacket. The two men consulted it carefully for a moment, and then turned and examined the numbers on the doors of the nearby houses. A few seconds later they had selected their destination: Count Ferenczy's residence.

The first man returned the notecard to his pocket while the other rapped on the door. Within moments the door opened, spilling light into the street, and the two men were admitted by a butler. I admit I felt a momentary pang of envy for the warmth and shelter, then the door closed and we were alone again in the quiet street.

Events continued in this vein for nigh on another hour.

Occasional figures would emerge from the gloom, select the house in question, murmur a few words to the butler and then be permitted inside. Clearly, the Count's advertisement in the newspapers had worked. These people, I gathered, were prospective buyers of the Moon Star, come to witness its unveiling.

"I hope we can stop those machines before it's too late," I whispered to Bainbridge, who glanced over at me, a question in his eyes. These were the first words spoken in hours, and I rather think my statement caught him a little off guard.

"Too late?" he asked.

"There's more than the diamond at stake here," I replied, levelly. "Think on it. The Count's guests must be among the richest denizens of the Empire. If they are able to even consider the purchase of such a magnificent gem, well – consider the nature of the jewellery that they themselves will be wearing this evening, or the contents of their wallets."

"Good Lord!" exclaimed Bainbridge, a little louder than perhaps he'd intended. "You're right. It won't be just the stone they're after. Whoever's behind the automata will be unable to resist such rich pickings. There'll be no need for them to burgle the houses of these people – the Count has conveniently brought them all together under one roof!" He gritted his teeth and frowned, as if silently cursing himself for not seeing it earlier. "We must be ready," he said, firmly. "We must stop at nothing to protect these people who've walked unwittingly into a trap."

"Quite so," I said, my gloved fingers closing on the handle of the revolver in my pocket. I would assist Bainbridge any way that I could, although in truth I feared that my weapon would prove ineffective against the machines. Then again – what weapon existed that could stop a man of iron? I had grave doubts that anything we could do would prove effective.

Soon, I knew, we were likely to find out.

* * *

It was around thirty minutes later that I became aware of the imminent danger. It began with the far-off clanging of metal against stone: a repetitive pattern that grew steadily louder. Soon enough, these ominous footsteps were joined by the angry hiss of escaping steam, and we knew then for certain that the iron men were upon us.

I glanced at Bainbridge, who gave a single nod and hefted his pistol, bracing himself for what was to come.

They came from the same direction as the other visitors, the far end of the street – four of them. They were hulking metal monsters, larger than a man and twice as fearsome. I had read about them, of course, and had listened studiously to Bainbridge's reports, but nothing could have prepared me for my first proper sight of the machines. Their red eyes were like beacons in the gloom, and I shuddered as I considered what the next few moments would bring. How could we ever stop such things?

The iron men moved with single-minded intent. They approached the door to the Count's property, where now a party was in full swing. Bathed in the light of the tall windows, their metal armour glinted with a polished sheen.

As described in the various police reports, they appeared to completely disregard their surroundings. Unlike most criminal gangs I had encountered, they did not post lookouts at either end of the street, and cared little for subtlety. They simply began pounding on the door, striking repeatedly with their fists until the wood itself began to splinter.

The miniature furnaces on their backs glowed with the heat of smouldering coal. This, of course, was the source of their power: pressurised, heated water that enabled their mechanical joints to move.

Within moments they had reduced the door to splinters and were forcing their way inside. I pulled my revolver from my pocket and stood, intent on tackling these monstrosities before they could do any real harm.

"No!" hissed Bainbridge, grabbing my sleeve and dragging me back behind the cover of a hawthorn bush. "Wait until they've gone inside."

"But all those people," I said, frowning. "We can't leave them to face those things alone. The Count has a full house."

"I know," said Bainbridge, levelly. "But once they're inside we have them trapped. Tackle them here in the street and they can get away. With them cornered we can block the exits and try to contain them."

I nodded, conceding the point, although I admit I was dubious as to whether these things could be contained at all. I watched, tense, as the last of them fought its way through the ruins of the door, disappearing within.

"Now! Go!" shouted Bainbridge, and all around us the bushes erupted as uniformed men burst forth from their cover and rushed the house. Bainbridge himself led the charge, orchestrating his men. "Block the exits," he bellowed, indicating for three of them to take up posts by the door. He led the others inside and I brought up the rear, my weapon ready.

Inside, chaos reigned. I found myself in a large reception hall, from which an impressive, galleried staircase swept up to the first floor. Civilians were screaming and fleeing in terror as the four iron men marched relentlessly towards their prize: a glass cabinet in the centre of the hall, within which the Moon Star rested upon a blue velvet cushion. It was immense – the size of a duck's egg – like no gemstone I had seen in all my years.

The noise was disorientating, and it took me a moment to get my bearings. It was only the report of a pistol to my left that brought me round, and I turned to see the bullet rebounding harmlessly from the shoulder of the nearest iron man. It whirled around, flinging out its arm and striking a civilian – a bearded man in black evening dress – who went down heavily with a spray of blood, rendered immediately unconscious.

Around me, there was a riot of truncheons and revolvers as the policemen charged the iron men. The machines were cumbersome and slow to react, but it mattered little; the policemen's attacks proved utterly ineffective. Their truncheons rebounded with dull clangs, bullets failing to pierce the thick iron plating and ricocheting dangerously into the fleeing crowd.

"Hold your fire!" I shouted, turning around my revolver and brandishing it instead as a club. "They're impervious to our bullets!"

I glanced at Bainbridge, who was across the other side of the hall, grappling with one of the automatons. It grasped his cane in both of its metal claws and lifted him a clear inch off the ground as he held on, struggling to reclaim it. Escaping steam hissed from small imperfections at the machine's elbows and shoulders as it hoisted him higher and higher, gears whirring. I watched, stunned, as it raised its arms almost fully above its head and heaved Bainbridge backwards, flinging him across the room. He soared through the air, arms flailing, and collided noisily with the display case containing the Moon Star. It shattered beneath the impact, sending broken shards shimmering into the air. Amongst these glittering fragments was the diamond itself, which tumbled from its perch, skittered across the marble floor, and spun off into the chaotic furore, finally coming to rest near the foot of the stairs.

Bainbridge slumped to the ground, dazed and semi-conscious, but apparently – miraculously – unhurt.

The iron man's gaze swivelled in the direction of the diamond.

"Oh no, you don't!" I bellowed, rushing at the machine and

presenting my shoulder, hoping to unbalance it and topple it to the floor. I barrelled into it, my shoulder striking it hard in the back. The iron man, however, simply disregarded my attack as a man would disregard a buzzing fly. It shrugged me off with a swipe of its arm, starting away in the direction of the jewel without even glancing back.

Smarting, I fell to the floor, clutching my shoulder as it blossomed in pain. My heart sank. We were done for. I could see no way of stopping the machines. All around me, our small contingent of policemen was being forced back, their weapons ineffective against the dreadful, metal monsters. Some of them lay unconscious on the floor; others were running for cover. Bainbridge was still picking himself up from amongst the ruins of the display case, and I was on my knees, my revolver hanging limp from my fingers, my upper arm burning with pain.

My efforts had proved futile. I watched, horrified, as the iron man reached the foot of the stairs, crouched low, and scooped up the precious stone in its skeletal fist. It straightened up again with a series of jerking, mechanical movements, and beckoned to its cohorts, gesturing to the door.

Once again, it seemed as if the machines would escape with their plunder, and there was nothing we could do to prevent it.

The four iron men trudged across the sea of broken glass, stepping over the heaped forms of three policemen and the civilian I had seen struck down a few moments earlier. Cursing, I hauled myself to my feet, meaning to assist Bainbridge, but froze when I heard a sudden shout from above.

"Now!"

I glanced up at the gallery, surprised to see the figure of a man, dressed in an evening cape and top hat, silhouetted against a moonlit window at the top of the stairs. He was flanked by a small army of youths, ranked in a long line that followed the balustrade around the edges of the landing. There were a dozen or more of them, each of them holding what appeared to be wooden pails, although it was difficult to make out any further details in the dim light.

At the command of the man – whom I took to be Count Ferenczy himself – the youngsters all hefted their buckets and overturned them in synchronised fashion, tipping gallons of freezing water down upon the gathered assembly below.

I bellowed in shock as the icy fluid sloshed over my head and shoulders, drenching me. Many of the constables around me issued similar, colourful curses, some of them in considerably more purple language. The water swilled across the marble floor, pattering down from the heavens like a terrible rainstorm.

"What the devil! I cannot begin to fathom –" I started, wiping water from my eyes, but stopped short as I realised with absolute stupefaction the truth of what had just occurred.

The four iron men stood rigid in the centre of the hall, steam gushing in great, swirling clouds from their doused furnaces.

For a moment everyone stood in silent shock, as if we were holding our breaths, anxious to see what would happen next. Then one of the uniformed men on the floor issued a heartfelt groan and stirred from unconsciousness, and the spell was broken.

Seemingly the first to regain my senses, I tentatively approached the nearest iron man. It appeared unmoving, as if frozen in mid-movement, its arm raised, a clawed finger pointing in silent accusation at the man at the top of the stairs. It was perfectly still and silent, as if now rendered completely incapable of movement. I noticed the cogs and wheels at its elbow and shoulder joints appeared to be seized in position.

I reached out a hand to touch it, but as my fingers drew within only an inch or two of the dull iron surface, the arm suddenly fell, dropping to swing loose by the automaton's side. I started in shock, fearing the thing had once again regained some semblance of life. I admit, I may have even issued a startled cry.

I stepped back, wary, as Bainbridge rushed to my side, clutching a constable's baton in his fist. We hesitated for a moment, waiting to see if it would react.

"It's dead," he said. "Just the weight of the arm, causing it to drop now that there is nothing to keep it suspended." He used the edge of the truncheon to nudge the shoulder of the stationary machine. It did not respond. The crimson lights that had previously burned in its eyes were now extinguished, I noted. The scent of the damp coals was thick and pungent.

"Careful!" a commanding voice boomed from behind us. "It may still be dangerous."

I turned to see the Count descending the stairs with a flourish, his cape billowing behind him. His Hungarian accent was pronounced, but stately. He was still wearing his top hat and carrying a cane. He appeared to be a middle-aged fellow, with a neatly trimmed black moustache and a long, puckered scar running across his left cheek, distorting his smile. He cut a somewhat eccentric figure as he strolled casually through the wreckage towards us.

The Count motioned for us to stand aside and both Bainbridge and I took a step back to give him room. He circled the automaton once and then, using the end of his cane, reached up and rapped noisily three times on its head. The sound was a deep, hollow clang.

Around us, I noticed the uniformed men had begun to gather, watching proceedings with an air of hushed expectation.

Grinning, the Count seemed to contemplate the iron man for a moment, before discarding his cane nonchalantly to the floor and stepping towards the automaton. With a white-gloved hand he reached up and began fiddling beneath its chin.

"Whatever –" Bainbridge began, but the Count silenced him with a look, and continued with his work. A moment later he had unlatched what appeared to be a metal clasp, and with a flourish, he levered the machine's entire head backwards to reveal – to my utmost surprise – the head of a man.

"Good Lord!" exclaimed Bainbridge. There were cries of consternation and alarm from around us.

The man's face was haggard and gleamed with a patina of sweat. His blonde hair was stuck to his forehead and his eyes were narrowed, his expression fierce.

"But…" I stammered. "It's… it's a man!"

The iron man's pilot spat at the Count in futile protest, wrinkling his nose in apparent disgust.

"But not a particularly pleasant one, Watson," replied the Count, in a familiar, satisfied tone.

"Holmes?" I exclaimed, confused. "Is it you?" The revelations were coming thick and fast, and I was beginning to doubt the veracity of my own mind.

The Count reached up and removed his top hat, making a show of flinging it across the room with a flick of his wrist. He pulled the white gloves from his hands, finger by finger, and then, with a sudden gesture, reached up and peeled away the moustache from his upper lip. The puckered line of the scar came with it, the smile relaxed, and I saw at once that it was, indeed, Holmes. Once again he had adopted the use of face paint and trickery in order to deceive us. I could hardly believe that I had fallen for the same trick twice in such a short span of time, but Holmes was nothing if not an expert in misdirection. I knew he must have had his reasons for keeping us in the dark.

"But why?" I asked, flabbergasted.

Holmes threw back his head and gave forth a long, hearty laugh. "To lure them here, of course, my dear Watson. I knew these 'iron men' – or rather, whoever was pulling their strings – would find the lure of the diamond irresistible. It was all the bait I needed to be able to put my theory to the test."

"What of the Count Ferenczy?" asked Bainbridge, his brow creased in concern. "What does he think about you co-opting his name?"

Holmes smiled patiently, presenting his palms as if in supplication. "There never was a real Count Ferenczy, Inspector. I fear I have misled you. It was always me, incognito."

"You could have let us in on it, Holmes," I said.

"Not a bit of it, Watson," replied Holmes. "My plan hinged on the deception. It had to appear, to all intents and purposes, that I was a genuine visitor to this country, here in London with a precious stone to dispose of."

"Astounding," muttered Bainbridge, shaking his head in admiration. "How did you know? How on earth did you fathom that these machines were, in fact, operated by men?"

"A simple deduction, Inspector," said Holmes, one corner of his mouth twitching in a smile. "Automaton technology is not yet at a sufficient point in its development for anyone to be able to engineer such miraculous machines. In all the many accounts of the iron men that were provided by witnesses, the machines were described as operating under their own free will. Even a cursory examination of the subject, however, would suggest that simulacra such as these are far beyond the means of any living engineer. This is true even of the Turkish and the French, who presently excel in the field.[1]"

---

[1] At the time, of course, Holmes was correct in his assertion. Many years later, however, Bainbridge – then Chief Inspector – would relate to us the details of the "Affinity Bridge" affair and the work of Pierre Villiers, the French scientist who had developed an advanced form of artificial man. These remarkable automata were installed in the houses of the rich elite,

"So it had to be men in suits of armour?" I prompted.

"Indeed," replied Holmes. "And their immense strength could be accounted for by virtue of the fact the suits are steam powered, allowing their movements to be assisted by a series of cogs, gears and pistons." Holmes gestured at the nearest iron man. The pilot's face was flushed red with barely contained rage. "As you can see, without that power the suits are too heavy for a mere man to operate."

"And the water, thrown from above, was enough to extinguish the burning coals that fuelled that power?" I asked.

"Precisely!" said Holmes, animated. "Exactly that, Watson!"

Bainbridge still looked somewhat confused. "But who are these... children?" He pointed, and I turned to see a large gang of urchins had gathered around the foot of the stairs. They were none of them no older than twelve or thirteen, and they were dressed in street rags. I recognised them immediately.

"The Baker Street Irregulars," I said, grinning.

Holmes nodded. "Who else?"

"The what?" said Bainbridge. "I fear you've lost me."

"A gang of street urchins that Holmes maintains on his payroll," I said, with a smile.

Bainbridge shook his head and sighed, as if resigned to the fact he would never fathom the ways of my friend. That, of course,

---

or employed in libraries, factories and restaurants as servants and workers. At the time they caused quite a stir and it seemed as if they would mark the onset of a revolution. Villiers' experiments with illegally obtained human organs, however, led to exposure and investigation by Her Majesty's agents, Sir Maurice Newbury and Miss Veronica Hobbes, and eventually Villiers' death at the hands of his duplicitous partner, Mr. Joseph Chapman. The automata were deemed unsound and removed from the market. It is thought that some, however, were hidden away by enterprising owners during the ensuing purge and even now remain in operation, maintained as illegal curios and objects de art.

was one of the many things one had to accept when they counted Mr. Sherlock Holmes amongst their friends.

"What of the stone?" I asked, suddenly. In the excitement I feared we'd all forgotten the priceless jewel, and it remained unaccounted for.

Holmes chuckled. "Paste, Watson. Nothing but paste."

"So there never was a Moon Star?" I asked.

"Indeed not, Watson. Naught but a fabrication. A cunning trap. Speaking of which…" Holmes turned to the unmasked man in the iron man suit. "Who are you working for?" he asked, firmly.

The man pursed his lips and spat again, this time successfully landing a gobbet of spittle on Holmes's cuff.

"The damned impertinence!" cursed Bainbridge, the disgust evident in his voice. He turned, searching out the nearest of the other, stationary iron men, and made a beeline for it.

All around us, the constables were beginning to restore order, helping their bruised colleagues to their feet, organising carriages for the injured, sending for the owner of the property. I felt a surge of pride for the sturdy British policeman, always handy in a crisis and happy to muck in. They'd given a solid account of themselves in the battle, and had made an effort to ensure the civilians were evacuated to safety. I made a mental note to say as much to Bainbridge when everything was done and dusted.

I watched Bainbridge with interest as he approached the other iron man. Mimicking Holmes's earlier tactic, he felt around beneath the chin of the machine's helmet until his fingers found the clasp. He released it with a sudden jerk, pulling the helmet free.

The face beneath – belonging to a red-faced, auburn-haired man in his thirties, with a crooked, broken nose – eyed Bainbridge bitterly.

"Tell us for whom you're working!" demanded Bainbridge, leaning closer, his tone firm. He'd clearly run out of patience, and was not about to accept any further delays.

The man shook his head, his lips pursed.

"Then I can assure you of one thing," said Bainbridge, bristling. "That each and every one of you will be standing trial for attempted murder. You'll face the gallows."

"Attempted murder?" stammered the red-faced man, who was clearly concerned by this new development. "Robbery, more like. It was only robbery!"

"I think you'll find the witnesses who saw you set upon me in Holborn the other evening might argue otherwise," said Bainbridge, levelly.

I saw the man swallow and glance at the exposed face of his fellow conspirator, as if searching for salvation. "We wouldn't have hurt you," he said, desperately. "We were only trying to scare you off." His voice had grown high and reedy with fear.

Bainbridge paced back and forth before him, his hands clasped behind his back, his face like thunder. It was an astonishing show. "You went to great lengths to scare me," he said, shaking his head. "Smashing your way into a derelict building, driving me onto the roof… I somehow think the jury will find it an easy verdict to agree. You'll all swing."

The man in the iron man suit looked frantic. "I… I… we…" he stammered indecipherably.

"Now tell me," said Bainbridge, ceasing his pacing and leaning in so that his nose was almost touching that of the other man, who flinched, but could not move away. "And I'll make sure they go easy on you," he added, quietly.

"Asquith!" the man blurted out, without further hesitation. "Percival Asquith! He put us up to it. He told us where to go, what we were looking for. He said there was no chance anyone would catch us in these things, and that he'd give us a share of the profits."

"Bloody liar!" spat the man behind me, the first time he had spoken since he'd been unmasked.

Bainbridge glanced at Holmes and I, and then turned to one of his men. "Sergeant!"

"Yes, sir?" said one of the policemen, turning away from the small group of civilians he'd been addressing to give Bainbridge his full attention.

"Secure the suspects and get them to a cell," ordered Bainbridge.

"Yes, sir! Right away, sir!" replied the sergeant.

"Mr. Holmes, Dr. Watson," continued Bainbridge, beckoning them to the door, "would you care to accompany me?"

"I wouldn't miss it for the world," I replied, with a broad grin. Holmes clasped me firmly on the shoulder, confirming his support, and together the three of us left the house in Pimlico in search of Percival Asquith, our final, elusive quarry.

CHAPTER TWENTY-FOUR

Percival Asquith's club – known to its members as the Nightingale Society – was behind an undistinguished door on Shaftesbury Avenue, and if it hadn't been for the address card that Asquith had given Bainbridge a couple of days earlier, I doubt we should ever have found it.

Like so many of the gentlemen's clubs that catered to those with a more sophisticated or aristocratic appetite, the existence of the organisation was known to only a select few. It was felt – I gathered – that by insisting on such secrecy from their members, clubs such as the Nightingale would be able to maintain a more elitist air, and as such, any undesirable elements could be kept far at bay. The upshot of all this, I'd long ago concluded, was that the clubs' owners were able to charge an extortionate fee from their members.

Holmes rapped loudly and insistently three times in quick succession, calling loudly for attention until the door was opened and an exasperated butler peered out, his eyes narrowed. It wasn't the subtlest of entrances, but it was effective – the man seemed intent on avoiding a scene on the street, and when his gaze fell upon Bainbridge's papers and the steely expression on Holmes's face, he ushered us in, quickly closing the door behind us.

"Can I be of service, gentlemen?" he asked, in hushed tones. "I must say – it's most unusual for us to receive a call from Scotland Yard, here at the Nightingale." He pronounced these last four words as if reminding us that we could have no possible business inside.

Bainbridge had little time for the man's haughtiness, however, nor the man's obvious desire to avoid being overheard by his clientele. He raised his voice, adopting a firm, commanding tone. "It is equally unusual for a club such as the Nightingale to harbour a villain in its midst, is it not?"

The butler bristled, as if physically affronted. "A… villain?" he mumbled, apparently shocked by the accusation.

"Quite so," said Bainbridge. "Now, if you would care to show us through, we'll see to the matter directly."

The butler appeared somewhat lost for words. Quietly, he led us across the austere reception hall and into the opulence of the main drawing room, where a scattering of members stood about in small groups, or otherwise lounged on Chesterfields, sipping whisky and locked in conversation or hands of cards.

We hesitated on the threshold. "Mind you, sir," said the old, white-haired fellow, wagging his finger at Bainbridge, "we don't want any trouble here at the Nightingale. We count royalty amongst our members, and they come to us to escape their day-to-day pressures in the company of other, like-minded folk. If there truly is a villain in our midst, we'd appreciate it if you could approach the matter with some discretion."

"You'll have no trouble from us, I can assure you, so long as the gentleman in question is willing to help with our enquiries," said Bainbridge.

"I should imagine any member of the Nightingale should be

willing to assist the police," said the butler, tartly. "Whatever the circumstances."

Bainbridge all but rolled his eyes as the butler retreated with a satisfied nod.

I admit – I was not so optimistic.

The club was well appointed, with dark mahogany-panelled walls and tasteful dried-flower arrangements placed strategically around the room. A large marble fireplace dominated the space, and a hearty fire flickered and spat in the grate. Above the mantel hung two crossed swords and a shield, depicting heraldry with which I was unfamiliar – presumably the club's coat of arms.

Bainbridge pointed out Percival Asquith, who was sitting with another man before the fire. He was smartly dressed in a black evening suit, with a starched white collar and a red carnation in his buttonhole. He was a willowy, clean-shaven man with neatly trimmed blonde hair, and was clutching a glass of brandy in his left hand. He appeared to be deep in conversation.

Holmes cut quite a figure as we crossed the room, still dressed in the elaborate finery of Count Ferenczy, his cape draped around his shoulders. In his hand he carried the helmet of one of the iron men, brought with us from the house in Pimlico. Heads turned to regard him with interest.

"Mr. Asquith?" said Bainbridge, as we approached. "I would speak with you urgently."

Asquith did not so much as raise his eyes to see who had spoken, but gave a little, dismissive wave of his hand as if to shoo us away, and continued his conversation. The arrogance of the man was astounding.

Bainbridge cleared his throat and remained standing before the fireplace, to the side of Asquith's chair. His face reddened as Asquith continued to ignore him.

I glanced at Holmes, whose face showed not a flicker of

emotion as he calmly studied Asquith. The moment stretched. Then, suddenly, he stepped forward, raised his arm and dropped the iron man helmet onto the low table between Asquith and his companion.

It landed with a terrible, hollow clang, shattering an empty brandy glass and causing everyone in the room to suddenly give up their conversations and turn to see what was occurring.

"What –" began Asquith, enraged. He turned accusing eyes on Holmes, and was about to issue what I imagined to be a foul-mouthed challenge, when his eyes caught sight of the object. They widened in stunned surprise.

"I think, Mr. Asquith, that you have a great deal of explaining to do," said Bainbridge, with some measure of satisfaction.

Asquith looked from Holmes to Bainbridge, panic evident in his expression. His face flushed. Realisation dawned. "I… well…"

"The game's up, Asquith," said Holmes, quietly. "We know everything."

"Percival? What's wrong?" said Asquith's friend, starting out of his seat. "Who are these people?"

"I'm sorry, Frederick," said Asquith, quietly, with the tone of a man resigned to his fate. I saw Bainbridge visibly relax, his shoulders dropping, and I, too, released my grip on the revolver in my pocket.

Asquith, however, had other ideas. He sprang suddenly from his seat, overturning the table, and Holmes leapt back to avoid being caught either by it, or the shower of broken glass.

Asquith moved like a cat, taking two strides to the fireplace, reaching up with both hands and yanking free one of the two swords that resided there. He twisted, swinging it wildly, the tip passing only inches before Bainbridge's face.

To his credit, Bainbridge simply took a step back and exhaled slowly. "Put the weapon down, Mr. Asquith," he said, slowly. "You're only making matters worse for yourself."

Asquith, however, was wild-eyed and frantic, beyond reason. He was a desperate, cornered man, and he knew there was no way out. "I'll run you through!" he shouted in reply, jabbing the sword at Bainbridge. "All of you!"

By this time there were shouts and jeers coming from all around the room, although I was not clear whether they were aimed at Holmes, Bainbridge and myself as trouble-making interlopers, or at Asquith for bringing the club into such terrible disrepute.

I pulled my revolver free from my pocket, levelling it at Asquith. "I'll shoot if I have to, man," I called. "Lower the sword, now!"

Asquith jerked suddenly, arcing the sword through the air towards me. In response, my finger depressed the trigger, and I realised in horror that my bullets had all been spent ineffectually on the iron men earlier in the evening.

The sword descended, as if in slow motion, and I tried to throw myself to the ground to avoid the blow. I struck the back of a chair, however, and I admit, at that point in the proceedings I thought I was done for. I closed my eyes, waiting for the blade to strike.

Yet the blow never came. Asquith's sword clanged loudly against metal, and I twisted awkwardly to see Holmes brandishing a poker he had snatched up from the fireplace. He had intercepted Asquith's attack, and they now faced one another, poised and ready.

Asquith howled in frustration, and with both hands still on the pummel of the weapon, swung it back behind his head and brought it down in a sweeping arc towards Holmes. My friend danced backwards, again raising the poker to parry Asquith's attack.

Myself and Bainbridge fell back, giving Holmes room to manoeuvre. He adopted a classic fencing poise, his weapon arm raised high, his torso exposed and inviting attack. His eyes traced Asquith's every movement.

Asquith, desperate and breathless, lunged forward with his blade, aiming for Holmes's belly. Holmes dropped his arm and twisted to his right. Poker met sword, deflecting the attack and sending it wide. Without missing a beat, Holmes struck out with his left foot, pivoting round and catching Asquith roundly in the chest.

Asquith stumbled backwards and almost fell, but caught himself on the back of a Chesterfield and was able to right himself in time to parry a sideswipe from Holmes's poker. Once again, the two men faced off against each other, circling before the fireplace.

Holmes was gritting his teeth, his expression fixed with determination. I fumbled for cartridges in my jacket pocket and slipped them hastily into the chambers of my service revolver. I raised my arms and tried to draw a shot, but knew it would be too dangerous to discharge the weapon there and then. I risked hitting Holmes, or the bullet going wide and striking an innocent civilian.

Men were beginning to gather in a wide circle around us, observing proceedings with interest. It seemed unlikely now that any of them would attempt to intercede; they appeared more concerned with deriving entertainment from the scene, shouting challenges and cheering as the two men fought.

I watched, helpless, as Asquith came on again, this time employing a downwards chopping motion, aimed at Holmes's head. Holmes, however, was wise to these desperate manoeuvres and side-stepped easily, allowing the blade to pass harmlessly a few inches from his face. Asquith, however, had overstretched, and Holmes saw his chance. He snapped out a fist and caught the other man hard across the chin.

Asquith bellowed and fell back, dropping the sword. His hand went to his face, and he looked as if he were about to swoon, shaking his head as if to clear the resulting dizziness. Holmes pressed his advantage, flinging the poker back into the fire and following through with a right hook to Asquith's kidneys.

Asquith doubled over and dropped like a sack of potatoes,

gasping for breath, spittle flecking his lips. Bainbridge saw his chance to intercede. He rushed forward and grasped the arms of the semi-conscious man, pinning them behind his back. "Someone fetch me some twine!" he barked, straining to keep Asquith upright.

Holmes fished around in his jacket pocket for a few seconds before withdrawing a thin silk cord. He tossed it to Bainbridge, who deftly snatched it out of the air and set about securing the villain. Moments later Asquith was trussed and bound.

"There you have it, Inspector," said Holmes, mopping his brow with a handkerchief. "The duplicitous wretch behind the iron men robberies."

"Indeed, Mr. Holmes," replied Bainbridge, grinning. "My thanks to you, for your assistance."

Holmes gave a cursory nod, and glanced over at me expectantly. My hand, still clutching the revolver, was trembling. I slipped it into my jacket pocket.

"Watson," said Holmes, "be a good fellow and ensure that some of the Inspector's constables are on the way."

"Very well," I said, with a sigh, starting towards the door.

"And then, I feel," went on Holmes, "a pot of tea before the fire at Baker Street is long overdue. Wouldn't you agree?"

"Indeed I would," I replied, with a broad grin. I felt suddenly as if a burden had been lifted from my shoulders. "And a slice of Mrs. Hudson's Madeira cake, perhaps?" I ventured.

Holmes threw back his head and gave a long, heartfelt laugh. "Quite so, Watson," he said, still chuckling. "Quite so."

CHAPTER TWENTY-FIVE

I could still barely believe the events that had unfolded over the last few days, and I brooded upon this as I sat in silence with Holmes later that evening, drinking brandy and staring at the dancing flames in the grate.

Holmes was puffing thoughtfully on his pipe, attired in his ratty old dressing-gown. He looked more relaxed than I'd seen him in months. Nevertheless, something about these twin cases had affected us both deeply, and I couldn't help but wonder what subtle mechanisms were now hard at work inside my friend's mind. He seemed unusually pensive, despite his peaceful countenance.

He'd spent the last hour explaining his movements over the previous two days, including a detailed account of how he'd scoured the city's many tobacconists in search of imported German cigarettes, and placed adverts in the London newspapers soliciting buyers for the fictional Moon Star diamond.

He talked also of his interludes posing as Gerber, and how he'd used this assumed identity to draw the villains out, encouraging each of the Maughams to take increasingly bold steps in the knowledge that, when they finally overreached, he, Bainbridge and I would be on hand to step in and arrest them.

I felt a prize fool for having had the wool pulled over my eyes for so long, but nevertheless a great deal of admiration for my friend. He was a wily devil, and had clearly seen to the heart of the matter – of *both* matters – in no time at all. While Bainbridge and I were still floundering about in search of evidence and motive, Holmes was working away behind the scenes, laying traps and luring the perpetrators in.

I wondered how Bainbridge was getting on back at the Yard. Bainbridge seemed to me to be a good man and a solid policeman, and I could tell that Holmes, too, held him in high regard. He lacked the insights of my friend, and neither did he have an affinity for the deductive methods employed by Holmes, but he clearly understood the need for thoroughness, and, when the situation called for it, action as well. I had a feeling he would go far in his chosen profession, but that it would be something of a bumpy and uncomfortable journey. Men like Roth – in my experience – did not enjoy being proved wrong. Bainbridge would have a fight on his hands.

Of the others, we could only speculate. It seemed as if Tobias Edwards – the *real* Hans Gerber – would indeed inherit the entirety of Sir Theobald's estate, once his true identity had been properly established and he'd stood trial for the wilful destruction of his uncle's last will and testament. Even if he was ordered to serve a prison sentence for his crime, Holmes assured me he was still likely to inherit upon his release, being the last surviving member of Sir Theobald's family.

Gerber's cousins, on the other hand, were destined for the gallows. The thought did not offer me a great deal of comfort.

For my part, I had badly misjudged Miss Annabel Maugham, allowing myself to succumb too readily to her feminine charms.

She had seen me for the gullible fool that I am, and had used that to her advantage, manipulating both Edwards and myself by masquerading as a vulnerable woman in need of our protection. As it transpired, she proved to be one of the hardest, coldest women I had ever met. It was a testament to her acting ability – or perhaps my naïvety – that I had been taken in for so long.

Holmes, of course, would never allow himself to become embroiled in such nonsense. I saw now the reason for his calculated coldness, his unwillingness to share in the emotions of others. To him, such things were a distraction, a form of weakness that sought to keep him from the clarity for which he yearned. Indeed, in the hands of those of dubious morality such emotions became a tool, used to manipulate others, to bend those unfortunates to their will. Which, of course, was precisely the approach adopted by Annabel Maugham in her dealings with Mr. Edwards and myself.

Whatever the outcome, I can honestly state that I regretted having ever laid eyes upon the woman. Aside from causing me to feel boyishly naïve, she had embarrassed me before Holmes, and for that, I could never forgive her.

Of course, I did not wholeheartedly agree with Holmes's uninvolved approach, as successful as it had proved during the years of our association. To leech the humanity from every situation and to set oneself apart from the people involved was, in my eyes, to somehow diminish oneself, too. Logic played a part, of course, but to remove all else from the equation? I found such a notion terribly disheartening. If it wasn't for the people involved – if we didn't set out to help those less fortunate than ourselves – why on earth did we bother to embroil ourselves in the affairs of others?

Perhaps this need to recognise the humanity in people was nothing but a symptom of my soft heart, or a sign of the doctor in me, but I suppose I secretly understood that, beneath the veneer, beneath the pomp and maddening opacity, Holmes was a decent sort of fellow. Probably the most decent I had ever known. His method, which he put above all else in his pursuit of the truth, represented a great sacrifice, and one that many could never recognise or know. To those subjected to his cutting remarks, his arrogance, his impatience, he was simply "that Baker Street detective", the hard-nosed eccentric who would strong-arm his way into a police investigation and show everyone up. But I understood that, in so doing, Holmes had removed not only the illogical from the situation, but much of himself, too. He had suppressed his own needs for the benefit of the case.

To Holmes, the world was nothing more than a puzzle that needed to be solved, the people in it mere pawns. I didn't much care to consider the world in those terms, and I believe that was why he often kept me around – because, when he needed me to, I could remind him of the human element, of what he had forgotten, or perhaps never had in the first place.

Additionally, I knew that, despite having my fingers burned by women such as Annabel Maugham, I would gleefully immerse myself in such situations again and again, and would no doubt continue to make the same mistakes *ad infinitum*. Holmes, I think, could never understand that about me, but then that was just another on his long list of puzzles to be solved.

I sensed movement, and looked over to see Holmes knocking out the dottles from his pipe on the arm of his chair. He brushed them dismissively onto the carpet.

"I say, Holmes," I said, finally breaking the silence that had grown up between us over the last few minutes. "You haven't yet explained how you came to the conclusion that Percival Asquith was the man behind the iron men robberies." I took a sip from my brandy. "What gave him away?"

"His desperation," said Holmes. "His need to be heard. The fact he had invested his entire family fortune in those ridiculous machines, and they did not work. He stood to lose everything."

"Quite so," I said, frowning. "But that doesn't explain why he should go to the extraordinary length of faking the theft of his own prototypes and waging a campaign of terror upon the streets of London."

Holmes chuckled quietly, amused by my evident misreading of the situation. "Oh, but it does, Watson. Of course it does. Above all else, Asquith desired publicity. He spoke to Inspector Bainbridge of going to the papers, of proclaiming to the whole of London that his fabulous machines had been stolen and were being put to nefarious use by some foul agent." He began refilling his pipe, stuffing tobacco into the bowl and tamping it down with his thumb.

"Perhaps so…" I offered, still confused. "Yet I fail to see what good such publicity might have done him, given the circumstances."

"Ah, Watson," said Holmes, affectionately. "Think on it for a moment. Asquith was close to ruin. His machines were not viable, and he had failed to secure any investment in his business. No one believed he'd ever get the things to work. But if, suddenly, working examples of his designs were stolen and seen publicly to be operational…"

"Then he'd have investors clamouring to throw their money at him! And, since his prototypes had been 'stolen', he wouldn't have to show them to anyone, meaning those sorry investors would never be able to ascertain that the machines were really just men in iron suits," I exclaimed. "Good Lord, Holmes!"

"Precisely, Watson," he said, approvingly.

"What, then, of the jewellery thefts?" I said, suddenly. "Why go to such trouble, and why put those poor people through so much?"

"It had to seem realistic, Watson. People had to believe the iron men were real. I suspect if Asquith had been successful in his deception, he might have unleashed a new breed of iron man upon the city, hunting down the 'misappropriated' models and returning the stolen jewellery to its owners, to much pomp and acclaim," said Holmes, shaking his head at the sheer temerity of the man.

"Or perhaps it was done for insurance, Holmes," I ventured. "Perhaps Asquith was hedging his bets, ensuring he still had something if his plot to attract new investors failed."

"Perhaps so!" said Holmes brightly, clearly taken with my idea.

"Well, I hope the blighter languishes in a prison cell for many years to come," I said. "Family fortunes, it seems, can be dangerous things." I gave a satisfied sigh. "I can't say I'm sorry to see the back of those blasted iron men, or those traitorous Maughams. I'll be happy to return to my practice tomorrow, and a little normality."

"It is tomorrow upon which you welcome the return of Mrs. Watson, is it not?" asked Holmes, around the mouthpiece of his briar. He struck a match, bringing the flame up to the bowl and puffing gently until it took. Smoke billowed around him as he settled back in his chair, casting the spent match into the fire.

"Indeed it is," I confirmed. "I miss her dearly, Holmes. Although I fear I may have familial reparations of my own to make upon her return. I've achieved little of what I promised while she's been out of town."

"Ah, but what you *have* achieved, Watson!" proclaimed Holmes, chuckling.

"Quite so, Holmes, quite so," I said, wistfully. "Although I cannot testify that Mrs. Watson will feel the same way…" I paused, looking at Holmes, who appeared to be struggling to contain a sudden outburst. My lips quivered, and then, unable to prevent myself, I let out a roar of laughter. Holmes, himself almost hacking on the smoke he had just inhaled, waved me quiet and put a finger to his lips.

"My dear Watson, the hour is late. Think of Mrs. Hudson." This, of course, served only to send us into further paroxysms of laughter. I collapsed back in my chair, gasping for breath. I felt as if the world had suddenly been lifted from my shoulders.

When our brief period of levity had passed, I stood, crossing to the drinks cabinet and replenishing my glass. "Holmes?" I asked, holding up the brandy bottle. He shook his head, content with his pipe.

"So what next?" I asked, returning to my seat by the fire. The warmth was having a soporific effect, and I knew it would not be long before I was forced to retire. Holmes had kindly offered me the use of my old room for the night. "I do hope you're not planning to indulge in another of your damnable black moods," I added.

Holmes smiled. "Fear not, Watson!" he said, brightly. "Inspector Bainbridge has already requested my assistance with another little problem – involving the carcass of a giant ape brought back from the Congo, if I'm not mistaken – and there's always the violin to keep me company."

"You know you only have to call, Holmes," I said.

"Why would I call? You are, as I've said, a creature of habit, Watson. I know you'll call here at Baker Street when you have the time and inclination." He clamped his pipe between his teeth, and reached under his chair, withdrawing his old violin and bow.

"Indeed I will, Holmes. Be sure of it," I confirmed.

Holmes leaned back in his chair, propped the violin beneath his chin, and attacked the strings suddenly and fiercely with the bow, eliciting a cacophonous response from the instrument. I frowned at the discordant tune as he continued in this manner. I feared he seemed intent on continuing on in that vein until breakfast.

"Oh, do you have to, Holmes? It's nearly two in the morning!" I said, glancing at the clock. "And besides," I continued, waving him to be quiet, "think of Mrs. Hudson."

If the violin had not already woken the poor woman, I was convinced that the ensuing raucous laughter surely would.

ABOUT THE AUTHOR

George Mann was born in Darlington and has written numerous books, short stories, novellas and original audio scripts. *The Affinity Bridge*, the first novel in his Newbury & Hobbes Victorian fantasy series, was published in 2008. Other titles in the series include *The Osiris Ritual*, *The Immorality Engine*, *The Casebook of Newbury & Hobbes* and the forthcoming *The Revenant Express*.

His other novels include *Ghosts of Manhattan* and *Ghosts of War*, mystery novels about a vigilante set against the backdrop of a post-steampunk 1920s New York, as well as an original Doctor Who novel, *Paradox Lost*, featuring the Eleventh Doctor alongside his companions, Amy and Rory.

He has edited a number of anthologies, including *Encounters of Sherlock Holmes*, *The Solaris Book of New Science Fiction* and *The Solaris Book of New Fantasy*. *Further Encounters of Sherlock Holmes* will be released in 2014.

READ ON FOR A SHORT STORY FROM

THE CASEBOOK OF NEWBURY & HOBBES

FEATURING CHARLES BAINBRIDGE

THE HAMBLETON AFFAIR

London, November 1901

"You never did tell me about the Hambleton Affair, Newbury."

Sir Charles Bainbridge leaned back in his chair, sipped at his brandy and regarded his friend through a wreath of pungent cigar smoke. Around him, the gas lamps flickered momentarily in their fittings, as if a sudden breeze had passed through Newbury's Chelsea living room. Unperturbed, the chief inspector crossed his legs and stifled a yawn.

Across the room, Newbury was leaning on the mantelpiece, staring silently into the fire. He turned towards the older man, the flames casting his face in stark relief. He nodded. "Indeed not. Although I will warn you, Charles, it's not a tale with a heart-warming end."

Bainbridge sighed. "Are they ever?"

Newbury smiled as he started across the living room to join his friend. "No, I suppose not." He paused beside the drinks cabinet, his expression suddenly serious. He placed a hand on his left side, just above the hip.

Bainbridge furrowed his brow. "The injuries are still troubling you?"

Newbury shrugged. "A little. It's this damnable cold weather." He sucked in his breath. His tone was playful. "I heartily commend to you, Charles, to avoid getting yourself injured in the winter. The experience is rather detrimental to one's constitution."

Bainbridge chuckled and took another draw on his cigar.

"Still, I suppose it would do no harm to relate my little tale," said Newbury, before taking the last few strides across the room and lowering himself gingerly into the chair opposite the other man. His black suit crumpled as he shifted to make himself comfortable. He eyed his friend.

Tonight, Newbury considered, the chief inspector was wearing his age. His white hair was swept back from his forehead and his eyes were rheumy and rimmed with the dark stains of too many sleepless nights. It was clear that he was in need of a rest. Newbury smiled warmly. "You look tired, Charles. Are you sure you wouldn't rather turn in for the night?"

Bainbridge shook his head. "No. Not yet." He raised his glass, a forlorn look in his eyes. "Tonight is the anniversary of Isobel's death. I'd rather keep from dwelling on the matter, if it's all the same." He took a swig of his brandy, shuddering as the alcohol assaulted his palate. "I still think of her, you know. In the quiet times." He shook his head. "Besides, I can't bring myself to abandon a decent brandy." He smiled, his bushy moustache twitching. "Come on, you've put this one off too many times before. Give it up!"

Newbury nodded and placed his own glass on the coffee table between them. He took up his pipe from the arm of the Chesterfield and tapped out the dottles in the palm of his hand. Discarding these, he began to fill the pipe from a small leather tobacco pouch that he searched out from amongst the scattered debris on the tabletop. A moment later he leaned back, puffing gently on the mouthpiece to kindle the flame. He had a haunted expression on his face.

"It was the spring of 'ninety-eight. April, to be precise. Just a few months before Templeton Black and the disaster at Fairview House, if you recall."

Bainbridge looked sullen. "All too well."

"Indeed. Well, I had just drawn a close to a particularly disturbing case involving a series of brutal murders at an archaeological site, when I received a letter from a man named Crawford, the physician of the Hambleton family of Richmond, North Yorkshire. I had schooled with Sir Clive Hambleton at Oxford, briefly, and while I couldn't claim him as a friend, I knew him as a man of integrity and science. Anyway, the letter went on to describe the most bizarre of affairs." Newbury paused whilst he drew on his pipe, and Bainbridge leaned forward in his chair, urging him to go on.

Newbury smiled. "It appeared that Hambleton had a new wife – a young wife of only eighteen years, named Frances – who had taken up residence with him at Hambleton Manor. Life had proved harmonious for the newlyweds for nearly twelve months, until, only a handful of days before the letter was dated, she had simply vanished from her room without a trace."

Bainbridge took another long slug of his brandy. He eyed Newbury warily. "Well, it sounds pretty clear to me. She'd finally realised that she had inadvertently committed herself to a life of drudgery in rural Yorkshire, with an older man as her only companion. It doesn't sound like the sort of matter I would usually associate with your field of expertise. Had she taken flight?"

Newbury shook his head. "No. Not as simple as all that. But I'll admit that was the first thing that crossed my mind upon reading the missive. Until I read on, that is." Newbury cleared his throat.

"It seemed that, after dinner, Mrs Hambleton had retired to her room, as was typical of her daily routine. Only on this occasion, she failed to reappear in the drawing room an hour later. Believing that she had likely fallen into a light doze, her husband made his way up to her room to look in on her, only to find that the bed was undisturbed and that his wife was nowhere to be found."

Bainbridge frowned. "You've lost me, Newbury. I still can't see how it could be anything other than the woman's desire to take flight from her circumstances."

"Quite. And Hambleton initially believed the same. Until he discovered that her belongings were all still *in situ* and had not been disturbed since that morning. Clothes were still in the dresser. Jewellery was still on the dressing table. Precious childhood mementoes were still in a box beneath the bed. Not to mention the fact that the lady had no money of her own.

"Distraught, Hambleton interviewed the servants, none of whom had seen the lady leave the premises. He had them tear the place apart looking for her, but she was nowhere to be found in the house or the grounds. It seemed that, somehow, Hambleton's new wife had simply vanished without a trace."

"Kidnap, then?"

"It remained a distinct possibility, and the local constabulary was indeed called in to investigate. But they could find no evidence of any wrongdoing, and the days that followed brought none of the expected demands from the imagined kidnapper in question. The entire affair remained a mystery, and Crawford, concerned for his charge, had been forced to watch as Hambleton had fallen into a deep funk from which he could not be roused. It was as if the life had gone out of him, leaving behind nothing but a shadow of the former man."

Bainbridge eased himself back in his chair and clamped his cigar between his teeth. "Quite a singular case. I can see now why the man was drawn to write to you. What else did he say?"

"The letter stated that Crawford was aware of my reputation as a man who had experience of the occult and, since there appeared to be no other explanation for what had become of Mrs Hambleton, asked if I would pay a visit to Hambleton Manor to investigate. At the very least, he hoped that I would be able to rule out any occult interference. Hambleton himself, of course, knew nothing of the letter." Newbury shrugged. "Of course, I'm a rational man and knew there had to be a rational explanation for the lady's disappearance, but one finds it difficult to resist a challenge. I set out that very morning, taking the twelve o'clock train from Euston to York." Newbury puffed thoughtfully on his pipe. After a moment he took it from his mouth and waved it at his companion. "Feel free to pour yourself another, Charles. You'll forgive me for not getting up?"

Bainbridge nodded. "Of course. You stay put, Newbury. I'll fetch the decanter over." The chief inspector placed his glass on the table beside Newbury's and pulled himself to his feet. He crossed the room, retrieved the bulbous, flat-bottomed vessel and returned to his seat. He removed the glass stopper with a light *clink* and began sloshing the brown liquid into his glass. He looked up. "Well, keep going man!"

Newbury laughed. "All this police work is starting to show on you, Charles. Patience certainly isn't one of your strong points."

"*Starting* to show! By God, Newbury, after thirty years at the Yard I'd expect even the most fresh-faced shoeshine to be able to discern *that* much."

Newbury grinned. He retrieved his glass from the table. "I hadn't had time to send a telegram ahead to alert Crawford of my impending arrival, so there was no escort awaiting me at the station when the train finally pulled in at York that evening. Collecting my bag from the steward, I took a cab immediately out to Hambleton Manor, which proved to be a pleasant – if brisk – drive through the countryside. The light was starting to wane by this time, and my first sight of the house itself was almost enough to cause me to reconsider my initial thoughts about the case. The place was a rambling wreck, more a farmhouse than a country estate, and appeared so dilapidated that I had to allow for the possibility that my earlier reasoning may in fact have been correct. At that point I admit I would not have been surprised to discover that the young Mrs Hambleton had indeed fled the estate in sheer desperation at her circumstances."

Bainbridge coughed noisily and placed the stub of his cigar in the ashtray. "I take it from your tone that this was not to be the case?"

"Quite so. In fact, as the hansom drew up outside of the house it became clear that the structure was not in such an alarming state of disrepair as it had at first seemed. Certainly, it was in need of urgent cosmetic attention, but the building itself appeared to be sound and the welcome I received from the manservant, Chester, was enough to immediately put me at my ease. I clambered down from the cab and followed the wispy-haired old chap into the house.

"Once inside I was taken directly to the drawing room to meet Crawford, whom – judging by his expression – was more than a little relieved to see another friendly face. He pumped my hand rather vigorously and bade me to take a seat.

"I could tell almost immediately that Crawford was an honourable man. He was clearly concerned for his old friend, and the strain of the situation had begun to show in his face. He was in his mid-forties, with a shock of red hair and a full moustache and beard. His skin was pale and he was obviously tired. He sent Chester away to fetch tea. I asked him where Hambleton was and he offered me a rather sheepish look. He said that he'd sedated him an hour earlier and left him in his room to get some rest. Apparently it was the only way that Crawford had so far managed to force his friend to sleep."

"Sounds like a rum job for a medical man. Was there no housekeeper who could have helped with all that?"

Newbury shook his head and regarded the bowl of his pipe thoughtfully. "I think they were all a little in awe of the man. Later I would witness the manner in which Hambleton bustled around the house barking directions at his staff, giving orders like he was running some sort of military operation. Which I suppose he was, in many respects, marshalling his troops to search the local area for evidence of his missing wife." He paused. "Still, I'm getting ahead of myself." He smiled, and Bainbridge nodded for him to continue.

"With Hambleton asleep in his room, Crawford took the opportunity to fill me in on the circumstances of the case. He explained that Hambleton had barely spoken a word for days, and spent all of his time waiting on news of his missing wife, or sitting in her room staring at her belongings, as if they could somehow reveal to him what had become of her. It was soon clear from Crawford's testimony that Hambleton was on the verge of a complete breakdown.

"After Crawford had finished recapping the details he had already disclosed in his letter, I explained that I had not had any real contact with the family since my time at Oxford, and asked Crawford to fill in any gaps. He went on to explain that Hambleton had inherited the family fortune – such as it was – after his father had died a few years earlier and had invested heavily in farming and agriculture. He was currently engaged in a project to develop a method of better preserving fruit and vegetables after harvesting, and until recently had spent long hours locked away in his workshop; time, Crawford was not afraid to add, that he felt

Hambleton should have been spending with his wife. Nevertheless, Crawford was quick to establish that Hambleton did in fact dote on his young wife, and that if truth be told the doctor was worried about how Hambleton would be able to carry on without her.

"Soon after, Chester returned with the tea, and our conversation moved on to more practical considerations. I promised I would do all that I could to help resolve the sorry situation, and that, first thing in the morning, I would examine Mrs Hambleton's room for any signs of evidence that may have been missed. Crawford promised that I would be reacquainted with Hambleton later that evening over dinner, and while the doctor was yet to enlighten his friend about my visit, he was sure that Hambleton would be pleased to see an old friend from Oxford." Newbury smiled. He eyed Bainbridge over the rim of his glass as he took a sip. "Can you begin to imagine how Hambleton *really* felt about my unannounced visit?"

Bainbridge shrugged. "Well, I'd imagine he'd be less inclined to reminisce about his schooldays than Crawford seemed to be suggesting, but glad of the extra help in searching for his missing wife, no doubt."

Newbury shook his head. "I fear that could not be further from the truth. I parted from Crawford after tea and Chester kindly showed me to my room. It was small but pleasant enough, furnished with oak panelling and an ostentatious four-poster bed, but with a wonderful view of the grounds. I unpacked my case and took a while to refresh myself, before heading down to the dining room to meet the others for dinner.

"No sooner had I approached the door to the dining hall, however, than I became aware of a heated debate being played out on the other side. Unsure what else I could do, I hesitated on the threshold, awaiting an opportunity to politely make an entrance.

"It seemed that Crawford had finally informed Hambleton

about his invitation and my subsequent arrival at the house, and the news had not been received well. I heard Hambleton cursing the doctor. 'She's left me, Crawford, can't you see that? I need to be left alone to my misery.' Crawford then uttered some sort of bumbling reply, and I decided that was the point at which to make my entrance. I strolled through the door as if oblivious to the tension between the two men, and made a point of greeting Hambleton like an old school friend would."

"Did he alter his temperament upon seeing you?"

"Not at all. He greeted me gruffly and without emotion. He refused to look me in the eye, and showed no real sign that he recognised me from our time at Oxford together. It was as if he saw me as an interloper, come to interfere and ogle at him as he wallowed in his misery. He hardly spoke a word throughout dinner, and then made his excuses and repaired to his room, claiming he needed an early night to be fresh for the morning." Newbury shrugged, pausing to gather his thoughts. "Crawford had certainly been right about one thing. Hambleton was indeed in a funk, and a dire one at that. The man looked as if he hadn't slept for a week. His hair was in disarray, he had neglected to shave, his shirtsleeves were filthy and he bore the haunted look of a man who was carrying the weight of the world on his shoulders. It was clear that he truly cared for this girl, and that he blamed himself for whatever had become of her, to the exclusion of all else."

"So how did you handle the man? It can't have been easy trying to help someone in that state of mind, no matter how understandable their disposition."

"I decided to carry on regardless. At that point in proceedings I was still unsure whether I'd actually be able to shed any light on the case, but with no other means to help the poor fellow I decided to follow Crawford's example, and together we retreated to the drawing room to plot our next move. Over a brandy we discussed how we could get to the bottom of the situation. We both felt that our influence on Hambleton could only prove beneficial, and that, whatever had happened to his wife, it was clear he was in need of answers. If we were able to shed even the tiniest sliver of light on the subject, we should do our damnedest to try. I reiterated my intention to search the lady's room at first light. Then, downing the rest of my brandy and offering Crawford all the reassurance I could muster, I retreated to my bed to take some rest.

"It was at this point, however, that things began to take a turn in an entirely different direction."

Newbury stared at the flickering gas lamp on the wall, lost momentarily in his reminiscences. Bainbridge edged forward in his seat. He was caught up in Newbury's story now, anxious to know what happened next.

"How so?"

Newbury smiled. He ran a hand over his face before continuing. "Wearily I made my way to my room, tired from my long journey and more than a little distracted by the shocking appearance of my old school friend. I spent my usual hour reading before settling in for the night – a rather lurid novel entitled *The Beetle* – and a short while later fell into a light doze. Sometime after that I found myself rudely awakened by a terrible banging sound from elsewhere in the house. I sat bolt upright in bed, unsure what to make of the despicable racket. It was as if someone was beating panels of metal sheeting, and the sound of it quite startled me from my bed.

"Pulling my robe around my shoulders, I took up a candle and crept from my room, anxious to understand the nature of the bizarre noise. The hallway outside of my room was dark and deserted. The entire episode had the quality of an intangible dream and I wondered, briefly, if I weren't acting out the fantasies of a nightmare, inspired by the gothic novel I had indulged myself with just a few hours earlier. Yet the banging was so loud and persistent that I knew it had to be real. I crossed the hall, feeling the chill draught as it swelled up the stairwell. The sound was coming from deep within the bowels of the house, far below where I was standing. I wondered why there was no sign of Crawford or any of the staff. Surely they must have been awoken by the thunderous sounds?"

"Remarkable. Did you find out what it was?"

Newbury laughed. "Yes. Indeed. And I fear it was nothing as sensational as you might have imagined, Charles. At the time, however, I admit I was perplexed. I made my way down the stairs in the darkness, my candle guttering and threatening to leave me stranded alone in the shadowy hallway at the foot of the stairs. Then, startled, I heard the shuffling sound of approaching footsteps and all of a sudden Chester was upon me."

Bainbridge frowned. "The manservant? Had he set upon you in the darkness?"

"No, no. But he certainly gave me a fright. His face loomed out of the gloom like some sort of ancient, other-worldly spirit. He was dressed in a robe and his candle had been extinguished, burned down in its holder. He appeared to be heading towards the stairway, returning from a brief sojourn elsewhere in the house. He asked if he could help me with anything, evidently unclear as to the reason for my appearance in the hallway at such a late hour. Puzzled, I enquired about the banging sounds, which were still ringing loudly beneath us – underneath, I realised, the ground floor of the house itself. I surmised that there was obviously a large cellar somewhere far below.

"Chester, who seemed entirely nonplussed by the intolerable sound, shook his head and smiled. 'Nothing to be alarmed about, sir. The master often works late into the night. Best to leave him to his labours.' He put his hand on my arm as if to shepherd me back to bed. Unsure how else to respond, and realising there was little

I could do about the noise, I resigned myself to a sleepless night and retraced my steps, following Chester up the creaking stairs and along the galleried landing to my room. After I had heard Chester retreat to the servants' quarters I lay awake for some time, disturbed by the noise, but also suspicious of the manservant and the reasons for his midnight stroll around the house."

Bainbridge stroked his moustache thoughtfully and searched around in his jacket pockets until he located his walnut cigar case. Withdrawing a cigar, he snipped the end with his silver cutter and flicked the brown cap skilfully into the ashtray. Then, taking up one of Newbury's matches, he lit the fat tube with a brief flourish and sat back in his chair, regarding the younger man. "For how long did Hambleton continue with his bizarre nocturnal pursuit?"

"Hours. There was little peace that night, and if truth be told, I rather abused Crawford's patience by taking the opportunity to rise late the next day. I was still groggy from lack of sleep and I admit I found myself a little out of sorts.

"The others were finishing their breakfast when I finally made my way down to the dining room, and even though I was suffering from a terrible bout of lethargy, I was keen to discover more about the nature of the work that had kept Hambleton busy so late into the night."

"I suspect he looked done in, after spending most of the night beating metal?"

Newbury shook his head. "That was one of the strangest things about the entire episode. Hambleton looked fresh-faced and clean-shaven, as if he'd had a good night's rest and had risen early for breakfast. He was sitting at the table finishing a plate of eggs and bacon when I entered the room. I remember it distinctly, the manner in which he eyed me warily as I took a seat beside him. Of course, the first thing I did was enquire about the banging and the nature of his work in the cellar."

"And was he forthcoming?"

"Only in as much as he acknowledged that he *had* been working through the night and apologised for keeping me awake. I pressed him further on the matter, politely at first, but he was loath to give away any real details. I held firm in my questioning, and eventually he relented. His explanation tallied with what Crawford had told me the previous day. He said he was working on a machine that would aid in the preservation of fruit and vegetables after picking, a means by which to maintain the freshness of the produce before it found its way to market."

"Did he show it to you?"

"No. He was dismissive of the whole enterprise. Told me it was 'far from finished' and that there was 'very little of consequence to see.'"

"How odd. Did this not raise your suspicions about the man in any way?"

"I certainly had a sense that there was more going on at Hambleton Manor than I had initially suspected. Nevertheless, I was also acutely aware that Hambleton was suffering a great deal of distress following the disappearance of his wife, so perhaps I was a little more forgiving than I may have been in different circumstances.

"Feeling that I should not press the matter any further, I finished my breakfast – indulging in copious amounts of coffee to stave off the fatigue – and agreed with Crawford that he would show me to the missing woman's bedchamber directly. Hambleton, for his part, did nothing but stare at his empty plate as we left the room.

"As we crossed the hall I felt the tension dissipating, and Crawford gave an audible sigh of relief. 'He's not his usual self. Poor man. Please forgive him his brevity of conversation. At any other time I'm sure he would be delighted to reacquaint himself with an old school friend, but with Frances gone…' The doctor clearly felt he needed to apologise for his friend and patient. I allowed him to do so, offering platitudes where necessary. I am much too long in the tooth to let such minor offences concern me.

"I still had little notion of what had occurred at the house, and hoped that the coming day's investigations would yield quick, obvious results. That way I could be on my way back to London as quickly as possible. One sleepless night was already enough for my constitution." Newbury shuffled uncomfortably in his seat, putting a hand to his side. He grimaced with obvious discomfort.

Bainbridge smiled warmly. "I'm sure it won't be too long before you're fully recovered, Newbury. I take it you're now a little more accustomed to sleepless nights?"

Newbury laughed. "Quite right. Quite right." He sucked at his pipe.

"So did the lady's room reveal everything that Crawford hoped it would? Evidence of foul play?"

Newbury shook his head. "Not a bit of it. I went through the place in minute detail. There was nothing of any consequence. No markings, no untoward smells, no evidence of occult activity. Hambleton had been right; the room was completely undisturbed, as if Lady Hambleton had simply disappeared into thin air. There was evidence that her husband had searched the place, of course, but nothing to suggest that she had taken flight. That is, nothing to suggest that she had *planned* to take flight. There was still the slight possibility that she had fled the house on a whim, bearing none of her effects, but that seemed increasingly unlikely. Having been driven along the approach to the house in a hansom the previous day, I found it difficult to believe that anyone could have been able to flee the grounds without being seen, or else without requiring vehicular assistance of some kind. If the lady *had* run away, it was clear to me that she must have had an accomplice.

"Nevertheless, I spent a good hour searching the room,

attempting to build an impression of Lady Hambleton and the manner in which she went about her business. You can learn a lot from a victim's personal effects, Charles, something your chaps at Scotland Yard could spend a little more time considering."

Bainbridge shook his head in exasperation.

"Of course, Crawford was getting desperate by this point, and was very insistent in announcing his theories. 'You see, Sir Maurice. The disappearance simply has to have a supernatural explanation. There's no other way to satisfactorily account for it', or words to that effect. I admit his zeal was growing somewhat tiresome. I typically find in situations such as these that the simplest explanation is usually the correct one, and I counselled Crawford that he would do well to keep that fact in mind. While the circumstances were clearly unusual, I was confident that the missing woman had not been abducted through supernatural or occult endeavour, and I resolved to put my finger on the solution before the day was out."

Bainbridge leaned forward to dribble cigar ash into the glass tray on the table. "Ah, so we are nearing some answers."

Newbury smiled and shook his head. "Alas, my hopes of resolving the mystery so quickly were soon dashed. I had a notion that someone in the house knew more than they were letting on, so I next took it upon myself to interview each and every member of the staff. Crawford and I arranged ourselves in the drawing room and, in turn, each of Hambleton's servants were called upon to give account of the events leading up to Lady Hambleton's disappearance. It was a day-long endeavour, and to my frustration we came away from the exercise with nothing of any real import or relevance to the case. Most of the staff proved anxious to stress that they were unaware of any furtive behaviour and that nothing out of the ordinary had occurred in the household on the day that Lady Hambleton went missing. The cook had prepared meals to her normal routine; the maids had stripped and made the beds in typical order. Even Chester, whom I had reason to suspect after finding him wandering the halls the previous night, provided a satisfactory explanation of his activities when pressed."

"Which was?"

"Simply that he'd been woken by the banging from the cellar and had risen to ensure that his master was not in need of his services. Having received no response to his query and finding the door to the cellar locked, he had come away to return to bed. He added that this was not an unusual occurrence and that while Hambleton himself often kept unsociable hours, he in no way expected his staff to accommodate him in such pursuits. His explanation seemed eminently reasonable and seemed to fit with the facts of the matter. In giving his account of the day that Lady Hambleton had disappeared, he accounted well for his whereabouts, the details of which were corroborated by at least two other members of the household staff.

"I admit at this juncture in proceedings I was very nearly dumbfounded by the lack of evidence, but I knew I still had one further line of enquiry to pursue. I needed to see what Hambleton was building in his cellar.

"By this time the day was drawing to a close. Hambleton himself had been out on the grounds of his estate for much of the afternoon. I suggested to Crawford that when Hambleton returned from his excursion we should question him like the other members of the household, allowing him to give his account of the hours leading up to Lady Hambleton's disappearance, and also to enlighten us further as to the nature of the device he was constructing underneath the house. Crawford, of course, was utterly appalled by this notion and rejected the idea immediately. He felt that it was not only a grave imposition on our host, but an unwise course of action, to submit a man in such a terrible state of anguish to probing questions about the loss of his wife. He went on to argue that, as a doctor, he was concerned about the health of his charge and that forcing the man to recall the events of that day would likely be enough to break him."

"Pah! I think this man Crawford was a little wet behind the ears." Bainbridge shook his head with a sigh.

Newbury laughed. "Perhaps so. But at the time I went along with his argument. I'd already resigned myself to spending another night at the manor, and I hoped that the evening might present an opportunity to discuss the matter with Hambleton to the same end. Tired, and unable to do anything more until Hambleton returned, I took myself off to my room to gain what rest I could before dinner.

"I slept for two or three hours, before being woken by a loud rap on my door. Chester had come to inform me that dinner would be served within the hour, and that the master had returned to the house and was taking a brandy in the drawing room. A little dazed from the rude awakening, I thanked the manservant and then stumbled out of bed. Fifteen minutes later I was washed, dressed and on my way to the drawing room, having decided that joining Hambleton for a brandy would be a most excellent idea.

"As it transpired, however, Hambleton had finished his drink and was now on his way to his room to change for dinner. I passed him on the stairs and he stopped momentarily as I bid him good evening. We eyed each other warily. 'I hear from Crawford that your search for supernatural activity on the premises has yet to bear fruit?' I couldn't help but catch the sneer that accompanied this gruff comment. I explained that I now felt beyond any doubt that there were no supernatural or occult elements involved in the disappearance of his wife, and that I was doing all I could to aid in her recovery. At this he seemed genuinely surprised, as if he'd expected me to react defensively to his offhand remark, and I could sense an immediate mellowing in his attitude towards me, as if, for the first time, he had realised that I was genuinely there to help. He smiled sadly, and said that he'd see me shortly for dinner, but that I could find Crawford in the drawing room in the meantime.

"I thanked him as he set off in the direction of his room once again, but I couldn't help thinking how far removed this person was from the distraught wreck of a man I'd seen that morning over breakfast. Evidently his turn around the estate had done him some good.

"I joined Crawford in the drawing room. He was sitting in a large armchair knocking back the brandy at a rate I had rarely seen in a gentleman. He was no longer sober, and I could tell from the manner in which he looked up and greeted me that he had been there for some time. The man was evidently at his wits' end, even more so than Hambleton had seemed that evening. It occurred to me that I hadn't yet taken the opportunity to question the doctor. I took a seat opposite him and poured myself a small measure. Then, when the opportunity presented itself, I steered the topic of conversation around to his relationship with the family and his arrival at the house. I asked him how long he'd been here at the manor and whether he'd also been the physician of Lady Hambleton following her marriage to Sir Clive."

Bainbridge coughed and glowered accusingly at the end of his cigar. His moustache twitched as he considered the facts. "Very interesting indeed. So you'd come around to wondering whether Crawford himself was involved in the disappearance. Did he give a satisfactory account of himself?"

"He did, although it manifested as a rather garbled slurry of words, as the man was by then too inebriated to sensibly string his sentences together with any meaning. Nevertheless, I managed to decipher the gist of it. He claimed he'd arrived at the house the day after the disappearance, following an urgent telegram from Hambleton requesting his help. And while he had indeed been acting as physician to the missing lady, he claimed he'd had little cause to treat her as yet, as she was young and in perfect health. I had no reason to doubt his claims – the facts were easy to corroborate. I believe his state at that time was derived simply from his frustration at being unable to help his old friend.

"A short while later Hambleton appeared again, dressed for dinner. It was clear by that time, however, that Crawford was in no fit state to eat, so together we carted him off to his room to sleep off the brandy. As a result, dinner itself was a relatively low-key affair, and although Hambleton was beginning to open up to me, he would talk only about our old days at Oxford together, or tell inconsequential stories of his family. When pressed to answer questions regarding his missing wife or his work in the basement, he retreated once again into an impenetrable shell and would not be drawn out.

"With Crawford incapacitated and Hambleton unwilling to talk, I found myself once again at a stalemate. I repaired to my room for an early night. I knew that I had to see what Hambleton was building in his cellar, and I was now near-convinced that it had something to do with the strange disappearance of his wife. There were no other obvious lines of enquiry, and no evidence to suggest that Lady Hambleton had fled the house in a fit of pique.

"That night, I managed to find at least a few hours' sleep before the banging recommenced to startle me from my dreams. I lay awake for some time, listening to the rhythmic hammering that, in the darkness, sounded like some dreadful heartbeat, like the house had somehow come alive while I slept. I stirred from my bed but hesitated at the door. I'd planned to make my way down to the cellar to surprise Hambleton and make sense of what he was doing under the house, but it occurred to me that Chester was probably prowling the house in the darkness, and with Crawford likely still unconscious from the alcohol he had consumed, I thought it better to wait until morning. I planned to get away from the others at the first opportunity and slip down into the cellar to examine the machine. If all was well I would at least have the comfort of knowing that Hambleton was truthfully not involved in his wife's untimely disappearance." Newbury leaned forward in his chair and rubbed a hand over his face. He sighed.

"The next day brought startling revelations, Charles. Perhaps some of the strangest and most disturbing things I have ever seen. But it started typically enough.

"I'd fallen asleep again in the early hours of the morning and woken in good time for breakfast. Expecting to find Hambleton and Crawford in the dining room, I shaved, dressed and hurried down to greet them. I hoped to find an opportunity to steal away while the others were occupied, so that I may find the door to the cellar and investigate what lay beyond. To my surprise, however, Hambleton was nowhere to be seen, and Crawford, looking a little green around the gills, was taking breakfast alone. Or rather he was staring at his plate as if indecisive about whether he should attempt to consume his food or not. He looked up as I came into the room. 'Ah, Sir Maurice. Sir Clive has had to go out on urgent business and extends his apologies. He said he would return by midday and that he hoped everything would soon become clear.'

"Of course, two things immediately crossed my mind. First, that Hambleton's absence from the manor would provide me with the opportunity I had been waiting for, and second, that his message could be deciphered in two different ways: that either he hoped Crawford and I would shortly find an answer to the mystery, or, as I was more inclined to believe, that it was Hambleton himself who had the answer, and that he hoped to be in a position to reveal it to us shortly. I had the sense that things were about to fall into place.

"I took a light breakfast with Crawford, who stoically attempted to hide the after-effects of his over-zealous consumption of the previous evening. He ate sparingly, with little conversation, and then declared he was in need of fresh air and planned to take a walk to the local village if I wished to join him. Of course, I refused on the grounds that I needed to press on with my investigations and stressed that he should feel at liberty to go on without me. He bid me good morning and took his leave, assuring me that he would return within a couple of hours to help with the matter at hand.

"Being careful not to alert Chester to my plans, I finished my tea in a leisurely fashion, and then, when I was sure that I was alone, I made haste to the cellar door. It wasn't hard to locate, being situated under the staircase in the main hall. I tried the handle, only to find that the door had been locked. Unperturbed, I fished around in my pocket for the tool I had secured there earlier. Glancing from side to side to ensure none of the servants were about, I set to work. I spent nearly five minutes tinkering with the mechanism, attempting to get the latch to spring free. Alas, the lock proved beyond me, as I was far from an expert in such matters in those days. Frustrated, I returned to the drawing room to consider my options."

Bainbridge was confused. "Didn't you put your shoulder to it?"

Newbury shook his head. "You must remember, Charles, that I had no actual evidence of wrong doing. While I had cause to suspect that whatever Hambleton was up to down in that cellar may have somehow been connected to the disappearance of his wife, I had no empirical basis for that belief. None of the staff suspected their master of anything more than a little streak of eccentricity and an inability to keep normal hours. If I went ahead and smashed the door off its hinges, I would have been declaring my suspicion then and there that Hambleton was somehow involved in the disappearance of his wife. If I'd been proved wrong… well, the recriminations would have been difficult to counter. I had no formal jurisdiction in that house. And more, if I was right about Hambleton's involvement, but unable to find any clear evidence in the cellar to support my claim, then the game would have been up and the villain would have been provided with the perfect opportunity to cover his tracks. It was certainly a quandary, and in the end I decided to sit it out and bide my time.

"As it transpired, however, the case was soon to resolve itself.

"Crawford was true to his word and came bustling into the drawing room around eleven, his cheeks flushed from the exercise. He looked as if the walk had done him good, and he had regained his usual composure. When he saw me sitting by the window with a book on my lap, he offered me a quizzical expression and came to join me, casting off his walking jacket and taking a seat nearby. 'Any developments, Sir Maurice?'

"I assured him I had not been resting on my laurels, and that, while I didn't yet have any evidence to show, I felt that I was drawing closer to a solution. Well, I don't mind telling you, Charles, that while I had indeed managed to spot the culprit in the matter, I had in no way been able to foresee the manner in which the crime had been perpetrated." Newbury paused to smile. "Or indeed the reasons why.

"Anyhow, I asked Crawford to give an account of his morning stroll. He was animated, full of energy. He said he had walked to the local village as planned, enjoying the brisk stroll and the fresh morning air, but had been surprised upon his arrival to find all manner of commotion in the village square. It soon unfolded that a young man had been found dead on the moors – a village lad, the son of the postmaster – and that everyone had gathered to gossip about what had become of the boy. He was seventeen years old and much liked by the community. It seemed a senseless killing. Nevertheless, someone had clearly taken a dislike to the boy, and just a few hours earlier his corpse had been recovered from amongst the heather; battered, bruised and broken.

"Crawford was obviously appalled by such goings-on, but clearly saw no connection to the case in hand. I, on the other hand, believed I now had all the information I needed. This was the motive I had been looking for, and all that remained was to await Hambleton's return. Then, I was convinced, I would have all of the evidence I needed to build my case."

"So what, Hambleton killed this boy on the moors? But why? Did he have something to do with Lady Hambleton's disappearance?"

"In a manner of speaking. But it was much more complicated than all that, as you'll soon hear.

"It was only a short while before Hambleton himself returned to the manor. Crawford and I, sitting silently in the drawing room, were alerted to his arrival by the sound of his horse whinnying noisily in the driveway. We both clambered to our feet. Of course, Chester was the first one out of the door, crossing the hall before either of us had even made it out of the drawing room. And indeed, it was Chester who was to inadvertently give his master away. Coming out into the hall, both Crawford and I heard the manservant exclaim upon seeing his master. 'Sir? Are you hurt?' Hambleton's reply was sharp. 'Don't be ridiculous, man. It's not my blood. Here, take the reins.'

"Glancing cautiously at each other, Crawford and I made our way out into the bright afternoon to get a measure of the situation. Chester was leading the horse away across the gravelled courtyard.

Hambleton, still wearing his hat and cape, was spattered with blood. It was all over him; up his arms, over his chest. Even flecked over his collar and chin. His gloves were dripping in the stuff. He gave us a cursory glance, before pushing past us and into the hall, his boots leaving muddy footprints behind him.

"Crawford was appalled. 'Look here, Sir Clive. What's the meaning of all this blood? What the devil have you been up to? This morning you said that you hoped everything would become clear, but as yet, things continue to be as murky as ever!'

"Hambleton stared at his friend for a long while. His shoulders fell. It was as if a light had gone out behind his eyes. 'Very well, Crawford. I had hoped to at least find myself some clean attire, but I suppose it is time. You too, Newbury. You've probably worked it out by now, anyway.'

"He led us across the hall, stopping at the door to his cellar. There, he fished a key out from under his coat, smearing oily blood all over his clothes. He turned the key hastily in the lock and then, pulling the door open, revealed a staircase, which he quickly descended into the darkness. Crawford hesitated on the top step, but I was quick to push past him and followed Hambleton down into the stygian depths of the workshop. A moment later I heard Crawford's footfalls on the stairs behind me." Newbury sighed and took a long draw on his brandy. Bainbridge was on the edge of his seat. He'd allowed his cigar to burn down in the ashtray as Newbury talked, and he was watching his friend intently, anxious to know how the mystery would resolve itself.

"The workshop was a sight to behold. It was a large room that must have filled a space equal to half the footprint of the manor itself. It was lit by only the weak glow of a handful of gas lamps and the crackling blue light of Hambleton's bizarre machine, which filled a good third of the space and was wired to a small generator that whined with an insistent hum. Valves hissed noisily and the machine throbbed with a strange, pulsating energy; a huge brass edifice like an altar, with two immense arms that jutted out on either side of it, terminating in large discs between which electrical light crackled like caged lightning. And in the centre of all this, prone on the top of the dais, was Lady Hambleton. Her face was lit by the flickering blue light, and it was clear that she was no longer breathing.

"Hambleton stepped up to take a place beside her.

"Crawford, appearing behind me from the stairway, gave a terrible shout and rushed forward, as if to make a grab for Hambleton. He stopped short, however, when Hambleton raised his hand to produce a gun from beneath the folds of his coat. He waved it at Crawford. 'Don't come any closer, Crawford. I don't want you to inadvertently come to any harm. This is only for your own good.'

"Crawford was incensed, but stayed back, putting himself between me and the gun. He caught my eye, trying to get a measure of how I planned to respond to the situation. He turned back to Hambleton, his voice firm. 'What's going on, man? What's happened to Frances?'

"Hambleton sighed and lowered his gun. He met Crawford's eye, and spoke to his friend as if I were not there in the room with them at all. I listened to his terrible tale as he recounted it.

"'I knew the danger of marrying a young wife was that she may quickly grow tired of an older man, or at least weary of my company as I grew only older and more stuck in my ways. I loved Frances more than it is possible to say. I love her still.' He glanced at his wife, serene on the contraption behind him. 'I had miscalculated just how soon she would begin to look for companionship elsewhere, however, and had not expected after only twelve months to find her making merry with the postmaster's son in the stables. I was enraged, and stormed out of there with fire in my belly. The boy had scarpered and I had refused to see Frances for the rest of the day. That night, however, we had a blazing row over dinner, and Frances had declared her love for the boy, claiming that I was a terrible husband who had trapped her in a drafty old house and paid her no attention. This cut me dreadfully, and I found myself seething as she fled the room.' Hambleton offered Crawford a pleading look, as if willing him to try to understand. 'That is when the insanity took hold of me. I knew I was losing her, and I couldn't stand it, couldn't stand the thought of another man laying his hands on her. In a fit of madness I waited until the servants were all engaged elsewhere in the house and stormed up to her room, dragged her to the cellar and activated the machine.'

"Crawford's voice was barely a whisper. 'What is the machine?'

"'An experimental preserving device, designed to maintain the integrity of food after harvesting. It holds things in a form of stasis field, a bubble of energy that preserves them indefinitely, preventing them from decaying or altering in any way.' He paused, as if choking on his own words.

"'I threw Frances into the stasis field in a fit of rage, believing that I was saving her from herself, that it was the only way to stop her from leaving me forever. Too late, when the madness and rage had passed, I realised I had not yet perfected the means to bring her out of it again. All of my experiments with fruit and vegetables had ended in disaster. The integrity of the flesh had not been able to withstand the process of being withdrawn from the preserving field. Anything organic I put in there would simply fall apart when the field was terminated. Frances was trapped. Frozen in time, unable to be woken, unable to live her life. I couldn't bring myself to end it, and for days I've been searching for an answer, a means to free her from this God-forsaken prison I've created.'

"Crawford edged forward, and Hambleton raised his firearm

once again. Tears were rolling down his cheeks. 'Oh no, Crawford. You don't get to save me this time. This time I deserve my fate. Besides, it's too late now, anyway. I killed the boy this morning; practically tore the poor bastard apart. There's no going back now. The only choice I have is to submit myself to the stasis field, to join the woman I love in the prison I have created. Goodbye, Crawford. Do not think ill of me.'

"Hambleton turned and threw himself onto the dais beside his wife, his gun clattering to the floor. Crawford cried out. The machine fizzed and crackled, static energy causing my hackles to rise. A moment later Hambleton was overcome, and he collapsed into a peaceful sleep beside his wife."

Bainbridge looked aghast. "So what did you do? How did you get them out?"

"That's just it, Charles. We didn't. There was no way to free them from their fate. Neither Crawford nor I had any notion of how to engage the controls of the machine, and although we spent hours reading through Hambleton's notes, we could find no evidence of a method by which to safely deactivate the preserving field. Hambleton had been telling the truth. They were frozen there, in that bizarre machine, and there was nothing at all we could do about it.

"At a loss for how else to handle the situation, Crawford and I sealed up the basement and went directly to the local constabulary. We told them that we'd all been out walking on the moors and that Hambleton, overcome with distress about his missing wife, had thrown himself in the river. We'd tried to save him, of course, but he'd been swept away and lost. The police set about dredging the river for his body, but of course there was nothing to find. The servants could not dispute the facts, either, as only Chester had seen his master return from the village that morning, and he was loyal until the end."

Bainbridge shook his head. "My God. What a terrible tale. What became of them?"

"A while later Hambleton was declared dead and the house passed on to his nephew. Chester retired from service and Crawford had the door to the cellar panelled over before the new incumbent could move in. The missing lady was never found, presumed dead on the moor, having fled the house of her own volition."

"So, they're still there? Trapped in that cellar, I mean?"

Newbury nodded. "For all I know, yes, they're still there. Perhaps there will come a time when technological achievement is such that the machine can be deactivated and the two disenchanted lovers can be reunited. For now, though, their story ends there, in a basement beneath a manor house." Newbury paused. He eyed his friend. "As I've said before, Charles, revenge can make people do terrible things."

Bainbridge eyed Newbury over the rim of his brandy glass. "Hmm. Well there's a lesson there for all of us, I feel. And for you in particular, Newbury."

Newbury frowned. "How so?"

"I don't think revenge has got anything to do with it. Women, Newbury. Women can make people do terrible things." His eyes sparkled. "Better keep an eye on that assistant of yours, eh?" He winked mischievously.

Newbury flushed red. "Right, you old fool. That's quite enough of that. Time you were getting some rest. I'm in need of my own bed, and you're keeping me from it."

Bainbridge laughed. "Right you are, old man. Right you are." He placed his brandy glass on the table and rose, a little unsteadily, to his feet. He crossed the room, took up his coat and hat and, his cane tapping gently against the floor as he walked, bid his friend goodnight and made his way out into the fog-laden night. Newbury watched from the window as the chief inspector clambered into a waiting cab. Then, hesitating only long enough to bank the fire, he extinguished the gas lamps and made his way slowly to bed.

GEORGE MANN

THE EXECUTIONER'S HEART

A NEWBURY & HOBBES INVESTIGATION

When Charles Bainbridge, Chief Inspector of Scotland Yard, is called to the scene of the third murder in quick succession where the victim's chest has been cracked open and their heart torn out, he sends for supernatural specialist Sir Maurice Newbury and his determined assistant, Miss Veronica Hobbes.

The two detectives discover that the killings may be the work of a mercenary known as the Executioner. Her heart is damaged, leaving her an emotionless shell, driven to collect her victims' hearts as trophies. Newbury and Hobbes confront many strange and pressing mysteries on the way to unearthing the secret of the Executioner's Heart.

Available Now

TITANBOOKS.COM

GEORGE MANN

THE REVENANT EXPRESS

A NEWBURY & HOBBES INVESTIGATION

In the next instalment of George Mann's *Newbury & Hobbes* series, we join Sir Maurice Newbury on his fateful journey to St. Petersburg in the aftermath of the "Executioner" affair, pursued by those who would see him dead…

Available July 2014

TITANBOOKS.COM

GEORGE MANN

THE CASEBOOK OF NEWBURY & HOBBES

VOLUME I

A collection of short stories detailing the supernatural steampunk adventures of detective duo, Sir Maurice Newbury and Miss Veronica Hobbes in dark and dangerous Victorian London. Along with Chief Inspector Bainbridge, Newbury and Hobbes will face plague revenants, murderous peers, mechanical beasts, tentacled leviathans, reanimated pygmies, and an encounter with one Sherlock Holmes.

Available Now

TITANBOOKS.COM

GEORGE MANN

ENCOUNTERS OF SHERLOCK HOLMES

BRAND-NEW TALES OF THE GREAT DETECTIVE

The spirit of Sherlock Holmes lives on in this collection of fourteen brand-new adventures. Marvel as the master of deduction aids a dying Sir Richard Francis Burton; matches wits with gentleman thief, A.J. Raffles; crosses paths with H.G. Wells in the most curious circumstances; unravels a macabre mystery on the Necropolis Express; unpicks a murder in a locked railway carriage; explains the origins of his famous Persian slipper and more!

Featuring original stories from
Mark Hodder • Mags L Halliday • Cavan Scott • Nick Kyme • Paul Magrs • George Mann • Stuart Douglas • Eric Brown • Richard Dinnick • Kelly Hale • Steve Lockley • Mark Wright • David Barnett • James Lovegrove

Further Encounters of Sherlock Holmes (February 2014)

TITANBOOKS.COM

JAMES LOVEGROVE

SHERLOCK HOLMES

THE STUFF OF NIGHTMARES

A spate of bombings has hit London, causing untold damage and loss of life. Meanwhile a strangely garbed figure has been spied haunting the rooftops and grimy back alleys of the capital.

Sherlock Holmes believes this strange masked man may hold the key to the attacks. He moves with the extraordinary agility of a latter-day Spring-Heeled Jack. He possesses weaponry and armour of unprecedented sophistication. He is known only by the name Baron Cauchemar, and he appears to be a scourge of crime and villainy. But is he all that he seems? Holmes and his faithful companion Dr Watson are about to embark on one of their strangest and most exhilarating adventures yet.

A brand-new original novel, detailing a thrilling new case for the acclaimed detective Sherlock Holmes.

TITANBOOKS.COM